GONE
WITH THE
WHISKER

Center Point
Large Print

Also by Laurie Cass and available from
Center Point Large Print:

Borrowed Crime
Wrong Side of the Paw
Booking the Crook
Cat With a Clue
Pouncing on Murder

**This Large Print Book carries the
Seal of Approval of N.A.V.H.**

GONE
WITH THE
WHISKER
A BOOKMOBILE CAT MYSTERY

LAURIE CASS

CENTER POINT LARGE PRINT
THORNDIKE, MAINE

This Center Point Large Print edition
is published in the year 2020 by arrangement with
Berkley, an imprint of Penguin Publishing Group, a
division of Penguin Random House LLC.

The text of this Large Print edition is unabridged.
In other aspects, this book may vary
from the original edition.
Printed in the United States of America
on permanent paper.
Set in 16-point Times New Roman type.

ISBN: 978-1-64358-606-9

The Library of Congress has cataloged this record
under Library of Congress Control Number: 2020931009

For Jon, whom I nominate annually for Best Husband of the Year, in spite of his unfortunate music preferences.

CHAPTER 1

Every summer when I was a kid, my mom and dad and older brother and I piled into the family car and headed north to visit my aunt Frances. It was a long drive from Dearborn up to Chilson, and it was even longer if road crews were working on I-75, shutting down lanes of traffic and creating backups that ran for miles. This was when my dad would mutter, "There are four seasons in Michigan. Fall, winter, spring, and construction."

At five years old, I hadn't grasped what he was talking about, but at nearly thirty-five, I had a much better understanding of the concept.

"This project wasn't supposed to start until after the Fourth," Julia said, glaring at the brake lights lined up ahead of us.

I glared along with her. "When I called the road commission last week, that's what they told me." I rolled my shoulders in an attempt to loosen my neck. As a six-year resident of northwest lower Michigan, I'd lost my tolerance for sitting in traffic five and a half years ago.

This wasn't anything close to the gridlock of southeast Michigan, but time spent waiting for the oncoming lane of cars to get through and our side to get waved forward was time the bookmobile wouldn't be able to spend with its patrons. The Chilson District Library Bookmobile carried me, aka Minnie Hamilton, Julia Beaton, my part-time bookmobile clerk, roughly three thousand books, magazines, CDs, DVDs, puzzles, board games, and video games and—

"Mrr," Eddie said.

And the bookmobile also carried Eddie, the black-and-white cat who had followed me home from a walk through the local cemetery a little over two years ago. At the time, I had not been a cat person, but it hadn't taken me long to become attached to the furry little guy. I'd dutifully placed ads in the paper for a lost cat, I'd talked to cemetery neighbors, and I'd called area veterinarians and the local animal shelter. No one, thankfully, had come forward to claim my new buddy, and we'd been fast friends ever since.

But like any relationship, we'd had our ups and downs. A definite down had been the day Eddie had managed to sneak aboard the bookmobile's maiden voyage. That had not boded well for my relationship with my then-boss, Stephen, who had been a stickler for any and all rules, one being no pets in the library, of which the bookmobile was an extension.

Eventually it had worked out, and now Eddie was a permanent fixture on the bookmobile, to the point that he got Christmas cards from elementary school classrooms, adult foster care homes, and other librarians. I tended not to tell him about his fame—he already had such a good opinion of himself that I hesitated to inflate his ego any further—but I had a sneaking suspicion he knew.

Julia put her feet on top of Eddie's carrier, which was strapped to the floor on the passenger's side, and toyed with the end of her thick strawberry blond braid. "If this keeps up, we're going to miss the next stop altogether."

She spoke with a slight drawl that hadn't been there last time she'd talked. Julia, now in her early sixties, had grown up in Chilson and left for the bright New York City lights right after high school graduation. A few decades and a suitcase full of Tony Awards later, she and her husband had come home, and she'd been bored to tears within weeks. She'd taught an acting class at the local community college, but teaching wasn't her strong suit, and when my aunt Frances had mentioned a job on the bookmobile, Julia had marched on over to the library and essentially begged me to hire her.

We'd hit it off straightaway, and the deal sealer had been when she'd met Eddie and instantly started talking to him as if he could understand her, which was exactly how I talked to him.

The newfound drawl indicated that she was playing a role. It could have been one she'd played, one she hadn't, or one that had never existed. Some days I tried to guess; other times I gave it up as a lost cause. This time around was a mystery, but I'd known her long enough to guess what she was thinking. "Do you know a way around?"

A wide, slow, Grinch-like smile curled onto her face. "Why, yes, I do." She pointed left, to a northbound road that quickly disappeared around a curve and up a hill.

I studied it. "I'm not driving the bookmobile on some narrow asphalt road that turns into a gravel two-track that peters out into loose sand where we'll get stuck and need a huge tow truck to yank us out."

Julia looked at me with puppy dog eyes. "You wound me, Minnie, truly you do. But that's Dozier Road. Isn't that the route you laid out?"

I had, indeed, planned to take Dozier around the construction zone, but hadn't found the time to make sure the road was bookmobile friendly. My last two months, and especially the last two weeks, had been so full I'd kept shifting reroute scouting to the next day. And the next. And the next. And now here we were. The location of today's stop was a one-time deal because the parking lot of the regular stop, a church, was being repaved. I'd scouted out our temporary location ages ago—it was little more than a wide spot on a dead end road—but checking the reroute hadn't popped to the top of my priority list.

Tapping my fingers on the steering wheel, I considered possibilities. The bookmobile was thirty-one feet long and weighed twenty-three thousand pounds. Which was big, but smaller than a lot of recreational vehicles, especially ones hauling a vehicle behind. As we sat there, listening to the twin dulcet tones of the bookmobile's motor and Eddie's snores, we watched a semi rig laden with rough-cut lumber trundle down the Dozier Road hill, around the curve, and air brake to a stop sign.

"That had to come from the sawmill," Julia said.

I leaned forward to look, and sure enough, the door of the truck's cab was labeled Palmer's Wood Products. Their sawmill was on the other side of the hills to our left, so there was a 99.9 percent chance the truck had come all the way down Dozier Road. The big vehicle roared past us and I would have sworn the driver was whistling a happy tune as he passed the long line of stuck-in-place cars.

Julia watched it go by. "If he did it, we can," she said confidently.

"Mrr!"

"Thinking," I murmured. The vote of a cat didn't count for driving route decisions, let alone the vote of a cat who couldn't possibly see what was going on because he was in a carrier on the floor. And technically Julia's vote didn't count either, because the bookmobile was my program, funded through my unexpectedly successful fund-raising efforts, and its operation was the responsibility of one Minnie Hamilton, all five foot and zero inches of me, along with my unmanageable curly black hair and total lack of fashion sense.

But Julia was right—if that lumber truck could make it, the bookmobile could. Though taking Dozier wouldn't help anyone reach the east side of Tonedagana County, which was the end point of our current road, it would get us to today's temporary stop.

And time was ticking away.

"We're doing it," I said, flicking the left blinker.

Julia whooped with delight. "An adventure! I'll tell Graydon you should get danger pay!"

"Please don't."

Graydon Cain had only been our library director since January. To date he was an excellent boss, but we would likely all be better off if he remained unaware of certain things. Julia and I had an unofficial rule that what happened on the bookmobile stayed on the bookmobile, and I fervently hoped the rule would be followed forever.

We bumped off the relatively smooth asphalt of the main road and onto the far narrower cracked asphalt of Dozier. I took a deep breath, loosened my grip on the steering wheel—because worrying about how this would play out wouldn't help anything now that the decision had been made—and asked, "What are you doing for the Fourth?"

Julia and her husband were without children of their own, but between them they had what seemed like zillions of sisters, brothers, and nieces and nephews, some by blood, others by tight bonds of friendship. Their circle was now expanding to include great-nieces and great-nephews, which meant I'd recently surrendered any hope of keeping track of names and exact relationships.

"Grilling in the backyard for twenty," Julia said. "No fireworks this year. Too many dogs and infants. How about you?"

"Not sure yet." Since I'd moved to Chilson, I'd spent the Fourth of July with my best friend, Kristen Jurek.

Kristen, who I'd met the summer I was twelve, was a force of nature. She owned Three Seasons, an outstanding restaurant that had been featured on more than one television show. The restaurant opened April-ish and closed October-ish, and then she took herself off to Key West, resting and tending bar until the snow melted. Complicating her life even more, she'd married Scruffy (not his real first name) Gronkowski a few weeks earlier, and since Scruffy was still working in New York with his famous television chef father, Trock Farrand (not his real name first or last), their living arrangements involved lots of plane rides.

Not that I could throw any housing stones. My own living arrangements were far from simple, especially this summer. For six years I'd moved every time the weather had turned. October through April I'd stayed with my aunt Frances in her elderly rambling house, but come springtime she cheerfully kicked me out to make room for her boarders and I happily went to Uncle Chip's Marina to live on the most adorable houseboat ever. Sure, it was tiny, but I had a relatively inexpensive lakefront abode, my summer neighbors were great, and the guys who hung out at the marina's office, the marina rats, were amusing almost all the time, even if their conversation did center on sports.

But now everything was different. This April, Aunt Frances had married her across-the-street neighbor, Otto Bingham, and moved into Otto's house. In May, our cousin Celeste had taken over the boardinghouse, and though Eddie and I were now on the houseboat, I wouldn't be moving back to the boardinghouse in October. Instead I'd be moving in with the funny and smart (and occasionally irritating) Rafe Niswander.

Though I'd met Rafe on Chilson's city beach ten minutes after I'd met Kristen, it had taken me more than twenty years to realize he was the love of my life. When he reminded me of what a slow learner I could be, I told him that things might have been different if he didn't have the regrettable habit of acting far stupider than he actually was. Rafe had multiple college degrees and was a fantastically good middle school principal, but from the way he sometimes acted, you'd think he'd have a hard time chewing gum while breathing.

But the real reason I hadn't understood how I felt about Rafe was I hadn't been ready. Now I was, and any day we got to spend together was a day worth remembering.

Julia cleared her throat in a way that sent a clear message she was about to ask something I wouldn't want to answer. "How's Katrina?"

My Rafe-induced smile dropped away. I tried to stifle a sigh, but was pretty sure I wasn't successful, because I heard Julia snort. "Katrina," I said, " is . . ." Then I stopped, since I didn't want to get too deep into family issues. "Did I tell you about her summer job search?" I asked.

Katrina was my slender seventeen-year-old niece, currently between her junior and senior years of high school, and the first of three children created by my brother and his wife. She was smart, funny, had lovely brown hair, and four Christmases ago had been thrilled to find herself taller than her aunt Minnie.

My brother and his family lived in Florida, and

apparently they'd actually listened to my annual moaning about the lack of summer workers in Chilson, because a few weeks earlier they'd called about having Katrina come stay with me for the season.

I'd been delighted. How fun to have Katrina for the summer! I'd get to know her so much better! We'd develop a solid relationship that would endure to our old age, and who knew, maybe someday she'd want to move up here to the land of lakes and hills and life in the slow lane!

After numerous text messages, phone calls, and sending of photos showing the tight quarters in which she'd be living on the houseboat, the arrangements had been solidified and I'd fetched Katrina from the Traverse City airport two weeks ago.

Out of the corner of my eye, I saw Julia shake her head in answer to my job search question. "All you've said was that she was looking."

And looking was all she'd done for more than a week. First off, I'd encouraged her to apply at restaurants. "I've never worked in a restaurant before," she'd said. "No one will hire me."

"Just go in and apply," I said. "Every restaurant in Chilson has a Help Wanted sign in the window." Except for Kristen's restaurant. She paid her staff well and treated them like family, which was to say horribly, but she must have been doing something right, because they came

16

back year after year. I said to Katrina, "Any restaurant will be happy to train you."

But she'd hesitated and delayed and balked and three days ago she'd announced that the smell of cooking food—any kind of food—gave her a headache.

Exasperation had blossomed in every cell of my body and my question of "Why didn't you say so in the first place?" was answered by a shrug and a sullen silence. Now, as I told Julia all of this, I was beginning to catch a glimmer of humor.

"The mysteries of the teenage mind are many," Julia said, smiling. "Kind of makes you understand why your brother and his wife were willing to part with their darling daughter for the summer, yes?"

I laughed. "Could be. But there are lots of retail jobs downtown." Though without tips, the pay wouldn't be nearly as lucrative. "She's applying at the toy store, Older Than Dirt, and Benton's. If none of those work out . . ." I shook my head. "There are other places. She's bound to find something."

Julia nodded and, wisely, said nothing.

We came to a stop sign, made a left turn, then soon another left onto the dead end gravel road where our one-time spot awaited us.

"Look at that," Julia said. "We have people waiting for us!" As I parked the bookmobile, Julia waved at the two bookmobilers waiting by

17

their cars; Nicole Price and Violet Mullaly, and a third, Rex Stuhler, who was leaning his bicycle against a tree.

I worked through the opening routines as Julia opened the door. "Sorry we're late," she said. "Construction."

The one-word explanation seemed to suffice. All three nodded and I let out a tiny sigh of relief. Though Rex was a decent guy, Nicole and Violet were among the more critical of our patrons. I could handle criticism, of course, but I didn't like inviting it onto the bookmobile.

Nicole came aboard. "Morning," she said shortly, her stern face set in firm lines. She headed for the new fiction, her red hair bouncing as she went. Violet muttered something that might have been a greeting as she came up the steps, gave Nicole a hard glare, then wandered over to the video games. Rex bounded inside and greeted Julia and me with a smile. "Had a great bike ride this morning." He nodded to the south, to the end of the road. "Went down that way for a bit. It's pretty down there, if you like trees, which I do, so I'll probably go that way again." He looked around. "Is my little buddy riding along today?"

I gestured toward the front, where Eddie was flopped on the console. "Waiting for you."

Rex went up and patted him on the head. "The bookmobile is here, and so is the bookmobile cat. All's right with the world."

"Mrr!"

It was hard to disagree with that, so no one did.

On the Fourth of July, I woke to find Eddie nestled into the crook of my elbow. With my eyes still shut, I used my free hand to feel around for the exact location of his head. More than once I'd opened my eyes to the sight of big yellow ones staring me down at a point-blank range. It was not an ideal way to start a morning, so I'd learned to scout out the exact arrangement of his body parts first thing.

"Mrr," he said sleepily. The distance of his voice indicated it was safe to raise my eyelids, so I did, which was when I saw, through the white lacy curtains at the window, that the sky was that gorgeous blue color you dream of all winter long.

"Not a cloud in sight," I said with satisfaction, doing my best to slide out of the bed without disturbing its feline inhabitant. After a quick shower and a toweling of my stupidly curly hair, I slid into appropriate layers: shorts, T-shirt, and a fleece sweatshirt that would come off as soon as the temperature bumped to the seventy-degree range. I made the bed around Eddie and bounced up the few steps into the houseboat's main room.

"Happy Fourth of July!" I said cheerfully.

"Go away."

My cheeriness dimmed a bit, but I determinedly pushed it back up. It had become clear to me over the last two weeks that Katrina was not a morning person. Of course, my oldest niece didn't seem to be a night person, either. What she mostly seemed to do was sleep, something I'd heard teenagers did, but since I'd never done so, I hadn't expected my own flesh and blood to have the habit.

I studied the top of her head, her hair waving smoothly across the pillow, and tried to judge her actual level of sleepiness. When Katrina had arrived, I'd assumed she would sleep in the other berth in my tiny bedroom, but instead she'd wanted to bunk down in a sleeping bag on what used to be my dining table. The table lowered to the level of the bench seats and, with the addition of some pillows, was apparently a comfortable sleeping area.

Though the loss of dining space was awkward at times, I was making do, and was even making progress in learning to avert my eyes from the piles of Katrina-related clothing and other miscellaneous belongings. If the piles started to expand and/or migrate, there would have to be a conversation, but so far, things were staying put.

"We're due at Aunt Frances and Otto's house in less than an hour," I said.

Katrina groaned and yanked the sleeping bag over her head. "Do I have to go?"

Until this summer, my aunt role had been giver of cool presents and teller of stories that made their father look bad. As aunt in loco parentis, however, things were different.

"Yes," I said firmly. "I told your parents you'd get the full Up North summer experience, and that includes morning-to-midnight Fourth of July activities. Up and at 'em, there's fun to be had!"

Grumbling about the unfairness of her life, Katrina oozed out of bed and shuffled into the bathroom.

"Mrr." At some point, Eddie had migrated to the boat's dashboard, his current favorite spot. Usually he faced out to watch seagulls swoop up and around, but now he was facing down-boat, looking toward the bathroom door.

"Yeah, I know." I folded up the sleeping bag. "She didn't say good morning to you, did she? Give her time. There are no pets at her house and she doesn't understand the rules."

Eddie blinked, then rotated and flopped down.

Katrina showered, I waited patiently, and by a small miracle we arrived at our intended destination only five minutes late.

"You're here!" Aunt Frances wrapped her arms around me in a huge hug, and once again I cogitated the fact that my aunt and I shared no physical traits whatsoever. She was tall and long-limbed and had short straight hair, once light brown, now mostly gray. For years she'd run the boardinghouse in the summer and taught woodworking at a nearby community college during the school year. But now that Aunt Frances was married, the boardinghouse was under Celeste's management, and it was unclear whether or not she would return to teaching.

"Of course we're here," I said, returning the slightly unusual hug. "Did you think we wouldn't?"

My aunt transferred her hug to Katrina, who, for the first time that morning, was smiling. Then again, it was hard not to smile in the presence of the powerfully optimistic Aunt Frances.

"Breakfast is almost ready," she said, leading us to the kitchen, which had been renovated while she and Otto were on their honeymoon. The new version was light and airy and spacious, with a new bump-out window seat that looked out over a backyard lush with blooming flowers of whose identity I was completely ignorant.

Otto, at the cooktop, smiled as we walked in. "Good morning, ladies. And a very Happy Birthday to you, Minnie."

"Seriously?" Katrina stared. "Your birthday is the Fourth of July?"

"Yep." I bounced a little on the balls of my feet. "Best birthday possible. National holiday, parades, cooking out on the grill, fireworks. When I was little, I thought it was all for me."

From behind me, a male voice said, "What, you mean it's not?"

I turned and grinned at Rafe, who also

enveloped me in a hug, but one with a slightly different flavor. "I didn't hear you come in."

"That's because I was here already. On time, you see?" He tapped the top of my head gently with the point of his chin.

"Five minutes hardly counts as late," I said, tipping my head up for a kiss.

"Says the woman who is nose deep in a book if I'm more than ten seconds late to meet her for anything," Rafe said to the room in general before leaning down.

Post-kiss, I watched Otto stirring something in a small saucepan, a something I deeply hoped was buttered maple syrup with pecans that would soon be spread over fluffy pancakes. Aunt Frances had cooked my birthday breakfast all the summers I stayed with her as a kid, and she'd continued doing it when I moved here as an adult. The menu had shifted from the Mickey waffles of my youth, and we weren't in the boardinghouse, but Aunt Frances was here, I was here, and having Otto and Rafe and Katrina here made the morning even better.

When breakfast was over and the dishes washed, we'd shifted to the fun topic of what to do with the rest of the day.

"Minnie gets to pick," Rafe said, drying his hands on a kitchen towel. "You only get to turn thirty-five once."

I beamed at my beloved, who really should

have known better. If the world had been a perfect place, we would have piled into a huge semitruck and visited bookstores across northern lower Michigan, filling the trailer as we went. But as much as I loved books, there were two small problems with that dream day. One, I lacked the financial resources to fund that kind of a trip, and two, I didn't have any place to put that many books.

But even if the world wasn't perfect, it was still a pretty nice place, and I knew exactly what I wanted to do.

An hour later, the five of us were walking down a narrow dirt trail, each of us carrying backpacks laden with a picnic lunch, water, and in my case, emergency reading material. I suspected that Katrina had stuffed a copy of *People* magazine into hers, but since she didn't seem to be talking to me on a voluntary basis, I decided not to ask.

We were headed down to the Jordan River Valley, to a section of trail I'd long wanted to hike. Otto was walking ahead with Katrina, and I was next to Aunt Frances, with Rafe close behind. The current trail was a fairly steep downhill that wound through a second growth forest of maple and beech trees, and I was mostly making sure I kept my footing and didn't slide to the bottom in an untidy heap.

"Did I tell you about Celeste?" Aunt Frances asked.

I picked my way over a miniature crevasse, probably the result of a recent thunderstorm. "What about her?"

"After all those promises, she's not doing it. Not at all."

To the inexperienced ear, this would have made no sense. I, however, understood the meaning behind the ambiguous words.

"Not doing what?" Rafe asked.

I hadn't realized he was close enough to overhear. *Hmm.* I looked over my shoulder. "Not doing the Saturday breakfast. You know, when the boarders cook for each other?"

"Ah." He lost interest and dropped behind us, and I focused on my aunt's dilemma, which wasn't so much a dilemma as an acceptance of change. My aunt's summer boardinghouse had been more than a boardinghouse; it had also been, unbeknownst to most, a matchmaking enterprise.

The applications for summer spots had always far exceeded the places available, and one year, on a whim, Aunt Frances had chosen her visitors based on how she thought they might pair up for long-term relationships. Every year it had worked like a charm—although it hadn't always appeared so at first—and now she'd started getting applications from offspring of some of the first pairings.

One activity that eased people together was the Saturday morning breakfast. This was the one day of the week my aunt hadn't cooked breakfast for her boarders, instead requiring the boarders themselves to cook for the group. Everyone knew that going in, but what they didn't know was that they would be paired up with the potential mate my aunt had selected. "Nothing like cooking a large meal," she'd said often, "to show compatibility."

Now, I asked, "Celeste isn't doing it at all?"

"Not so far as I can tell," my aunt said. "I know I should let her run things her own way, but she's going to ruin the boardinghouse. She's going to make it something else entirely. I would never have handed it over to her if I'd known she was going to pull this kind of stunt!"

The voice of my normally calm, cool, and collected aunt had risen. Otto looked back and I met his gaze, arranging my face in a gesture that I hoped said, "Help!"

He slowed and said, "Minnie, I haven't asked how the library finances are moving along. Have there been any developments?"

I sent him a grateful glance. I'd talk to Aunt Frances about Celeste, but that conversation should take place in private. Otto, a retired accountant, had taken an interest in the large bequest bestowed on the library by the late Stan Larabee. Though Stan's estranged family had

26

contested the will, the case had recently been settled.

"The library board is still considering options," I said.

Otto nodded. "Understandable. With that amount of money, you don't want to rush into decisions."

"Everyone else," I said glumly, "is ready to go on a spending spree."

Otto laughed, and his Paul Newman–like appearance became even more pronounced. "Let me guess," he said. "The staff and the Friends of the Library disagree on how the money should be spent."

"You are one of the smartest people I know."

"Smart enough to marry your aunt." He looked at her, love writ so clearly in his expression that I looked away. Not because I was embarrassed at the display of emotion; more because the look she sent back mirrored his own and I felt like an intruder.

I hung back, letting the two of them go ahead with Katrina, who chattered to them with no evident inhibitions. Since dwelling on the fact that the relationship with my niece was far from ideal wasn't a happy way to spend my birthday, I thought instead about the recent weddings with which I'd been involved.

Aunt Frances and Otto had married in April here in Chilson and spent a long honeymoon in

Bermuda. The wedding itself had been small and the party afterward large, with half the town attending. I'd stood up as maid of honor, and Leo Kinsler, the former boarder whose stories of Aunt Frances had instigated Otto's move north, stood up as best man. My dad had given the bride away, and there hadn't been a dry eye when they'd exchanged vows.

Kristen and Scruffy's mid-May wedding had been large, the reception even larger, and the food so spectacular that the local guests were still talking about it. It was harder to tell about the out-of-town guests, but the parking lot of Three Seasons seemed to have more New York license plates than in previous years.

I sighed happily at the memories. Kristen, gorgeous in flowing white. Scruffy, even more impeccably clad than normal in a summer tux. The wedding cake decorated with lifelike fondant roses. The appetizers of crab cakes, rumaki, teeny tiny waffles topped with real maple syrup and bits of real whipped cream, shrimp on top of tiny tortillas with a slice of avocado between, something I'd been told was spanakopita, half strawberries with the cutest little ice cream cones imaginable stuck into them and filled with custard, and—

"Are you mad at me?"

I started at Rafe's question and almost tripped over a tree root. "Why do you think I'm mad?"

"You're not talking."

"That's evidence of anger?"

He shrugged. "You haven't said a word to me since Frances mentioned Celeste, so it only follows that talking about Celeste made you think about the boardinghouse, which made you think about the houseboat, which made you think about how you're jammed in there all summer with Katrina when it would have been a lot better if I'd been able to finish the house and we could all be staying there instead of the two of you being in such close quarters, which can't be easy."

The trail was now relatively flat, and Rafe was walking next to me, his long legs taking one step to every step and a half of mine. His straight black hair glinted in the sun, and his slightly reddish skin, an inheritance from native ancestors, seemed to almost glow. I felt a burst of love for him and wondered if my face looked anything like my aunt's had. "That was a very long sentence," I said.

"Yes."

He didn't say anything else, which made me laugh. "Did you know," I asked, "there's a betting pool going for when you get the house done?"

Rafe stopped. "That can't be. I'm the one who sets up pools, not the subject of them."

"Yeah, well, not this time." He would eventually find out I was the one who started the pool, but with any luck, it wouldn't be soon.

"Absolutely no one had you down for finishing in April." I'd been collecting money for months and the kitty had grown to the point that I was keeping it at the library in a locked drawer. And every week someone handed me more cash and whispered a date.

"Huh." He started walking again. "Don't suppose you'd tell me the day you have down."

I smiled at him fondly. "Nope."

"Don't suppose you'd let me put some money in."

"Not a chance."

"How about the average date? The last date? How many people entered?"

Grinning, I shook my head to all of his questions. It was a rare thing for me to have so much information he didn't have, and I was finding the sensation enjoyable. Which should have been disturbing, but wasn't.

He heaved a tremendous sigh and took my hand. "Then I guess we'll just have to go on with enjoying your birthday."

"Guess so," I said, and felt my heart swell with love.

The sun had slid down over the line of hills that separated Janay Lake from the majestic Lake Michigan. A small channel connected the two lakes, and Chilson was strung along the northwest end of twenty-mile-long Janay Lake.

The waterside location had allowed the city council to, over the years, construct a public marina, an adjacent park complete with gazebo, and a performance shell that hosted everything from chamber of commerce awards to traveling professional shows. Tonight the stage would be crowded with a local community band who'd be playing music to accompany the fireworks, and I'd been looking forward to the evening for weeks.

Up at my aunt's house, we'd stuffed ourselves with hamburgers, corn on the cob, and potato salad, and we'd walked the long way to the park to work off some of our intake.

"I haven't gone to fireworks since I was little," Katrina said, watching as Rafe and I spread blankets on the grass. "Fireworks are for kids and old people. They're all the same. Boring."

I glanced at Aunt Frances, but she was hand in hand with Otto, chatting away with our right-hand neighbors, a quartet of downstaters in their fifties. Though I assumed Katrina meant fireworks were boring, not little kids and the elderly, I wanted clarification. "You don't think fireworks are fun?"

"Booooring," she said, drawing out the word.

Rafe looked at her, looked at me, and smiled, since he knew what was coming.

"Only boring people find life boring," I said.

Katrina rolled her eyes and flopped down

onto the middle of the blanket. "You sound like Grandma," she muttered.

For a moment I was horrified. Then I took a deep breath and calmly said, "Grandma has been around the block a time or two. You might want to listen."

"Whatever." She rolled onto her stomach. "And from now on, my name is Kate, okay? I'm tired of stupid jokes about the hurricane." My niece pulled out her phone and was mentally gone from the here and now.

Kate? Did her parents know about this? I was thinking seriously about ripping the phone from her hands and pitching it into the lake when my aunt tapped my shoulder.

"Enjoy the night," she said. "Things will work out."

I wanted to object, to say that life could be cruel and painful, to tell her that horrible things happened to people for no good reason, but since I'd just told Kate-not-Katrina that grandmas knew what they were talking about, I should probably listen to someone of the same age. Besides, my aunt knew all about life's hard knocks. And she also knew how wonderful life could be.

So I took her advice and went back to enjoying myself. Dusk was falling slowly and softly, as it did in the north so close to the summer solstice, and it was a sweet pleasure to sit and watch the sky darken, listen to the murmur of passersby, and smell the drifting scents of charcoal fluid and cotton candy.

As soon as it grew dark, the band started playing and the fireworks started exploding. It wasn't the exquisitely timed production that big cities could put on, but knowing half the band members more than made up for the timing issues.

I leaned against Rafe, and side by side, eating the popcorn Otto had bought for me as a final birthday present, we watched the sky. From a barge moored out in Janay Lake, small canisters zipped high and burst into explosions of white, red, blue, green, pink, and even purple. Huge bangs made toddlers squeal and adults wince. Sparkles snapped-crackled-and-popped into fireworks that blossomed into more fireworks that blossomed into even more.

It was a stupendous show. Once I glanced over at Katrina-now-Kate and smiled to see her staring up at the sky with a look of delight. I nudged Aunt Frances, who was sitting on my other side, and tipped my head in Katrina-Kate's direction.

My aunt nodded, mouthed, "Told you," and then came the grand finale with its torrent of booms and bangs and enough exploding fireworks to light the entire sky.

The last one hadn't finished fading when the crowd started applauding, and as always, I got a lump in my throat at the sound.

"Are you ready?" Katrina asked through the applause. "Because I have to be at work Monday morning and I don't want to mess up my sleep schedule."

"You got a job?" I blinked. "Where?"

"Oh, you know. Around." She stood, brushing off her shorts.

I got to my feet and motioned at Rafe, Otto, and Aunt Frances, who were in a conversation with our left-hand neighbors about local farmer's markets, to move aside so I could pick up the blankets. "Around where?" I asked. "And when?"

"Part time, is all. That toy store, the antique place with the weird name, and the old store that belongs in a movie from a hundred years ago."

I interpreted these to be the toy store managed by Mitchell Koyne; Older Than Dirt, which was owned and run by my friend Pam Fazio; and Benton's, a family-owned general store now under the competent hands of Rianne Howe.

"Did you tell your parents?" I asked.

Even in the dim light, I could see Katrina's scowl. "Why do they need to know?"

"Because they're your parents, and—"

"I don't care," Katrina said as she started walking backward through the crowd.

This worried me a bit, because she wasn't looking where she was going, but she was backing away from the water, not toward it, so I tried to stop worrying.

34

"I'm stuck here for the summer with no friends and nothing to do," my niece said, "so if I want to take ten jobs, I'm going to do it," she called as she continued backing into the dark. "I have to do something to keep from going nuts and—*oohh!*" She tumbled down.

"Katrina, are you okay?"

"My name is Kate," she said angrily from the ground. "And I'm fine. I just tripped over something." She sat up, looked at what she'd fallen over, and screamed. "He's dead! He's dead!"

Aunt Frances, Rafe, Otto, and I raced toward her, and I reached her first. "It's okay, sweetie, it's okay. Come on, stand up, let's see what's . . ."

Katrina sobbed into my shoulder. But it wasn't going to be okay, because she was right. She'd stumbled over a person, not a thing, and the man was indeed dead. Even in the dim light I could see that. The bullet hole in the back of his head was proof, and . . . and . . .

Around me, I heard Otto calling 911 and talking to dispatch, I heard Aunt Frances comforting Katrina, and I heard Rafe asking me if I was all right.

I stared at the man lying at my feet, his eyes glazed open, a man I'd seen only a couple of days earlier. "I know him," I whispered.

CHAPTER 2

The next morning I was bleary-eyed and feeling raw from turbulent dreams and disturbing thoughts. I couldn't fathom that Rex Stuhler, a bookmobile patron, was dead. At some point during the Chilson fireworks, someone had taken advantage of the show's bangs and explosions and shot him.

I'd seen Rex just two days ago, at the temporary stop. He'd been waiting for us when we'd arrived late, and he'd patted Eddie on the head. Rex was maybe fifty, and a voracious reader. His profession as a pest exterminator out of his home office meant he worked irregular hours, and the combination of those facts made him a bookmobile regular.

He was also one of those guys who loved gadgets, especially electronic gadgets, and when we'd teased him about preferring paper books over e-books, he'd whispered it was a secret he was trying to keep from his buddies, and what did he have to do to buy our silence?

At the time we'd laughed, but now I was having a hard time swallowing my tears. Rex didn't have to worry about anything any longer.

But life went on for those still living, and last night Rafe had asked me to pick up a box of drywall screws at the hardware store first thing. "Sorry," he'd said after we'd been questioned and dismissed by a sheriff's deputy and he'd walked us back to the houseboat, "but if you get those, I can keep working."

"No problem," I'd told him, putting my arm around a shivering Katrina. Her life in Florida had not prepared her for cool summer evenings in northern Michigan, but she continued to shrug off recommendations for always having a sweatshirt at hand. "I'll take care of it."

So now, though I deeply wanted to roll over and sleep for twelve hours, I yawned, yawned again, slithered out of bed to avoid waking Eddie, and got showered and dressed as quietly as possible.

Not that Katrina moved a muscle, other than those involuntary ones that kept her heart and brain going. As I wrote my whereabouts on the kitchen's whiteboard—*Hardware store, house, back by noon*—I listened to her soft, regular breathing. Last night, she hadn't taken well to my command to call her parents and tell them what had happened, but when I'd asked if she was going to text any friends about it and did those friends have parents who knew hers, she grudgingly saw the need.

My brother and his wife had been understandably shocked and concerned, and after Katrina curled up in her sleeping bag and went into coma mode, we talked into the wee hours of the morning. We eventually agreed there was no immediate need for her to go home or for them to fly up, but that I'd keep a close eye on her and let them know immediately if she was exhibiting signs of emotional trauma.

And now it was morning. Gently, I tucked the sleeping bag around her shoulders and hoped what I'd told Matt and Jennifer had been right.

"Kids are resilient," I told the blue sky as I stepped outside. At least that's what people said. But I wasn't so sure. Maybe kids were just resilient on the outside, same as adults. Who knew what was going on inside?

I made a solemn vow to watch over my niece, to take careful note of any changes in her behavior, and to deepen our relationship so that she'd feel free to talk to me about anything. In the long run, this would all work out, I was sure of it.

Well, almost.

But the future would work itself out in due time, so I tucked my worry about Katrina into a back corner and made up my mind to enjoy the morning. Which was easy to do, because the sun was shining, the birds were singing, and so many things in the world were amazing and wonderful.

A hop, skip, and a jump from the marina was the old, large, 1900s Shingle style house that was rising up from the metaphorical ashes of having been divided into apartments decades earlier. It had a deep front porch, lake views, and my vote for being the most beautiful house in Chilson. Plus, in a few short months it would be my own home. Rafe was already living there, because he didn't mind living in a state of perpetual renovation. And I might have been living there with him this very moment if it hadn't been for my recently discovered inability to tolerate the fumes of paint primer.

I walked on tiptoes as I went past the house, looking for signs of Rafe. There was no visual clue, but then I heard the drywall saw start up. I blew a kiss in his general direction and headed up the hill.

The hardware store was on the outskirts of downtown, a short walk from the marina, and by the time I arrived, my spirits had risen and I was darn close to one hundred percent awake.

In many places, hardware stores were closed on Sundays or opened late. In Chilson, as in many other northern resort towns, businesses had one hundred days to make money, more or less Memorial Day through Labor Day. Being closed on any one of those days was close to unthinkable. And here it was, barely eight o'clock on the fifth of July, and the hardware store was so crowded and noisy that I barely heard the door's bells jingle as I went inside.

I picked up a big box of number seven by two-inch drywall screws, walked away, went back for another box, then headed up to the counter, where a small group of men I didn't recognize clustered together. Not long ago I'd been intimidated by hardware stores, but thanks to Rafe's constant need for fasteners—a catch-all term I'd formerly made fun of, but now accepted as part of the construction vocabulary—I was on a first-name basis with the hardware store owner and his staff.

"Hey, Minnie." Jared, the owner, took the boxes and put them into the bag. "Sure you got enough?"

"I got double what he asked, so maybe."

"On the account?"

When I nodded, he started typing into the keyboard. Rafe and I needed to have a serious chat about money and construction costs and mortgages, but every time I brought up the subject, he diverted the conversation. It had to be soon, though, because I wasn't moving in until we were both happy with the financial situation.

"Probably one of those random killings. Bet it wasn't anyone from around here," a man to the left of me said, and I realized the male cluster was talking about last night's murder.

I shook my head, trying to wish away the image of Rex Stuhler's unseeing eyes.

"Downstater. Had to be." Luke Cagan, one of Jared's part-time employees, leaned against the counter, crossing his arms, which were covered with thick blond hairs.

The rest of the men nodded agreement and their cluster dispersed.

But I stood there, staring at the space where they'd been, because up until that moment my brain had been more occupied with the shock and aftermath of Katrina literally tripping over a murder victim. Up until now, I hadn't thought about the obvious implications.

Who, indeed, had killed Rex Stuhler?

Why had someone killed Rex?

And would that someone kill again?

I delivered the screws to Rafe, who accepted the double delivery without batting an eye, and looked around for an out-of-the-way place to sit. Rafe and a friend of his were installing drywall on the basement ceiling and there wasn't a role for me, other than having my phone at the ready to call 911.

Yes, I could have tried to be useful, but the couple of times I had done so during drywall work, things hadn't ended up well for me, Rafe, or the drywall. I could do other things, though, especially when it was a benefit to be efficiently sized. A five-foot-tall body fit far better into an attic space for placing insulation, for instance, and my compact-size fingers were much better than Rafe's big ones for installing tiny pieces of trim.

I spotted an upside down plastic five-gallon bucket that had once held paint, carried it near the work area, and sat on my new stool.

Rafe glanced at me through his upraised arms. "How's Katrina?"

"Asleep," I said. "At least she was when I left."

"She seemed pretty shaken up last night."

"Who's Katrina?" Bob asked. "Is she hot? And single?"

I wasn't sure exactly how Rafe knew Bob, but if I asked, I'd get a long story that may or may not have provided a real answer, so I imagined a story about a late blizzard and a lost puppy, which was almost certainly a much better explanation than reality.

"She's seventeen." Rafe pulled his screw gun from his tool belt.

"And my niece," I said over the noise of drywall screws being screwed in tightly.

Bob gave a heavy sigh, which fluttered his thick, dark blond beard. "So my bad luck is holding."

"Right now it's more important that you hold up your end of the drywall," Rafe said, installing screws faster than I would have thought possible for a guy who wasn't a professional contractor.

As I watched them work and listened to them banter, I thought about the other revelation I'd had last night, the one from my sister-in-law. My brother had gone to bed, but Jennifer and I had talked a little longer, and one of her questions had come across as so odd that I'd pursued it.

"Is Katrina acting . . . secretive?" she'd asked.

I'd been puzzled by the question. And curious

as to the reason behind it. "Why do you ask?"

Jennifer hemmed and hawed and eventually said, "Well, there was this boy . . ."

And so I learned that the reason behind my niece coming north had almost as much to do with her parents wanting distance between their eldest daughter and her erstwhile boyfriend as it did with aunt-niece bonding and summer employment.

Jennifer had sighed. "We should have told you, I know we should have, but somehow . . . somehow it never came up."

Last night I'd been too tired and emotionally fraught to deal with family drama, but now that I was awake and chipper, I was taking it out and looking at it.

Yes, they absolutely should have told me. So how was I going to react?

After thinking for a bit, I decided not to react at all. I'd gone through a few rounds of bad judgment myself, and since I wasn't a parent, my viewpoint of appropriate parental action was bound to be skewed. But now what did I do? Did I tell Katrina that her parents had told me about The Boy? Or did she assume I already knew?

I stood, still having no idea what my next steps should be, niece-wise.

"Headed out?" Rafe asked.

"Much as I'd like to sit here and watch other people work, I have a niece to tend to."

43

"Say 'hey' for me. She had a rough night."

I sent a kiss in his direction and left them to it.

Outside, the sky was starting to cloud up. I sent the sun and sky a fervent wish to stay strong and walked the two hundred feet to the marina. My tiny houseboat shared a short pier with a large Crown powerboat owned by Eric Apney, a forty-ish divorced downstater who made his living as a cardiac surgeon. He was an excellent neighbor, quiet and conscientious about following marina etiquette, and was sitting on his deck with a cup of coffee and a newspaper.

"Morning, Minnie," he said. "Been out running?"

"Sort of." I explained about the screw delivery, and he looked interested. There was something about other people's renovation projects that got a certain slice of the population to volunteer their time, sort of a small-scale version of the classic Amish barn-raising.

"Ceiling work?" Eric settled back into his chair. "Maybe I'll go up after lunch."

I grinned. Which was when Rafe and Bob would be done.

"Want some?" Eric gestured with his mug.

Since I hadn't had any caffeine in almost twenty hours, of course I did, but I tried not to look too eager. "Sure. That'd be great."

He got to his feet and went into the cabin, and I stepped aboard. The view from Eric's taller

"Sure." Holly's husband, Brian, a strapping man who towered over me when sitting, let alone standing, slid over and patted the seat beside him. "Make some space for Miss Minnie, Anna. You too, Wilson."

Anna, aged seven, and Wilson, a year older, were miniature versions of their parents. They obligingly made room and I fetched Katrina. Holly had already met her, but Brian and the kids hadn't, so I introduced her saying, "This is Katrina, my niece from Florida and—"

"Kate," Katrina said.

I blinked. I'd completely forgotten about last night's name change. "Sorry. Kate." I made the Terpening introductions, forgoing the description of Brian's mining job out west, which meant he was gone three weeks out of four, and instead told Anna and Wilson that Kate's dad worked at Disney World.

Anna's eyes went wide. "Does he get to ride the rides every day?"

Kate shrugged. "If he wanted to, I guess."

"Do *you* get to ride the rides every day?"

My niece shook her head. "I have school and stuff. But we used to go a lot when I was little."

Wilson started asking questions about Mickey Mouse, and I leaned behind him to look at Holly. "Did you hear about last night?" I asked quietly. "About Rex Stuhler?"

Holly nodded. "I heard a tourist found him.

What a horrible thing to happen on your vacation."

"It was Kate." I glanced at my niece. "We were leaving the fireworks and she literally tripped over him."

Holly's mouth opened, and at first no sound came out. Her jaw went up and down a couple of times before she could say, "The poor girl." She sent a soft, sympathetic Mom look in Katrina's direction. "Is she okay?"

Was she? I had no idea, not really. She seemed fine, but how could I possibly know for sure?

"Menus." Carol, our waitress for the meal, put two on the table. "Not that you need one," she said, glancing at me. "I'll bring you coffee. What would you like to drink, miss?"

Katrina/Kate tucked her chin toward her chest. "Coffee, please," she muttered.

I smiled. "Nicely done. I'll have you in espresso by the end of the summer."

"It's just I'm tired," she said. "I didn't get much sleep last night."

"How come, Kate?" Anna asked. "Was it too noisy with fireworks? Our dog doesn't like them at all."

Kate shrugged. "No, I was having night . . ." She stopped, looked at Anna's open, interested face, and said, "Having silly dreams."

I desperately wanted to put my arms around her and tell her it would all be okay. There she

48

was, being nice to a child she'd just met, keeping her pain inside, while I'd mostly been wondering why she wasn't talking to me.

But of course she wasn't. She barely knew me. Why on earth would she confide in an aunt she saw once or twice a year? And if she was suffering from a boyfriend breakup, that was one less person she could rely upon. Jennifer had said that Katrina/Kate had numerous friends, but not really a best friend. So who was she talking to?

Maybe no one. And that couldn't be good.

Katrina sighed and rubbed her eyes. "Hope that coffee comes soon. I'm still pretty tired."

I glanced at the Terpenings, and saw that the foursome was focused on the breakfast-or-lunch decision. Leaning forward, toward Katrina/Kate, I put my hands on the table. "Kate," I said softly, "I know how you feel. About finding . . . a body."

"Doubt it," she said stiffly.

I hitched a little closer. "It has happened to me." More than once. "Your dad doesn't know, and neither does your mom or grandparents." Mostly because I didn't want to deal with what would surely have been my mom's overreaction. "But Aunt Frances does."

"Yeah?" Kate looked me full in the face. "How long did it take for the nightmares to stop?"

"Honest truth?" I asked. She nodded, but I hesitated, not wanting to tell her that I still occasionally woke shouting out for help, still sometimes sat straight up in the middle of the night with my heart beating too fast.

"It gets easier," I finally said, "when the killer is arrested and put in jail."

"In jail?" she asked, staring at the table. "You know, that might help." She spoke with, if not animation, at least interest. "If that guy was in jail, I bet I could sleep. I mean, right now, he's still out there, when Mr. Stuhler is dead. If the killer was in jail, that'd be a sort of closure, right?"

"Sure," I said.

Kate looked at me. "How long did it take to arrest the killer?"

That depended on which murder she was talking about. "We found out—"

My niece cut right into that. "What do you mean 'we'?"

Uh-oh. "Well . . ." I stared at her questioning face, trying to form the appropriate words. "Um."

"Did you help the police? I bet you did." She leaned forward, talking fast. "You know the sheriff, don't you? And that really cute deputy? You know all of them. And I bet you looked into that murder yourself and helped put the killer in jail."

I patted her hands and smiled. "Not if you ask Detective Inwood."

"You're not denying, which means you did." Kate almost glowed. "You helped out with a murder investigation and got your own closure. The best ever kind of being proactive."

Um. "That's one way to look at it."

Kate grabbed my hands. "So help me get my closure. You'll help that detective and figure out who killed Mr. Stuhler and . . . and . . ." She blew out a fluttery breath. "And then I'll be okay to go to sleep again."

I held her hands tight, because her face was two shades paler than it had been yesterday afternoon, because her fingers were trembling, and because she was biting her lower lip to keep from crying.

"Absolutely," I said.

CHAPTER 3

The next morning, the first morning of Katrina's life as a retail clerk, I bounced out of bed early enough to get us a proper breakfast of doughnuts and bagels from Tom's, the local bakery. Tom, who had to be the skinniest baker in the history of the world, had a soft spot for the bookmobile and not only gave me a reduced rate on the bag of cookies I picked up every bookmobile day, but in the summer also let me in the back door so I didn't have to stand in line.

Being the morally upright person I aspired to be, that morning I stood in line like everyone else, and made friends with the people on either side of me. We'd reached the Facebook friend stage and were approaching an exchange of cell numbers when it was my turn at the counter. Five minutes later, I had a bright pink bag in hand, waved good-bye to my new friends, and hurried home.

When I got back to the houseboat, Katrina was in the shower, using far more water than I would have liked. I went all out and put the breakfast options on a plate and even found napkins that didn't have a restaurant name on them. Eddie had nestled himself into Katrina's sleeping bag, but when I removed the clear plastic lid from the cream cheese, he opened his eyes a small sliver.

"Not for you, pal," I said.

Katrina's hair dryer went on. Eddie's eyes flipped wide open. In one sudden motion, he leapt to his feet, off the sleeping bag, and onto the floor, where his scrambling feet found purchase on a small rug. The rug crinkled up under him, and for a second he looked like a cartoon cat, feet moving furiously without forward motion. Then his paws hit the floor and he shot forward like a rocket.

Of course, since it was the houseboat, he couldn't go very far, but he did go as far forward as possible; up on the dashboard, pressed against the windshield, back arched, fur fluffed, and growling the teensiest bit.

I looked at him. "I suppose you don't want me laughing at you?" Hair dryers did not pair well with my curly mass, and the boardinghouse was big enough that he'd been able to hide from the noise of Aunt Frances's morning routine, so Eddie had never dealt with up close and personal exposure to the evil things.

"Mrr!"

"Right." I padded up to him and scratched the side of his head, murmuring soothing phrases like "You're the best cat this houseboat has ever seen, she didn't mean to scare you, she doesn't know hair dryers are the enemy, you'll get used to it, I'm sure you will."

His fur soon de-fluffed and the two of us were sitting outside on the houseboat's deck, soaking up the morning sun, when Katrina came out, a glazed doughnut in one hand and a naked bagel in the other. "See you tonight," she said. "Not sure when I'll be back."

"You're leaving already?" I tried to sit up from the chaise lounge, but Eddie was making it difficult. "I didn't think you had to be there much before ten."

After breakfast yesterday, I'd sat down with Katrina/Kate and essentially forced her to write down her work schedule. Which was complicated, what with three part-time jobs and all, but after a while I started to see the pattern. We'd spent the rest of the day in mild accord and I'd been looking forward to chatting with her over breakfast, just like Aunt Frances and I did during the winter.

"Mitchell texted me and said I could come in earlier." Katrina shrugged. "Not sure I need to learn much more about toys, but I'm awake so I might as well go in." Then, before I could say another word, she'd hopped off the boat, onto the wood-decked pier, and was gone.

I looked at Eddie. "Now what?"

He jumped off my lap, pawed open the screen door to the houseboat—something I had no idea he was able to do—and slipped inside.

"Well." I stretched and stood. My intentions when I'd scheduled this as a vacation day had been to spend time with Katrina, but now that she was working, the day was empty of plans. I pushed away the temptation of my To Be Read book pile, wandered inside, and put the remaining parts of breakfast back into the waxed bag.

Five minutes later, Rafe had scarfed down a chocolate-covered doughnut and was slathering cream cheese on a pumpernickel bagel. "How is the teenager formerly known as Katrina doing this morning?"

"Still not talking about it. But she's not sleeping well." About three in the morning, her sobbing had pulled me out of a deep sleep. I'd gone up to talk to her, to give her a hug, to make it all go away, but she'd been snoring softly by the time I got there.

I hesitated, wanting to tell him everything, but also wanting to protect my niece's privacy. "Last night she had bad dreams and I'm sure they're related to the murder. She slept fine until two nights ago."

"What are you going to do?" Rafe asked through a mouthful of bagel.

Easy question. "Find out who killed Rex Stuhler."

Rafe swallowed and grinned, his teeth white against his tanned skin. "Surprised it took you this long to say that out loud. Want some help?"

"Depends," I said. "Will it be the good kind of help or the interfering kind?"

"Whatever kind you want." He held out his hand to seal the deal with a handshake, then pulled it back. "On the condition that you talk to your sheriff buddy, or at least your detective friends."

My buddy the sheriff was Kit Richardson,

a woman who seemed to intimidate almost everyone except me. At five foot nothing, I'd inured myself to intimidation early on in my career, otherwise I'd never have managed to achieve any professional goals. My detective friends were Hal Inwood, a sixtyish downstate transplant, and Deputy Ash Wolverson. Ash was a friend of Rafe's and was training to be a detective. I'd also dated him for a few months, but our relationship had never truly kindled and we'd parted as we'd started—friends.

"Deal." I extended my hand and Rafe used it to pull me in for a kiss. Which was nice, and went on for some time. But even good things come to an end, and when we eventually went back to the pastries, I told Rafe what little I knew about Rex Stuhler.

"He and his wife own a pest control company." I swallowed a bite of apple fritter. "He was about fifty, and he grew up around here somewhere, but I don't think it was Chilson. Petoskey, maybe?"

Rafe reached into the pink bag and pulled out a powdered doughnut. "All that will be in his obituary. It might be on Birtrand's website already."

The local funeral home was a few blocks away. I glanced in its direction. "Really? I didn't know obituaries would go up so fast."

"Sometimes yes, sometimes no. Depends on the family."

I frowned. "How do you know this?"

"Because I grew up next door to Birtrand's. I know more about being a mortician than anyone who isn't in the business should."

The idea creeped me out a little, so I nodded and went on. "The only other thing I know about Rex is he was big into bicycling and cross-country skiing. He'd been looking for books about establishing and running nonprofit organizations. He said he was helping create a group supporting a new nonmotorized trail connecting Chilson to Petoskey."

Rafe looked down at his dark gray T-shirt, which was lightly dusted with powdered sugar. He gave it a halfhearted brush, smearing the white, and said, "None of that sounds like it should have led to murder."

I sighed. "No, it doesn't."

But something had, and my niece was suffering, so I was going to do my best to figure out who had killed Rex. And a good start to doing that was to figure out the why of it.

I stepped inside the front door of the sheriff's office and looked around at the lobby. Empty. Was I the only one who ever walked in like this?

The deputy at the front desk slid open the glass door. "Morning, Minnie."

"Hey, Carl. Still on light duty?"

Carl rubbed his shoulder. "Had to have a third surgery a few weeks ago. If this one doesn't take,

I'm toast. This desk stuff is driving me nuts." He shook his head, then summoned a smile. "So what's up with you? Hang on," he said, tapping his nose. "You were with the kid who found the murder victim during the fireworks. You want to talk to Hal and Ash?"

I nodded. "Are they here?"

"Inwood's out on a call, but Ash is in the back. Just a sec." He slid the window shut and picked up the phone. I could see his mouth moving, then, still on the phone, he opened the window. "Go on back, he'll be right there."

The interior door made a buzzing sound and I reached for the handle. "Thanks," I called over my shoulder, and walked down the hallway. I made a right turn into a small windowless room and sat in what I'd long ago come to think of as my chair, in front of a bland laminate-topped table that looked like it had been born in a decade when every man except members of the military sported long hair.

I looked at the ceiling tiles, which for years had been discolored with a water stain that, to me, looked exactly like a dragon. Last fall, however, due to a leak in the fire suppression system, all the tiles had been replaced and the dragon was a thing of the past.

Ash came in, saw me looking up, and laughed. "The ceiling isn't as much fun now, is it?"

Sighing, I said, "Hard to believe I'm missing a stain."

"Yeah, sometimes you have to be careful what you wish for."

More like always. "Thanks for making time for me," I said.

"No problem."

He leaned back, and once again I was reminded what an incredibly good-looking man he was. Square jaw, great hair, and the legs of someone who spent his free time running and biking. He was also kind, smart, and funny. Why our short stint of being girlfriend and boyfriend hadn't sparked was a mystery we'd both shrugged off to the bizarreness of human chemistry.

"Have you or Kate remembered anything else from the other night?" he asked.

I looked at him blankly. Kate? Who was Kate? Oh. Right. "No. At least not yet." In the last couple of years I'd been entwined with a number of incidents that had introduced me to police investigations. One of the things I'd learned was that most people's memories worked like mine did, like a filing cabinet that didn't have folders, wasn't organized in any way, and had one big label of miscellaneous.

"Do you have anything new?" I asked. Then, because I knew I was about to get the can't-discuss-an-ongoing-investigation talk, added, "Anything that you can tell me about?"

"Well." Ash rubbed his chin, roughing the stubble. For me that noise was equivalent to the proverbial fingernails on a chalkboard, so maybe the answer to our nonspark was simpler and far more shallow than I wanted to think.

He gave his chin one last rub. "There's one thing I could tell you, because it happened in public. The afternoon and night of the Fourth, Rex Stuhler and his wife, Fawn, were on Janay Lake with friends. On a big pontoon boat. You know that parking lot where the city is letting food trucks park? Well, someone from the boat placed a food order and they dropped Rex off so he could pick it up. Only he never got there."

"This was during the fireworks?"

"The order was sent in about an hour before. But Rex sent a text to his wife that the food truck was backed up, and that he was going to walk around for a bit. That he'd let them know when he picked up the food, so no one thought too much about how late he was."

The implication was clear. "So Rex's wife—what was her name, Fawn?—was on the boat and didn't murder him."

"That's the way it looks."

I grinned. "Spoken like a true law enforcement officer. Reassuring, yet leaving your options open. You sure you don't want to go into politics?" An odd expression came and went on his face so quickly it took me a second to interpret.

My smile went even wider. "You're thinking about sheriff, aren't you?"

"Shh!" He made frantic quiet-down motions with his hands. "Don't say that out loud! Sheriff Richardson is a long way from retiring."

I stood. "Your secret is safe with me. And for the record, I think you'd make a great elected law enforcement official."

He gave me a pained look, which made me laugh, and smiling, I headed back outside.

The sheriff's office was just up the street from Chilson's main downtown blocks. I stood there for a moment, considering my options. I could drop into the toy store to see how Katrina—Kate—was doing, but there were two drawbacks to that. One, it would annoy her, and two, now that it was late morning, the sidewalks were packed with tourists.

Tourism was a critical part of the Up North economy, and I appreciated every dollar they spent in our town, but there were days that I just plain didn't feel like elbowing through the crowds, and today was one of them. So I headed up the hill to the boardinghouse, tracing a path I'd walked many times before, a path I would probably walk less and less in the future.

This made me sad, and I decided not to think about how life changes were never one hundred percent positive, that even changes you desperately wanted came along with things you'd miss. Instead I focused on how I was going to get into the boardinghouse without being seen by Aunt

Frances, who now lived right across the street.

Not that it *really* mattered if she saw me, of course. She was a reasonable adult, and if I wanted to stop by the boardinghouse she'd run by herself for decades, there was no reason to assume that if she caught me going in she'd buttonhole me afterward, quiz me on what I'd seen and heard, ask what was different, and roll her eyes at the answers.

Then again, that was pretty much what she'd done the last time I'd popped in to say hello to Cousin Celeste. If I'd been thinking ahead, I would have contacted Otto and asked him to get my aunt into the kitchen, where she couldn't see the street, or even better, out of the house altogether.

But I hadn't, and it was too late now, so I squared my shoulders and prepared myself for the doom that could soon await me.

I climbed the boardinghouse steps and onto the wide wooden porch. A swing at the far end swayed lightly. It was a bit ghostly, but then I saw the newspaper open on the swing's seat.

"Well, hello there, Minnie honey." Cousin Celeste popped out the front door. "How are you?" She nodded at the tray of drinks and cookies she was carrying. "It's like I knew you were coming. Have a sit."

"Um." I glanced over my shoulder at Otto and my aunt's house. "Have you seen Aunt Frances this morning?"

"She and Otto left about an hour ago on a tandem bicycle after loading what looked like a dandy picnic." Celeste set the metal Coca-Cola tray on a small table and sat in the swing, patting the seat next to her. "Now sit."

Feeling slightly disloyal, I lowered myself as Celeste handed me a glass filled with water, ice, blueberries, and strawberries. I took it, feeling a pang of loss for the lemonade my aunt had always served on the porch, but as soon as the berried water went down my throat, I forgot all about it. "This is wonderful!"

Celeste beamed, crinkling her weathered face into tiny wrinkles. Her long gray hair was tidied up in a braid that she'd rolled into a bun and secured with magic. Sitting or standing, we looked each other straight in the eye. It was immensely refreshing to know I wasn't the only person in our extended family who didn't have an excessive amount of height.

"Thought you'd like it." Celeste nodded decisively. "The guests can't get enough. After all, they've never been here and they don't know Frances used to serve lemonade."

Some might, if they read the scrapbooks from previous years, and sometimes the children of previous boarders came up to stay, but I kept drinking to avoid a response.

"I hear you were mixed up with that sad

business at the waterfront the night of the fireworks," Celeste said.

"Only peripherally." I told her what had happened.

"That poor girl!" Celeste put a hand to her throat. "Is she going back home?"

"She started working at the toy store this morning, so not today anyway."

Celeste smiled. "Ah, the resiliency of youth. Do the police know who killed that poor man?"

"They're working on it."

"Well, I'm sure they'll figure it out soon," she said comfortably.

For a moment we swung gently to and fro, then Celeste sighed. "Minnie, your aunt is a wonderful woman, but I need to talk to someone about her and I don't know where else to turn."

I'd known this was coming. It was, in fact, why I'd walked up here, when I would rather have returned to the houseboat and spent the rest of the morning reading. I half smiled. "Aunt Frances is driving you nuts, isn't she?"

"And how," Celeste said fervently. "I thought we had an agreement. She said she'd be hands off, that this place was mine to run and that whatever I wanted to do was fine by her, and that she wouldn't say a word about how I was running the boardinghouse." She stopped. "Well, I suppose that's true in fact. She hasn't *said* anything, but she stops and gives me that look. You know the one."

64

I did indeed. My aunt was an imposing figure, and not just because of her height. Years of teaching community college woodworking to classes of young men who thought they knew more than she had given her the ability to quell an unruly mob with a single glance.

"And she's sending me text messages." Celeste offered me a plate of butterscotch cookies. "Reminding me about things I've already done. I'm being polite as I can, but I'm afraid it's going to get worse."

I made sympathetic noises around bits of cookie, and braced myself for what was sure to come next.

"Minnie, I hate to ask, but can you talk to her?" Celeste turned, beseeching me with her light blue eyes. "Please?"

And there it was.

On the outside I smiled. On the inside I heaved a huge sigh. "I'll do what I can," I said.

"Thank you!" Celeste lunged at me and gave me a hug. "Thank you so much! I'm no good at confrontation. I know you'll straighten this out in no time."

"No problem," I murmured, as I wondered how in little green apples I was going to make both Celeste and my aunt happy.

Donna, one of the library's part-time clerks, frowned from behind the front desk. "What are you doing here?"

I looked around. "Are you talking to me?"

"Do you see anyone else?" she asked dryly.

The lobby, entry, and main room of the library were quiet and, except for the two of us, completely empty. A low patron count was normal on nice summer days, but this was a little ridiculous. And a bit eerie. Then I heard the distant voice of a child and an adult murmuring in reply, and relaxed. The zombie apocalypse had not overtaken the Chilson District Library and swooped away all our library-goers.

"So again I ask," Donna said, putting her elbows on the counter and her chin in her hands. "What are you doing here? You took the day off. So take yourself outside and go play."

I grinned. Donna was in her early seventies and had already retired from a full-time job. She had children and grandchildren and a husband who was within a year of retiring from his much-loved job as the local barber.

Donna was also an active long-distance runner, and the primary reason she worked at the library was to help fund trips to run marathons in faraway places. And for Donna, far away meant Norway, Ethiopia, and Argentina. And the trips weren't just to run. Last winter she'd traveled to Antarctica, and she and her equally adventurous daughter had enjoyed themselves immensely.

"Couldn't stay away," I said, spreading my arms. "I mean, look at this place."

The building around us had once upon a time been Chilson's elementary school. The town's young demographic had eventually expanded to the point where a new, larger building had been necessary and this handsome L-shaped brick building, filled with Craftsman details, had been shuttered.

For years it sat empty, deteriorating slowly but surely, and then, just before the roof collapsed, the library board put a bond proposal on the ballot to renovate the building. The people of Chilson had overwhelmingly voted in favor, and the school was transformed into a stupendously gorgeous library that was the envy of all.

Well, maybe not all. I'd heard the Library of Congress had a decent space. But what other small town library had a reading room with a fireplace and window seats? What other library had a vaulted ceiling over the main stacks? Who else had gorgeous metallic tile in the restrooms and lobby?

"It is nice," Donna said. "But it's nice outside, too." She tipped her head toward the massive oak front doors. "And while this building will stay nice, out there could change in the next five minutes."

"The Wi-Fi at the marina is painfully slow," I said. "I'm just here to look something up."

"Research? Ooo, let me play, please?"

I looked at her and decided I might as well get it over with. So I told her about the night of

67

the fireworks, and Rex Stuhler, how Katrina—
Kate—was having a rough time of it, and how
I was going to do my best to help track down
whoever killed Rex.

"The poor girl," Donna said sympathetically.
"But at least she has you. How many other aunts
have also found murder victims? You two could
create your own support group."

My penchant for finding dead bodies was not
something I wanted to discuss at length with
Kate, but I half nodded. "I was going to look on
the county's website to see where Rex and his
wife live."

"Foundation research. Good idea." Donna
rotated her large monitor so I could see, pulled out
her keyboard, and started typing. "Tonedagana
County, parcel search . . ." She clicked away.
"Do you know what township? Never mind, there
can't be many Stuhlers . . . okay, here we go.
'Owners Rex and Fawn Stuhler,' " Donna read
out loud. "So that's their property." She pointed
at a yellow rectangle on Ayers Road. "Let's see
what we can find out about the neighbors. If
they're people I know, I can ask about Rex."

A few clicks later, we learned that the parcels
to the west and south of the Stuhlers were
owned by the county. "Forestry parcels, is my
guess," Donna said. "The county forester sets
up parcels to get logged off every thirty years or
so. Makes the county a little money, and wow,

would you look at that?" She'd turned on the aerial photography layer, and the Stuhlers' roof practically popped us in the eyeballs. "That's a bright red roof."

It certainly was. "Who owns that?" I nodded at a smaller parcel to the north.

"Hang on . . . here we go. Somebody named Vannett. First name 'Barry.' "

"Do you know him?" I asked. Except for a short stint at college, Donna had never lived anywhere but Chilson. If she didn't know someone, or at least know of them, odds were approximately a hundred percent they weren't from here.

"Nope." She drummed her fingers on the countertop. "But the name sounds familiar. Let me think."

Meanwhile, something was twitching inside my own brain. "Hang on," I said slowly. "Isn't Ayers Road part of the route for that new bike trail?"

Donna shrugged. "I haven't been paying close attention. If it ever gets built, I'll be long gone. Those things take forever."

I asked Donna to let me know if she remembered anything about Barry Vannett, then wandered out into the sunshine, wondering who might know about the trail. All I knew was from the newspaper, which had reported that a group of local folks had banded together to plan a route connecting Chilson to Petoskey via back roads and county-owned property. I could talk to my friend Camille at the paper, but what I wanted was insider information.

"Got it," I said, making a 180-degree turn and marching the other way. I was on nodding-acquaintance terms with Jeremy Hull, director of the nonprofit Northern Lakes Protection Association. If Jeremy didn't have information on the trail, he was bound to know someone who did.

I entered the blue lobby of the Protection Association's office and saw Jeremy and his wife sitting together at his desk, picking apart the delectable treat that was an elephant ear, that classic deep-fried, cinnamon-sprinkled doughy goodness.

"Hey, Minnie." Jeremy waved a piece of ear at me. "You've met my wife, haven't you? Honey, Minnie Hamilton, the bookmobile librarian. Minnie, this is my wife, Honey Hull."

Honey and I murmured nice-to-meet-you's and Jeremy asked, "Don't suppose you're here to make a sizable donation to our new project. We're raising money to rework that undersized culvert on the Mitchell River."

"Sorry," I said, pulling the pockets of my shorts inside out. "Nothing here. I just stopped by to ask if you knew anything about that new trail they're proposing, the one that would connect Chilson to Petoskey . . ."

Jeremy was shaking his head. "I don't, but—"

"But I do." Honey smiled. "I'm on the planning

committee. If you'd like to help, we're holding a meeting next week."

"Um." I shifted from one foot to the other. I'd hit the jackpot! Too bad I didn't have a good explanation of what I wanted! "It's about Rex Stuhler. My niece is the one who found him the other night, and . . ." And what? But I needn't have worried.

Honey's face flushed a fast red. "That poor girl. But I knew something like this would happen, I just knew it. Rex didn't take him seriously, though. Fawn laughed it off, too. The whole thing makes me want to—" She broke off and covered her face with her hands.

Jeremy reached out to comfort his wife. "It'll be okay," he said.

"No, it won't," she choked out through sobs. "Rex is dead. It'll never be okay for him or for Fawn. And if they don't arrest Barry Vannett, then something is seriously wrong with the universe."

I inched closer. "Why would Barry Vannett be involved?"

Honey looked up. Tears streamed down her face, but she made no move to wipe them away. "Because," she spat out, "when Rex talked to Barry about an easement for the trail, Barry threatened him. Told Rex to get off his property, that the red roof had been the first sign of bad judgment, and that if he ever tried to get a trail across his farm again, he'd get a face full of shotgun."

CHAPTER 4

Rafe, Katrina, and I were eating together in the dining room. Which sounds grander than it was, because we were at a table of plywood plopped on top of sawhorses and eating sandwiches from Fat Boys Pizza accompanied by a side order of bread sticks with garlic cream cheese for dipping. The bread sticks were a request of my niece's, and I was pretty sure I was going to gain five pounds this summer due to a complete inability to stay away from the delicious little buggers.

"So, Kate, how was it working with Mitchell today?" Rafe asked.

Though Rafe had already switched from Katrina to Kate, I was having a harder time. I hadn't used the name on her birth certificate out loud all day, which I was considering a victory, but I was still translating in my head. I was also still having a hard time with Mitchell Koyne as anyone's boss, let alone my niece's.

Until last year, Mitchell had been one of those laid-back Up North guys who switched jobs with the seasons. Construction in the summer, snow plowing and ski resort work in the winter, and making do in the shoulder seasons by hauling firewood and setting and removing docks.

Though he was smart enough (in a goofy

72

Mitchell sort of way), his brains hadn't been accompanied by a single ounce of ambition. But then he'd started dating Bianca Sims. No one, including me, had thought the relationship would turn into anything serious. How could the energetic and ambitious Bianca, one of the area's most successful real estate agents, see anything in slacker Mitchell, even if he was suddenly waking up to the fact that he could have a career?

Kate reached for a napkin and wiped cream cheese off her mouth. "He seems nice. And his wife came in and introduced herself."

Yes, Bianca Sims was now Bianca Koyne, and had been for almost six months. They'd been married by the local magistrate, and the ceremony had been followed by a noisy, crowded party at the bowling alley.

"Were things busy?" I'd heard from the owner that the toy store had substantially increased its profits since Mitchell had taken over as manager. Truly, wonders never ceased.

Kate rolled her eyes. "It's my first day. How would I know?"

She had a point, but the eye thing seemed unnecessary. I shut away memories of my own teenage eye movements and tried to think of a question that couldn't possibly be answered by a gesture I was starting to despise.

We ate in silence for a few moments. How could conversation with a teenager be so hard?

Weren't teen girls supposed to talk all the time? Not that I had, but I'd always known I was different.

"Did you stop at the sheriff's office?" Rafe asked.

Katrina flinched, dropping a messy slice of tomato onto the plywood.

I handed her a fork, but she ignored it and used her fingers to tuck the red squashiness back between the layers of lettuce and turkey. "Yes," I said. "Hal wasn't there, but I talked to Ash." Even as I said the words, I realized I hadn't done what Rafe asked me to, namely let the sheriff's office know that I wanted to help find the killer. Huh. Well, I'd have to fix that later.

"He didn't have much time to talk," I said. "But he did tell me Rex and his wife, Fawn, were out on a boat almost all day on the Fourth, and most of the night." I explained about the food truck order. "Fawn was on the boat the entire time," I said, "so she's out as a murder suspect."

"What if she hired someone?" Katrina asked. When Rafe and I looked at her, she added impatiently, "To kill her husband. What if she paid someone to have it done?"

I dared not look at Rafe for fear the laughter that was bubbling up inside of me would escape, thereby damaging the tentative relationship with my niece. "Um," I said, but couldn't figure out what next to say.

Rafe reached down, grabbed yesterday's edition of the *Chilson Gazette*, opened it to the back pages, and shook his head. "Nope. Don't see anything under 'ASSASSIN.' But it's summer, maybe they're booked up like everybody else and aren't wasting money on advertising during the busy season."

Smothering a snort, I said, "Kate, no matter what they show in movies, I don't think it's easy to hire a killer. Especially in rural areas."

"I'm not saying it would be easy," she said loudly. "I'm just saying it's a theory and the police should take it into account." She stood. "You're not taking me seriously and that's crap. My opinion should matter just as much as anyone else's. More, because I'm the one who—"

Her voice broke. With a shuddering intake of breath, she rushed out of the room and into the foyer, where we could track her location by a slammed front door and the sound of her sandals flip-flopping down the steps.

I started to stand, but Rafe waved me to sit. "She needs a few minutes. Finish eating and then go after her."

Half up, I thought his advice through, decided he was right, and sat back down. "I'm really glad you're our middle school principal. You understand kids better than any adult I've ever known." I watched as he used the end of a breadstick to make a smiley face in the cream cheese. "Of course," I said, "it's likely you find kids so easy to understand because you never grew up yourself."

Rafe put a hand on his chest. "You hurt me, Minnie, you truly do."

As if. "I haven't looked for Rex's obituary yet. Did you?"

"Not up yet. So did you tell Ash you want to help with the investigation?"

"Speaking of the investigation," I said, "I found something interesting about Rex and Fawn's neighbor, Barry Vannett." It didn't take long for me to explain the proposed trail, Rex's involvement, the odd comment about a roof, and the threat Vannett had made.

Rafe looked at me over the top of his sandwich. "Don't think I didn't notice you didn't answer my question about telling Ash you want to help with the investigation." I was still working through all the negatives he'd used when he added, "So I'm going to guess you didn't tell Ash what you learned about Barry Vannett, either."

"Not yet," I said. "I will, though. Tomorrow morning on the way in to the library."

Rafe waved a bread stick at me. "If you don't, I'll have to, and you know how that will end up."

I did. With Rafe hanging out at the sheriff's office for half a day, not getting anything done at the house, which would make him cranky as all get-out.

"Promise," I said, and leaned over to give him a light kiss.

Then I went after my niece.

It had been easy to find Kate, as she'd gone back to the houseboat, let Eddie out, and flopped on one of the two lounges on the deck. Eddie had jumped onto the other lounge and I'd silently picked him up and sat down with him on my lap.

At first he didn't want to stay there, but I kept petting him and he eventually started purring and his muscles relaxed to the point where his body started to conform to the shape of my legs.

I was thinking various tumbling thoughts, about Kate and Rafe and the house and Eddie and the bookmobile and Mitchell and the library the next day and Rex and Fawn and Barry Vannett, when Kate sat up. "There's a movie theater downtown, right? Can we go?"

So of course we went, making the seven o'clock movie by the skin of our teeth, then since the other movie at the two-screen theater also looked good, we went to the nine o'clock showing, too. Kate and I strolled home the long way, talking about the movies, about other movies we'd seen, about movies we'd like to see, and we'd continued talking once we got back to the houseboat.

Which was why, when I woke up the following morning, I stared blearily at my alarm clock, then was instantly awake and throwing back the covers.

"Mrr!"

"Sorry, pal." I gave Eddie an apologetic pat on the head. "Kate!" I called. "Wake up, it's late!" I hurried into the bathroom, took the shortest shower in the history of Minnie showers, and was dressed and toweling my hair by the time Kate extracted herself from her sleeping bag.

"Why did you let me sleep so late?" she wailed, stomping into the bathroom, where her complaints came through the thin door. "It's my first day at Older Than Dirt. Pam will fire me if I'm late, I know it. She looks mean, I wasn't sure I even wanted to take the job, and now I'm going to be late!"

If she stopped yelling at me and focused on getting ready, she wouldn't be late at all, but I kept my mouth shut and opened the bag of leftover bagels.

Kate stormed out of the bathroom, tossed her pajamas onto her sleeping bag, snatched up her purse, and stomped out, completely ignoring my apologies and the cream cheese bagel I was holding out for her.

Eddie bumped his head against the back of my knee. "Mrr."

"Yeah, I love you, too. And I'd give you a nice long snuggle, but you're covered in Eddie hair and I'm dressed for work." My near-uniform

78

for summer was khakis, a dressy T-shirt, and an unstructured three-quarter-length-sleeve jacket. All slightly boring, but professional and practical. "See you tonight, buddy," I said, picking up my backpack and opening the door. "Have a good kitty day!"

"Mrr!"

I stopped, because Eddie's reply had sounded as if it had come from the top of the kitchen counter. He stayed off the forbidden space when I was home, but was walking out the door considered as being home?

Erring on the side of Eddie's wishes, which was the most sensible side because he eventually won any contest that mattered to him, I headed out into the day, an hour later than I'd planned.

This meant I didn't have time to keep my promise to Rafe to stop at the sheriff's office, but there were other ways of communicating. The sidewalks were still mostly empty at that hour, so I did some walking and texting and hit the Send button to Ash's phone with a satisfied nod.

I fast-walked the last few blocks to the library and dropped into my chair right on time. Then I sighed, because Kelsey was scheduled to work that day and I knew what that meant.

With my trusty ABOS coffee mug in hand—the Association of Bookmobile and Outreach Services—I hurried to the kitchen, because it was possible Kelsey was also running late.

But no. I stood in the doorway and watched glumly as Kelsey Lyons, one of our part-time clerks, pushed the coffeepot's Go button. Kelsey was a wonderful clerk, but she had the unfortunate belief that the only good coffee was coffee with enough strength to climb out of the pot by itself.

"Early bird gets the first brew," she said, smiling. "It's not often I get here before you do, Minnie, so thanks."

"Oh, man." Josh Hadden, our IT guy, stopped in the doorway I'd just vacated. Josh was stocky, with short black curly hair so similar to mine that some people took us for siblings. "Kelsey made the first pot? You sick, Minnie?"

"Running a little late. My niece and I were at the movies last night."

"In town here?" Josh eyed the dripping coffee. "I hear they finally got that digital projector."

I shrugged. "We sat, we watched, we left. It didn't seem any different to me."

Josh shook his head. "How is it you grew up with two engineers and learned nothing? But speaking of big purchases, has the library board decided what they're going to do with Stan Larabee's money?"

"They're still looking at options." And I was pleased I was out of the loop on those meetings. Sometimes not knowing anything was the absolute best.

"You've told them about the servers?" The coffee drip slowed and he held out his mug for Kelsey to fill. "Thanks. Because," he said to me, "I've been asking for new computer servers since I got here, and I still don't have any. Someday one of them is going to break down and we'll be in a world of hurt."

I nodded in what I hoped was a soothing manner. "You're absolutely right." And since I could tell he was about to launch into an explanation of exactly why we needed new servers, what kind of server we should buy, and from whom, I said, "And I'll go talk to Graydon about it right now."

Josh grinned. "You're the best assistant director this library has ever had."

Since I was the library's first assistant director, I knew exactly how much that meant. "Wish me luck," I said, and climbed the stairs to Graydon's second-floor office.

"Knock, knock," I said, leaning inside the open door to look at the thin-faced man at the desk. "Do you have a minute?"

Graydon looked up from his computer screen and smiled. "For you, I have two. Three, if you brought me coffee, but since I can see you didn't, you only get two minutes."

I made a face. "Kelsey coffee."

"And since you saved me from that horrible fate, you zoom up to five minutes." He nodded at the empty chairs across from his desk. "What's up?"

Sighing, I sat heavily. "I'll give you three guesses and the first two don't count."

He laughed. "Who's spending Stan Larabee's money this time?"

"Josh." I sipped the coffee. It was as vile as I'd anticipated, but it was caffeine, and that was the important thing.

"New servers?" Graydon leaned back.

"You're pretty smart," I said. "It's no wonder the board picked you as director."

"Only because you didn't apply."

I shifted uncomfortably. If I'd become director I would have had to give up driving the bookmobile, and I wasn't ready for that. "Anyway, I told Josh I'd talk to you about new servers, so I have to stay up here for a while."

"Stay as long as you'd like. I'm writing the June summary for the board, if you'd like to add anything."

"Even from here I can see that it's wonderful. Don't change a thing." When I was interim director, those reports had been the bane of my existence.

Graydon laughed. "You sound like my daughters when I ask for Christmas letter contributions."

It suddenly occurred to me that he could be an excellent source for parenting advice. I sat up straight. "You have multiple daughters, all at or over voting age. Can you tell me what it means when a seventeen-year-old girl talks to you a mile a minute at midnight, but slams the door on you in the morning?"

"Uh-oh." Graydon smiled. "You and your niece aren't getting along?"

"Only intermittently. With an emphasis on the 'inter' part."

I told him about the fireworks, about Rex, about her nightmares, and about the previous night. I talked and talked and he made many sympathetic noises. When I left, I felt better, but it wasn't until I'd gone back to my office that I realized he'd never answered my question about the door slam.

My text to Ash went unanswered for hours. It wasn't until I was thinking about what to pick up for dinner—and that at some point I'd have to actually cook something, but today wasn't the day to start that kind of habit—that he sent a reply.

Ash: *Looking at Vannett. Thx.*

Me: *No problem. Glad to help.*

Ash: *Glad you are. Just stay away from snow-storms.*

He'd added a winking emoji at the end. "Funny," I said to my phone, and turned it off. Eddie and I had endured a few bad hours last January at the hands of a killer, and it had taken me months to feel truly warm. Though Eddie had seemed to recover faster, he did seem to be shedding more than usual this summer. Maybe he'd grown extra fur, post-incident.

I picked an unusually long black-and-white hair off my sleeve and put it in my office wastebasket. One down, forty-two zillion to go. And then there were the hairs still on him. Life with Eddie was full of surprises, and one was where I'd find Eddie hairs. I also got the fun of leaving them in interesting places. My current favorite was the state capitol. A few months ago, I'd gone down to Lansing for a library conference, and when I'd had time to drive over to the historic building, I'd surreptitiously set free half a dozen tiny pieces of Eddie.

Smiling, I remembered the hair I'd dropped from an upper balcony and let waft down, down, down to the rotunda's glass floor. I'd also let one loose on the capitol's front lawn, right next to a group of protestors. What they'd been protesting, I couldn't remember, but it had something to do with agriculture.

Agriculture? My brain twitched. Hadn't Jeremy's wife quoted Barry Vannett as saying that Rex's trail would never cross his farm? Hmm.

I reached for my keyboard—librarians, start your search engines!—and went to the county's website. After a few clicks, I found that Vannett's property was indeed zoned as agricultural.

But so was a lot of other land. What could be different about Vannett's farm? What could incite conflict? What could . . . "You are so stupid," I said out loud, meaning me. Going back to the website, I found the phone number I wanted and dialed.

"Tonedagana County Planning Office, this is Trish," said a cheerful voice. "How can I help you?"

"Hi, Trish." I sat and studied the computer. "If I give you an address, can you tell me if anyone has applied for zoning permits on that property?"

"Sure," she said. "That's public information. I'll need a foya application, though."

"A what?"

She laughed. "It's an acronym for the Freedom of Information Act. FOIA, see?"

I did. And with a little direction from her, I also saw where to fill out the appropriate form, how to sign it, how much it might cost to get my request fulfilled, and where to send it. "This can all be done electronically?"

"Just started this year," she said. "Easy, right?"

It was. I thanked her and she said if I sent the FOIA application right away, she might be able to get to it before five o'clock. This meant I spent the rest of the day checking my e-mail repeatedly, but at two minutes to five, there it was.

I clicked it open and blinked. "Huh," I said out loud.

Barry Vannett was applying for a recreational marijuana growing license.

CHAPTER 5

Rafe aimed the yellow mustard bottle at his opened hamburger and gave a healthy squirt. "Okay, but what could a marijuana grow license have to do with murder? Medical marijuana has been decriminalized in Michigan for more than ten years, and the recreational stuff went the same way in 2018. So . . ." He shrugged.

A downside of having my boyfriend help me with a murder investigation was that he was helping me investigate a murder.

The three of us were sitting at one of the marina's picnic tables, getting ready to eat the burgers Rafe had grilled and the potato salad, chips, and dip that I'd picked up at the grocery store. It was a beautiful evening; the sun was still high in the sky, the wind was light, seagulls were squawking, and if I turned around and looked hard, I would have been able to see Eddie's face pressed up against a houseboat window.

"It's an anomaly," I said. "Something different. Things that are different cause disagreement. Conflict. Anger. All that. And even if marijuana isn't a criminal offense in Michigan, it's still a cash business. And there's bound to be a black market for it."

Rafe added pickles, onions, tomatoes, ketchup, and mayonnaise, guaranteeing that he'd end up with burger goo on the picnic table. "Okay. Money's always a murder motive, so that's a given. But how about a motive that isn't money-based?" He frowned. "There must be some."

"Sure," I said. "Let's say Barry Vannett wanted to grow marijuana and . . ." And what? From what I knew about the licensing process, if the township where Vannett lived allowed growing operations, all Vannett had to do was apply, assuming he wasn't a felon. Even if Rex had been appalled at the idea of marijuana next door, there wasn't much he could do about it.

Was it possible I'd zoomed off into assumption land? That I'd been wrong to say there could be nonmoney motives?

He was looking at me over the top of his burger, waiting for my response. So I changed the subject.

"Look, Kate!" I bumped my silent niece with my elbow and nodded toward the waterfront sidewalk, specifically at the two teenage girls with ice cream cones who were more focused on keeping their ice cream from dripping than they were on where their feet were taking them. I didn't think they'd actually fall into the water, but since I happened to know they were both good swimmers, I wasn't too worried. "There's Emily and Alyssa." The Gwaltny girls were regular library patrons, sisters who actually got along, funny, smart, and about Kate's age.

Kate shrugged and kept on dipping her chips.

"Let's go meet them," I said with forced cheerfulness, ignoring the look of warning from Rafe. "Come on."

"Do I have to?" she asked.

"Well, no, but I thought it'd be fun for you to meet some other teens. When I was up here at your age, I—"

"That was, like, a generation ago," Kate said, suddenly fierce. "It's not like that now, okay? Everything's different." She jumped up and ran off.

"Be back in a minute," I murmured to Rafe and went after my niece. Inside the houseboat, I looked around. No Kate in sight, which on a boat this size had to mean she was in the bathroom. "Kate?" I asked. "Are you okay?"

"I'm fine," came her voice from behind the door. "Just leave me alone."

"But—"

"I'm fine!"

I twitched at the intensity of her tone and was about to venture directly into the Not Leaving Alone category of aunting, when I heard an odd rustling noise. I looked left and right and up and down and finally found my cat, who was mostly under Kate's sleeping bag.

He wriggled out from underneath and stretched.

After moving roughly six inches closer to me, he sat upright and looked me in the eye. "Mrr," he said.

"Do you believe her?" I asked softly.

"Mrr."

"Yeah, I don't, either." Because there was no way Kate was fine. She'd suffered the trauma of falling over a murder victim, and was probably dealing with a variation of post-traumatic stress syndrome. I wanted to help her, I was trying to help her; I just didn't know how.

I sighed, called to Kate that I was going to finish eating, got a muffled "Fine" in reply, and headed out.

Rafe hadn't wasted any of the time I'd left him alone. In those ten minutes, he'd finished eating, gone up to the house for a small cooler, filled it with ice and adult beverages, brought it back down, and replaced me with someone else.

"Hey, Ash. Long time no see and all that." I settled down next to Rafe and made a come-hither gesture to my plate. Ash slid it over and I debated my next bite. Chip? Potato salad? Burger?

"How's she doing?" Rafe tipped his head in Kate's direction.

"She says she's fine." I picked up my fork and aimed it at the potatoes, opting to eat first the food more likely to make me sick if I didn't eat it soon.

"Takes after her aunt." Ash eyed an unopened bag of chips. "Is someone eating these?"

"Knock yourself out," I said. "And what do you mean, she takes after me?"

The two men at the table exchanged a glance. "But what I stopped to tell you," Ash said, opening the bag, "is about Barry Vannett."

I sat up straight and leaned forward. "You found a gun in his car, matched the ballistics to the bullet that killed Rex, and you've already arrested him."

Ash paused, looking at me over the top of a laden potato chip. "That's quite a sequence." He took the time to eat, chew, and swallow before he continued. "But no. None of that happened."

I deflated. While I hadn't been a hundred percent sure of Vannett's guilt, it would have made for a fast resolution. "What did?"

"The senior generation of Vannetts have a cottage on Janay Lake, and every year there's a big family reunion over the Fourth. A different family member is in charge every year. This year it was Barry's turn."

My deflation continued. I could picture the scene. Multiple generations of Vannetts running around from dawn to dusk and beyond, making memories of boating and s'mores and sparklers that would last a lifetime.

"So Barry Vannett is out as a suspect," I said.

"Looks like." Ash glanced at the houseboat. "You going to tell Kate? I could, but—"

"No, it's my job." I started to stand, but sat back down again, remembering the closed bathroom door. "It can wait a few minutes, though. Pass the chips, will you?"

My talk with Kate about the murder investigation didn't go as expected. When I told her that Barry Vannett had been eliminated as a suspect, but that the investigation was still continuing, she didn't accept the family reunion alibi.

"But that doesn't make sense," she said, crossing her arms across her chest. By the time I'd finished dinner and returned to the houseboat, she had left the confines of the bathroom and gone out to the houseboat's deck with Eddie and her tablet.

I sat on the vacant chaise—well, vacant except for a sprawling Eddie—and gave her the news, which she didn't like. "How does it not make sense?" I asked, trying to keep my expression interested, neutral, and not at all annoyed and disagreeable.

"Because," she said oh-so-patiently, drawing out the word into five or six syllables, "with so many people around, it would be easy for him to go out for an hour without anyone noticing. I mean, how far is the cottage to Chilson? A five-minute drive? Ten?"

She sat up and faced me. "Or maybe, since Barry is dead set against that trail, maybe the whole family is, too. So maybe it wasn't Barry who killed Rex, but maybe it was someone else in the family."

My mouth opened, then closed. "You're right," I said slowly. "You're absolutely right."

"I . . . am?"

"Yep. Do you want to tell Deputy Wolverson about this, or should I?"

She demurred on talking to Ash, so I texted him the theory. He didn't completely dismiss it, but it didn't sound as if he took it seriously, either. Not that I told Kate. What I told her was that the sheriff's office appreciated her ideas and to keep passing them along.

The next morning, I left for the library when Kate was still in her sleeping bag. I touched her on the shoulder. "Time to get up," I said. "You start at Benton's in an hour."

Benton's was the classic general store, from its wood floors to its tin ceiling, from its stick candy to its shiny brass cash register. It had been run by the same family since its birth, and was now in capable hands. Rianne Howe, a woman a few years older than myself, had been raised in Chilson, left for the big city, but had come home to run the family store.

"Mmm," Kate said, snuggling deeper into her sleeping bag.

She had my sympathy; the morning was cool and she had to be comfortably cozy in there.

"Mrr!" Eddie jumped from the floor to the

sleeping bag, landing on what looked like her midsection.

"*Oooff!*" Kate rolled over. "Fine, I'm awake, I'm awake!"

I laughed, but it was a laugh of sympathy. "At least I know it's not personal. He does that to me once a week."

"Rotten cat," Kate muttered, but she extracted one of her arms and rubbed the side of his head.

"He is pretty horrible. Sorry, pal," I said, "but it's true. Doesn't mean we don't love you."

So I headed up to the library feeling downright perky. I'd had a good night's sleep, my niece and I were talking, and my cat was wonderfully awful. Sure, the sun was covered with clouds and the air felt more like September than July, but that would pass. I sang cheery morning nonsense songs, waved at Cookie Tom on my way past the bakery, and spent a happy hour in my office reading librarian trade magazines.

"You look pleased with yourself this morning."

I grinned at Holly, who'd just come into the break room, a room I'd recently entered myself. "Easy to be happy on mornings I get to do this," I said, hitting the coffeemaker's Go button.

"Who made it?" Josh asked as he entered.

"You have a gift," Holly said. "Every time the coffee is fresh, there you are. Have you ever actually made a pot of coffee?"

It was a good question. For the majority of

his adult life, Josh hadn't been a coffee drinker, preferring to get his caffeine via diet soda from the vending machine. That had all changed when he'd bought a house and come to grips with his altered financial status. And now he had a serious girlfriend and they were talking about moving in together. It was a concept hard to wrap my tiny little mind around.

Josh slapped the pockets of his cargo pants. "Nope, don't have it."

"Don't have what?" Holly frowned and I wondered if this was going to turn into one of their sibling-like spats.

"For Minnie," he said. "An article about these new servers. A little more money than those other ones, but these would—"

Holly made a rude noise. "You're spending Stan Larabee's money, aren't you? New servers might be nice, but the ones we have work fine. The first thing we need to do with that money is buy more computers for the children and young adult sections. And get tablets with educational software so kids can check them out. They're doing it at the library in—"

"Not a chance," Josh interrupted. "Who do you think is going to look after all that? I already have too much to do. There's no way I can support more computers and tablets."

"If you're that busy," Holly said, "why are you in here half the time?"

If there was any chance of keeping the spat from becoming a full-blown argument, I had to do something fast. So I asked the first question that came to mind. "Do either one of you know anyone around here named Vannett?"

They turned and blinked at me.

"I know a Nate Vannett," Josh said. "He's a website designer, has a place next to that art gallery your buddy has stuff in."

Holly said, "There's a Faith Vannett who works at the eye doctor downtown. Is that who you mean?"

"If she's related to Barry, then yes."

"What's up?" Josh asked, adding more coffee to his coffee.

Holly studied me. "Does this have to do with Rex Stuhler's murder?"

"Not sure yet," I said. "If it does, I'll let you know."

Eventually.

At lunchtime, I hurried home for a quick peanut butter and strawberry jam sandwich—see Mom, I'm eating fruit!—encouraged Eddie into his carrier, and drove him up to the bookmobile, where I'd done the preflight check before I'd left the library. One of the things I'd wanted to do for ages was expand the bookmobile's summer hours, and now that Graydon had settled in as library director, he was taking over a lot of the

95

work I'd been doing when I'd been stuck as interim director. All that meant I was able to squeeze in an extra half bookmobile day and it was wonderful.

Julia was waiting in the parking lot, leaning against the side of her SUV, looking like a 1950s teenager with her hair in a ponytail, a bright white T-shirt, and rolled-up jeans.

"Nice look," I said, unlocking the bookmobile door.

"Yes, isn't it?" She checked her ponytail in the bookmobile's side mirror and slightly rearranged its pink polka-dotted bow. "I lost a bet with my husband and now I have to dress like I was when we met."

I eyed the bobby socks and flat sneakers. "In what universe did you wear clothes like that?"

"Playing an extra in *Grease*."

That explained the particulars of the clothing, but not the rest of it. "You going to tell me about the bet?"

She arched one eyebrow and gave me a slow smile. "Are you sure you want to know?"

"Well . . ."

"Mrr!" said Eddie from his carrier, which was still in my hand.

Julia leaned toward it and whispered loudly, "I'll tell you later, okay? But it involved a bottle of wine and a new negligee."

"All righty, then," I said, suddenly wanting to

change the subject. "This morning Josh was asking about new servers. Again. And Holly wants to buy more technology for the youth sections."

"This is about the Larabee money?" Julia climbed aboard ahead of me, sat, and accepted the cat carrier I handed over. "There you go, my feline friend," she said, strapping Eddie in snugly. "The board hasn't decided?"

"Not yet." We buckled our seat belts and I started the engine. "What do you think should be done?"

"I've been thinking about this," Julia said, her voice shifting to a serious tone. "And the only real answer is a full set of Sookie Stackhouse books."

"That would be nice," I agreed, "but even with all those books, there would still be a lot of money left." Thousands and thousands and thousands of dollars, actually. "What else?"

Julia waved off the question. "I'm part time. My opinion doesn't matter a tinker's you-know-what."

"It matters to me," I said.

She reached over and patted my shoulder. "And I love you for that, my dear, but I know my place in the world of the Chilson library and I'm quite happy not having an opinion. Safer that way."

I made a rude noise in the back of my throat. If she'd wanted to play life safe, she never would have left Chilson in the first place, let alone become a successful stage actor.

"Opinions get you into trouble," she said, squiggling comfortably in her seat as we reached the outskirts of Chilson and headed into the rolling, wooded countryside. "Did I ever tell you about the time the director of a *Streetcar Named Desire* production asked for my opinion on his directing?"

As she told the story, which ended with a thrown chair and a damaged stage set, part of my brain was thinking about Rex Stuhler and Barry Vannett. Was their difference of opinion on the proposed trail a deep enough motive for murder? Or were there deeper reasons out there waiting to be uncovered?

"Mrr!"

Julia looked down at Eddie. "You know what? That's exactly what I told him."

I grinned, getting an inkling of what she'd been like to work with onstage, and tried to focus on enjoying the rest of the tale. But it was not to be, because Julia diverted to a completely new topic.

"Speaking of opinions," she said. "Do you have any on Rex's murder?"

"Too early to tell." I glanced over and saw her looking at me. "What?"

She tapped her chin with an index finger. "Just wondering. Is it possible that we saw something, the last day Rex was on the bookmobile, that might be a clue?"

"I can't imagine what."

"Me either."

We sat in silence a minute, then Julia said, "Say, you were outside with Mr. Eddie for a while, answering the call of kitty nature. Did you see anything?"

I shrugged. "Just a couple of cars going by. I remember wondering where they thought they were going, it being a dead end road and all. Then, when they didn't come back right away, I figured they were hiking or something."

"Do you remember anything about the cars?"

For maybe the first time in my life, I wished I'd actually paid attention to vehicles. Even better, that I had a habit of memorizing license plate numbers. "The second one was an old sedan with a bunch of stickers on the back bumper." I'd been too far away to read any of them, but they'd all been bright pink. "And the car was kind of noisy." Eddie had flattened his ears as it drove past. "The first one was a truck, just crawling along. I remember thinking it was probably a new truck, and that the driver didn't want to get any gravel dings or dust on it."

"So we have a noisy car and a new truck, and no real reason to think they're connected to Rex's murder." Julia nodded. "We're halfway to solving this."

"Mrr," Eddie said.

The rest of the day flew past, as per usual on the bookmobile, and in the blink of an eye we were back in Chilson, lugging books from vehicle to library. The chore didn't take long with two people working, and soon Eddie and I were back at the houseboat. Which was empty. I opened the carrier, Eddie sauntered out, and I went to look at the whiteboard. To my surprise and delight, Kate had actually left a message.

Went up to Great-Aunt Frances and Otto's to eat. Back later.

Smiling, I erased her note and added my own. *Going for a walk, then over to the house. Back later.*

I nodded. "What do you think of that, Mr. Edward? My niece and I are communicating!"

Eddie didn't say a word, so I went on the hunt, and found him in the tiny bedroom closet, up behind my shoes. It had been his favorite place a year or two ago, but I hadn't seen him in there since.

"Is this another phase?" I asked, looking down at his curled-up self. "I'm fine with it, as long as you don't chew anything."

One yellow eye opened, then closed.

"Right. Well, I'm off for a walk."

Eddie sighed and curled himself a little tighter. For some reason, this made me smile, so it was with light spirits that I headed outside. It was a Wednesday, but it was also only four days after the Fourth of July, so it was a guarantee that the sidewalks of downtown Chilson were near peak capacity.

To avoid that, I walked the block parallel to the main street. One street over, the pedestrian and vehicular traffic was minimal. I felt a bit smug as I made long-ish strides past the parking lots and backs of buildings. From back here, the downtown's architectural mishmash was even more apparent. Our mix of hundred-year-old buildings and new buildings, brick and wood, expensive and not, all summed up to create a business district whose appeal could never have been planned. The main street was almost exclusively retail, and the side streets were filled with professional businesses that didn't need the higher foot traffic and retail stores that didn't want to pay astronomical rent.

Hang on a minute . . .

I made a hard left, walked past a resale shop and a chiropractor's office, and walked into Lakeview Art Gallery. The twenty-something woman at the counter looked up and her long honey-brown hair flowed over her shoulders and down her back. "Good even—oh, hey, Minnie. What's up?"

I smiled at Lina Swinney. As a former part-time bookmobile clerk, Lina would always have a special place in my life. "Just stopping by," I said. "Does Cade have anything new?"

Russell McCade, better known to his millions of fans as Cade, had, along with his wonderful wife, Barb, a home on nearby Five Mile Lake. Our first meeting had been unusual—I'd rushed Cade to the emergency room in the bookmobile—and the three of us had bonded over use of the letter *D*.

Cade painted gorgeous, lifelike paintings of lake scenes, cozy cottages, and sunsets. Many critics dismissed his art as mediocre works that pandered to the lowest common taste, but Cade just smiled and deposited the checks.

Lina tipped her head at an empty spot on the wall. "Someone bought it yesterday. But there's this cool new weaving piece from a new artist I bet you'll like." She hopped off her stool and led me into a side room. I admired the weaving's complicated mix of textures and colors, and since no one else was in the building, I asked oh-so-casually, "Do you happen to know Nate Vannett? I hear he works next door."

"Um, sure."

I turned and focused on Lina's face. Yep. She was blushing. "Hmm," I said, mock-frowning. "Do I detect a romance? Please say yes."

Lina's blush went deeper. "He's a friend of my brother's. I've known him forever, but haven't seen him much since my brother moved downstate. Then this spring he leased that place next door and . . ." She gave a goofy smile.

My return smile was also on the silly side, since my relationship with Rafe had taken a similar trajectory. "What's he like?" I asked. "Tall, dark, and handsome?"

She laughed. "More like shortish, blondish, and cute in a baby face kind of way. But he's . . . he's wonderful. He actually listens to me. I mean, really listens. To me! Can you believe it?"

I could, since I knew Lina was smart and funny, but I also knew what she meant. To have a friend who valued you inside and out was a wonderful thing. I made appreciative noises, then, since being belatedly clever was better than not being clever at all, I said, "I hear the Vannetts have a huge Fourth of July party every year. Were you there?"

"It was awesome," she said, nodding. "Their family place is like a ten-minute walk away from the waterfront, so it's really convenient."

"I hear Barry and his wife were hosting this year. Bet they were busy all the time."

"Oh, you know them?" Lina asked, frowning a bit. "You're friends?"

"Not exactly," I said, in complete truth.

"Good. I mean, Barry is Nate's cousin, but Barry is kind of a jerk. Technically, he and his wife were hosting, but she was doing all the work. Half the time no one knew where Barry was."

"Even during the fireworks?"

She rolled her eyes. "Especially then. That's the big Vannett family moment. Everybody's supposed to be down next to the dock, because right before the fireworks, there's a family reading of the Declaration of Independence. Everybody gets a section, but this year no one could find Barry to start it off. He showed up later, with this lame excuse that he had to do a beer run."

"But there was plenty of beer?"

"Well, he came back with some, but why would he need to buy more when there was a whole other cooler full?"

Lina went on to list reasons for Barry to be gone for an hour, reasons that ranged from a hatred of the writings of Thomas Jefferson to an affair. But never once did she mention the possibility of murder.

Thinking hard about fireworks and motives, I left the gallery and headed home. When I turned onto the Main Street sidewalk, I suddenly remembered why I'd avoided that street half an hour earlier. Even at eight o'clock at night, it was still wall-to-wall people, with vehicles jammed tight from intersection to intersection.

I eyed the mess, then shrugged and plunged in. Two steps later, something banged into the back of my legs. "Oomph!"

"Honey," said a man to a toddler, "watch where you're walking, okay?"

"Okay, Daddy," the kid said, eyes still looking everywhere but at the ground right ahead.

"Sorry," the guy apologized. "She's just excited about being here."

"No problem," I said, because he was being nice and the kid was cute. But I edged over toward the curb, where the pedestrian traffic was lighter. I didn't need to see the retail shops, the restaurants, or the fudge stores; all I wanted was to get back to the houseboat, take my cat on the deck, think about what I'd just learned, and when I'd figured everything out, I'd walk over to the house and talk to—

And then I was on one foot, teetering and off balance.

And then there was nothing to keep me from falling toward the street, toward the moving traffic, falling, falling, falling . . .

CHAPTER 6

I was falling directly into moving traffic. My arms flailed wildly and my feet had no idea what they should be doing. I hit the asphalt hard, and through nothing but sheer instinct I started rolling sideways, rolling away from the tires that were so very close to me.

My ears, which hadn't heard anything for quite a while, suddenly started working again, hearing all sorts of things. Brakes shrieking, people yelling, a child screaming. I rolled to a stop and lay there for a moment, face up, looking at the sky. Still cloudy.

Footsteps ran to my side. "Are you all right?" a woman asked.

A car door slammed. "She fell right in front of me," a male voice said, his tone tight and high. "There was nothing I could do."

In seconds, I was looking up at a circle of strangers. "I'm fine," I said, because I was pretty sure I was, but my voice came out quiet and no one heard me.

"Minnie! Look at me!"

I looked around and finally focused on a familiar face. "Hey, Pam. What's up?"

"Not you, apparently." Pam Fazio elbowed her way to my side. "Let's give her some room, folks, okay?" Pam, owner of Older Than Dirt, the antique/gift store where Kate was spending a third of her working hours, kneeled by my side. "I'm sure someone has already called nine-one-one. Do you need an ambulance?"

I sat up, brushed myself off, and with Pam's help, got to my feet. Everything seemed to be in working order, except my shirt had a new hole in the shoulder. I pulled out my phone and called dispatch, telling them to cancel everything, that it was just an accident. All was well.

The car's driver hovered until I swore on an imaginary stack of Bibles that I wouldn't sue him for almost running me over, and he eventually left.

"What was that all about?" Pam asked, brushing a bit of dirt off my back. "You just being your normal awkward and bumbling self?"

"I guess so."

"Maybe it's time to start paying more attention to what you're doing?"

"Start a habit like that now, at my age?"

Pam shook her head, which made her short dark hair shake, too. "Well, since I have two decades on you and don't have the habit, I suppose I shouldn't ask it of you."

I smiled. "Good to know you're aware of the hypocrisy."

"But honestly, Minnie, what happened?"

By now we were back on the sidewalk, and

the vehicular and pedestrian traffic had cleared as much as it was going to until late August. I nodded at the congestion. "I'm not sure. Maybe someone accidentally pushed me?" I shook my head, trying to loosen the memory, but it didn't come free. "But mostly likely, I just fell. I was trying to get around a woman pushing a stroller and I just . . . tripped."

Pam picked a piece of leaf out of my hair, told me to take care of myself, and headed back into her store.

Slowly, I walked back to the marina, feeling the bumps and scrapes that were going to make me horribly stiff in the morning, wondering about what had just happened. Had I really felt someone shove me into the road? Yes, I was pretty sure of it. But had it been accidental or intentional?

There was no way for me to know, so I decided not to think about it too much. By far the likeliest scenario was an accident. But just in case it wasn't and just in case someone knew I was helping the police with the murder investigation and wanted me out of the way, I decided to double down my efforts to find Rex Stuhler's killer.

And maybe I'd be a little more careful, too.

At the house that night, I very casually explained to Rafe that the new bruises on my arms and legs were a sad example of what could happen on the mean streets of Chilson, and immediately changed the conversation to next steps in looking for Rex's killer.

"There's a hole in your shirt." Rafe put three of his fingers through it, and I deeply wished I'd taken the time to go back to the houseboat to change.

"Old shirt," I said, pulling the fabric out of his reach. "I was thinking about the Stuhlers' pest control business. Are you familiar with any of those websites that review local businesses?"

Rafe squinted. "What, you think because Rex couldn't get a squirrel out of an attic fast enough someone killed him?"

"People kill over dumber things," I said. "And what if it was a skunk? What if the skunk sprayed all over . . . over . . . some historic papers, a signed letter from Abraham Lincoln, and now it's not worth anything. Or what if Rex had guaranteed an attic critter-free, but it wasn't, and someone had stored their, um, their Queen Anne furniture up there and raccoons got in and—"

Rafe held up a hand. "Don't spend all your brain power dreaming up unlikely but possible scenarios. I take your point and, yes, I can think of a couple of websites people around here use."

Grinning, I rubbed my hands together and, because of the recent abrasions, immediately regretted doing so. "Great," I said. "Where's your laptop?"

"You want to do this now?" Rafe pointed at the tool belt around his waist.

"No time like the present." Darkness was coming and Kate was about to spend another night dreaming of things that made her wake up crying. "Just tell me and you can go back to doing whatever it was you were doing." I hesitated. "Unless you need my help, of course."

"If it's the kind of help where you ask what I'm doing and why I'm doing it and slowing things down more than you speed them up, then I'm fine alone."

"You hurt me," I said, giving him a look of fake pain. "Truly and deeply."

"Oh?" He moved closer. "Where exactly does it hurt? Let me kiss it and make it better."

Which is what he did, so it was a few minutes before we extricated ourselves from each other and moved on to our appointed tasks. I found his laptop right where he said it was, on a counter in the kitchen, underneath a stack of newspapers and magazines.

I fired it up and typed in the first review site Rafe had mentioned. Nothing came up under the name of Rex's company, ABK Pest Control. "Rats," I muttered, then giggled at myself. Rats? When I was looking up pest control? Hah! Still giggling, I pulled up the other review site. This one included an entry for ABK. I scrolled down and read the comments that had been posted.

DaveR: Rex did a great job getting rid of the bats in our belfry. Okay, it was an attic, but they're gone and that's what matters. Thanks!

Suzie11K: One panicky phone call about the squirrel my cat brought in and Rex was here in less than an hour. He saved me from a heart attack. I love this man and if he wasn't already married I'd snap him up. Sorry, honey :)

There were more in that same vein, but then I read a post from *JNJ132: Don't ever call Rex Stuhler. He'll make your life so miserable you'll wish you hadn't been born.*

I stared at the harsh words. Studied the cryptic name of the poster. And knew exactly what I'd be doing first thing in the morning.

The sixtyish woman looked at me over the top of her computer. "Morning, Minnie. What brings you here so early? Coffee?" She nodded at the machine set on a counter near her desk.

"Polly," I said, "you are the answer to my prayers."

"That's what all the bookmobile librarians tell me," she said. "What can the chamber do for you today?"

Polly, director of the Chilson Chamber of

Commerce for twenty years, was a whirlwind of energy in summer and essentially hibernated in winter. She had privately lamented to me that with the tourist season expanding into spring and fall, the hibernation thing was getting harder to do, but she was hoping to continue her habits until retirement.

"Well," I said, opening the cupboard and choosing a slightly chipped yellow mug with the logo of Chilson's sesquicentennial, "I saw on your website that ABK Pest Control is a member of the chamber."

Polly sighed. "Rex and Fawn. It's so sad. Do you know if the police have found out who killed him?"

"Not yet, but last night I had an idea." I leaned against the counter, which on most people would have hit them at hip level, but on me nestled into the small of my back. "Do you keep a list of complaints against your members?"

Polly eyed me. "You mean like a Better Business Bureau?"

"Exactly." I wrapped my hands around the mug and sipped of the life-giving liquid. "Maybe it could give the sheriff's office a lead."

"Sorry," Polly said, "but we don't keep a list like that."

I deflated. I'd been so sure. "Do you remember anyone complaining about them?" I explained about the review site and the nasty comment.

"What was the name?"

"Of who posted? It was a combination of letters and numbers. Don't remember the numbers, but the letters were JNJ."

Polly nodded. "Well, there you go. I'd lay money that was John and Nandi Jaquay. JNJ, see? They blamed Rex for an infestation of raccoons that spent an entire winter in their summer cottage. Made a huge mess of the place, from what I hear."

"How was that Rex's fault?"

"Who knows." She shrugged. "People like to have someone to blame, I guess. John and Nandi kept e-mailing and calling, telling me to strike him from our membership."

"But you didn't."

"From one complaint?" She snorted. "But they were angry, that's for sure. And they seemed intent on ruining Rex's business."

I thanked her and went out into the morning sun, walking up to the library slowly as I thought through what I'd learned.

The Jaquays wanted to ruin Rex. How big a step was it from destroying a man's livelihood to murder?

I worked in the library all Thursday and did bookmobile runs on Friday and Saturday morning. After waving good-bye to Julia at noon and taking Eddie back to hearth and houseboat, I grabbed a quick lunch of peanut butter and jelly sandwich, washed it down with a few bites of cottage cheese straight out of the container since Kate wouldn't touch the stuff and wasn't there to see me commit food heresy, and stuffed a bottle of water and a book (because you just never knew) into my backpack.

"I'll be back soon," I called to Eddie from the kitchen. But he was doing his usual post-bookmobile routine, that of being flopped on his side on my bed, snoring like a steam engine.

"Sweet dreams." I blew him a kiss and headed out into the sunshine. The day was bright as a shiny penny and my heart was light as I rolled my bicycle out of my marina storage unit. Rafe was out fishing with some friends and we'd be meeting in a couple of hours, so I had plenty of time to explore the idea I'd dreamed up that morning.

What I'd learned about the Jaquays had been interesting, and I'd passed on that information to Ash, but I was still convinced that Barry Vannett, he of the nasty temper, was a likely candidate for Rex's murder. What was it he'd yelled at Rex? That if Rex came back to talk about a trail, he'd get a "face full of shotgun." So obviously, what I needed to do was learn more about the trail proposal.

My clever use of the Internet during a nonbusy bookmobile stop had turned up a website for a grass-roots trail advocacy group. *Chilson Connection* was both the website and tentative trail name, which had a theoretical route laid out.

I clicked on the map and saw that, yes indeed, the proposed route was zipping right across Vannett and Stuhler land and diving deep into the adjacent state forest. I also noted that the website talked a lot about conceptual design, construction design, and costs that made my mouth drop open.

But it was the site's home page that I found most interesting, because it told me all about a fund-raising event being held at an existing trailhead just outside Chilson that very day.

"Fate," I said to myself as I pedaled up the hill. Well, gasped to myself, really, because the hill was long and steep and my exercise the last few months had been more sanding and painting and much less running and biking.

The trailhead was only a mile outside the city limits, and I coasted into the parking lot glad I'd decided to bike and not drive. The parking lot was jammed so full that people were parking on the grass and on the road's shoulder. A tent with a banner proclaiming COUNTDOWN TO THE CHILSON CONNECTION was packed with people and all of them appeared to be reaching for their wallets.

Hmm.

I biked past, watching and thinking, and hours

later, was still thinking when Rafe arrived at the house with a cooler in hand. Since one of my hands was holding a paintbrush and the other was all painty, I declined to hug him, and instead tipped my head forward.

"This is the only part of you not covered in paint," he said, kissing the top of my head. "How do you do that?"

"It's a skill," I said, eyeing his cooler. "If only I could monetize it. Does that hold what's left of your beverages, or does it hold future dinner that someone is going to have to cook?"

"None of the above." He set it down and, with a flourish, opened the top and presented two foam containers. "Hot off the grill from the Round Table, two fish sandwiches made of fish caught by yours truly. Fries on the side, but I had nothing to do with those."

"How did . . . ?" Then I remembered that one of his fishing partners was the head cook at the Round Table. My beloved was quite the catch. Smiling at my own internal pun, I scrambled to my feet, since I'd been sitting on the floor to paint the living room's baseboard. In short order I'd cleaned up and we were on the front porch eating fresh fish and fries.

He told me a little too much about his day out on his buddy's boat and all the bad jokes they'd shared, and I told him about the Jaquays and their intent to ruin ABK Pest Control. I also told him about my bike ride and what I'd seen at the trailhead.

"So," I told him, opening a packet of malt vinegar and sprinkling liberally, "to me all that energy and enthusiasm about the trail means murdering Rex couldn't possibly have changed a thing."

"Did Vannett know that?" Rafe asked. "Maybe he thought Rex was the leader and the group would fall apart without him."

Possible, but it didn't seem likely. "I'm back to thinking Barry's marijuana application has something to do with the murder. Marijuana involves money, like we were saying before, remember? Legal or black market, it means cash, and that's always a great motive."

Rafe nodded. "Sure, but what's the connection in this case? What was Stuhler going to do, steal all of Vannett's plants? Burn them? Do we even know if Stuhler was against having a grow operation next door? Maybe he was thrilled with the idea."

"But—" I stopped myself. Because Rafe was right. We didn't know, and we needed to find out.

CHAPTER 7

The next morning, I dragged Kate out of bed and up the hill to the boardinghouse.

"But I was just here the other day," she protested. "Celeste and I had fruit-flavored water and oatmeal cookies on the front porch."

With her jaw jutting out like that, she looked so much like my brother that I had to hide my smile. "We haven't been up for breakfast all summer," I said, "and breakfast is different."

"How?"

I hemmed and hawed as I considered how much to tell her about past boardinghouse processes and the reconnaissance I was doing for Aunt Frances, trying to determine if those old processes remained intact.

"When Aunt Frances was running the boarding-house," I finally said, "Saturday was the only morning she didn't cook breakfast. The boarders paired up to cook and clean." Even though I'd never been a summertime boarder, I'd often dropped by for Saturday breakfast, just to watch the fun.

"Huh." Kate didn't sound impressed. "But today is Sunday. And it doesn't sound like much of a boardinghouse if you had to do your own cooking."

"One meal a week," I said. "With six boarders, no one cooked more than three or four meals all summer."

"What if someone was a horrible cook?"

"Then breakfast was horrible. But house rules were that cooks got compliments, not criticism." I smiled, remembering one memorable time when the eggs had been overdone, the bacon underdone, and the fruit hard as a rock. The dining room had been quiet except for the tinkle of knives and forks until the oldest boarder, a woman who'd retired from decades of teaching kindergarteners, finally said, "I love the way you two folded the napkins."

"The whole thing seems weird," Kate said, and this I couldn't disagree with. "Is Celeste doing the same thing?" she asked.

But since that was what we were here to find out, I couldn't tell her.

"There you are!" Celeste called from the front porch. "I was just about to call out the dogs!" We climbed the steps and she crushed us into a three-way hug. "You won't believe the breakfast that Amy and Zach are cooking. Hang on, where's that nice-looking young man of yours?"

It took me a moment to catch my breath after she released us. "I didn't know you wanted him, too."

"Well, of course." Celeste patted my cheek. "You two are a pair. A matched set. You don't get one without the other. Call the boy and get him up here. There's time, if he hurries."

And because I knew she wouldn't rest until I did the deed, I started texting. Celeste chattered as she escorted us inside, through the entryway and living room with its pine-paneled walls, massive fieldstone fireplace, and bookcases stacked with books, jigsaw puzzles, and board games, and into the dining room.

Kate immediately went to the sideboard to pour herself a cup of coffee from the carafe, and I allowed myself to be tugged forward by Celeste.

"This is my cousin Minnie," she announced to the foursome at the far end of the dining table. "She drives the bookmobile with her cat, Eddie. And that's her niece, Katrina."

"Kate," I said before I got the evil eye. "She prefers Kate."

"Hi, Kate," the four said, almost at the same time.

"And you too, Minnie," a middle-aged man said, nodding. "I hear you're the one to ask about scenic back roads. Yvette here is longing to get my pickup stuck in the most remote two-track possible."

The middle-aged woman on his left jabbed him lightly with her elbow. "Bert here likes to think I want to have my way with him. Don't say anything," she said in a stage whisper, "but he might be on to something."

An elderly woman with deep brown skin made a harumphing sort of noise. "You two need to get a room," she said, but her eyes danced with laughter.

"Canary, my dear," an equally elderly man said, taking her hand. "If they leave, and if Amy and Zach try that breathtakingly athletic kiteboarding they've been talking about, and if we can convince Celeste we don't need anything at all, the two of us will have the run of the entire house the entire day."

I beamed at the foursome, and continued throughout breakfast, beaming at the boarders, at the food, at Kate, at Celeste, and at Rafe, who showed up just as we sat down to eat.

Afterward, Kate hung back to help Canary and Walter, for that was the name of Canary's new friend, with putting together a thousand-piece jigsaw puzzle of Lake Superior, and Rafe and I walked back to the house for a fun day of sanding and painting.

"She's added books," I said to Rafe, who frowned. Clearly, he didn't understand. "In the living room. There are books mixed in with the board games and jigsaw puzzles."

Rafe did the one eyebrow thing. "You're complaining because there are books on the bookshelves? What kind of librarian are you?"

"The kind with an aunt who is having trouble letting go of the boardinghouse."

"Ah." He nodded. "You know what you should do, right?"

"Stay out of it."

"And are you going to do that?"

I grinned. "Not a chance."

"What's that noise?" Julia asked.

As the bookmobile was, at that point, driving over an asphalt road in need of repair, I couldn't hear much over the protestations of the springs and shocks and struts. Which were very expensive to repair. I closed my mind to the potential dollar signs and tried to listen for what Julia was hearing, because in the months she'd spent on the bookmobile, never once had she shown any evidence toward mechanical aptitude.

"What noise?" I asked. "All I hear are"—I paused to navigate around a particularly large pothole—"the normal abnormal road noises."

"I think it's him."

Out of the corner of my eye, I saw Julia pointing a dramatic finger at the cat carrier.

"What's he doing? Shredding his cozy pink blanket? Kicking the door in hopes of escape? Or has his snoring managed to reach a new level?"

"Worse," Julia said. "Don't you hear it?"

And then, just as I flicked the turn signal to enter a narrow driveway, I did hear the unmistakable noise of my cat in the early stages of hacking up a hairball and I knew from experience that things would soon get ugly.

"Hang on, Eddie," I called. "We're almost there and—"

"Oh, ew," Julia said, and I inwardly cringed at the noise emanating from the carrier.

"Sorry." I pulled into the driveway and braked us all to a stop. "You go in. I'll clean up the mess."

But Julia was frowning and not moving. "Whose is that?" She nodded at the battered vehicle parked to the side, its nose facing us. "Rupert drives an SUV."

We were stopping at the Wileys' because right before his heart surgery, Rupert had stopped at the library to order a stack of books, asking that we deliver them a week afterward. "I'll be ready," he'd said. "My wife will say I shouldn't be picking up something that heavy, but the doctor says it should be fine."

Since I hadn't wanted to get in the middle of a spousal argument, even between the very happily married Ann Marie and Rupert, I'd erred on the side of caution and told Rupert the bookmobile schedule would send us out there two weeks after his surgery, and if he didn't like that, then he should check out some extra books right then. Rupert had laughed his great big laugh, told me to bring a copy of *The Historian* when we showed up, and now here we were, with a big fat pile of books.

But the cars in the driveway didn't interest me nearly as much as a fast cleanup of Eddie's carrier. Luckily, the mess was small and easy to take care of with a couple of paper towels, and in moments both Julia and I were standing on the front porch of the Wileys' newish retirement home, our arms piled high with books.

"There you are," Ann Marie said, ushering us inside. "And none too soon. This old codger is driving me nuts. A copy of *David Copperfield* is just the ticket to keep him quiet."

"If the bookmobile had stopped by last week like I wanted," Rupert said from the living room's recliner, "I would have been quiet days ago."

His wife sighed so dramatically that Julia gave a nod of approval. "A week ago," Ann Marie said, "you couldn't lift a water glass. How do you think you could have held up one of those big fat books you like so much?"

From Julia's smile of delight, it was clear she was enjoying the argument. I, however, wanted to make sure the teasing didn't devolve into something nastier. "Whose car is that?" I asked, tipping my head to the front door.

"Courtney's," Ann Marie said, since Rupert was busy paging through the top book of Julia's stack, already deaf to what was going on about him. "Rupert's home health care aide. A nurse stops by every couple of days, but we hired a little extra help for a few weeks, until he gets on his feet again."

"My feet work just fine," Rupert muttered as he switched from *Middlemarch* to *The Goldfinch*.

"Feet, yes. The rest of you? Not so much." His wife crossed her arms. "Remember what happened two days ago with the peanut butter sandwich?"

As Julia made encouraging tell-me-more noises, I stuck my thumb in the direction of the kitchen and mouthed, "Bathroom?"

Ann Marie nodded, and I left Julia alone with the Wileys. If the story was good, she'd tell me later, and her recounting would only improve it. Change it, maybe, since Julia never let the strict truth get in the way of a good story, but I'd learned to live with that.

I crossed the formal dining room and saw the back of a thin woman I assumed was Courtney sitting at the oak kitchen table. "Hello," I said cheerfully.

At the sound of my voice, she jumped sky high. Her arm swiped across the table and medications skittered left and right and everywhere, bouncing like tiny balls.

"Oh! Oh!" She lunged to catch what she could, but only made things worse as she created an additional ripple of pill movement.

"I am so sorry." I hurried toward the corner of the room, where I'd seen a small disk roll underneath a plant stand. "I didn't mean to startle you. I'm from the bookmobile and wanted to use the bathroom."

"It's okay," Courtney said, although from her tone of voice, it was anything but.

Well, I could understand that. I'd just created a huge mess for her, and with a job like hers, she was probably on a tight schedule. "Here, let me help." I deposited a small handful of pills on the table and dropped onto my knees to continue the search.

"Thanks," she said, and the second time I handed over a colorful heap, I got a small smile.

She was younger than I'd first thought, probably in her early twenties. Her dark hair was pulled back in a tight ponytail, accentuating her sharp cheekbones and square forehead. "It's just that it takes me so long to count out a week of pills." She nodded at the multi-compartmented box on the table. "I'm not that great with numbers, my boyfriend says I have numerical dyslexia, so I triple-check everything."

And I could certainly understand that, too. Despite the fact I was the offspring of an engineer father and the sister of an engineer brother, math had never been my strong suit. I grinned and gave her a final handful of medications. "I feel your pain. I didn't become a librarian just because I love books."

Courtney sort of smiled. "Good to know I'm not the only one."

"You are so not alone. And sometimes I even wonder about my librarian career choice." I didn't, not ever, but she was looking uncomfortable, and when that happens, I often start babbling in a regrettable way. "Sometimes I think about other things I could do. Open a store, or become a police officer, for instance, because I think they need the help. The murder of Rex Stuhler, you heard about that? Well, there are things they should be considering and—" I stopped short.

Courtney looked up from her pill counting. "What's the matter?"

Out the kitchen window, I'd caught a glimpse of Eddie, who I shouldn't have been able to see, because for me to see him, he'd have to be perched on the windowsill of the side door, which wasn't wide enough to hold him. "Nothing," I said, because he'd disappeared—jumped or fallen?—and explaining Eddie would have taken far more time than either of us had.

I apologized one more time, we made mutual it's-been-nice-to-meet-you's, and I headed back to the living room in time to hear the end of the sandwich story.

A few hours later, the dinner dishes—I'd made tacos, and the grocery store spice pack instead of a homemade blend wasn't nearly as horrible as Aunt Frances claimed—were done, Eddie was contentedly sleeping on the houseboat's dashboard, and my niece was staring at me with a blank expression on her face. "You want to do what?" she asked.

"Walk up to Three Seasons for dessert."

"And I'd want to do that why?"

I looked at the ceiling. *Give me strength,* I asked anyone who might be listening. *I'm trying, I truly am trying.* I put the last spoon in the drawer, assembled a smile, and turned to face Kate. She was sitting on her sleeping bag, legs sprawled out long, and poking at her tablet, playing a brightly colored video game that seemed to involve a significant amount of muttering punctuated by mild invectives. When I'd once asked what game she was playing, she'd shaken her head and said I wouldn't know it. Which was undoubtedly true, but still.

"Because," I said as patiently as I could, "Kristen is making crème brûlée. With strawberries."

In past summers, Sundays had been dessert night. On Sunday evening, Kristen's busy restaurant weekend was at an end, and the two of us, and occasionally our mutual friend Leese Lacombe, spent the evening talking and laughing and, every so often, crying. But things were different now. Kate was staying with me, there was Rafe, and Kristen was married.

Kristen and the Scruff were staying at her father-in-law's summer place for the season and I'd stopped asking about their long-term plans, because they didn't seem to have any other than the certainty that someday the two of them would create a new cooking show unlike anything the world had ever seen.

I absolutely believed this would happen, but that didn't change the fact that I still wanted crème brûlée every Sunday, all summer long. Or in this case, Monday, because flexibility was good.

"Don't you want to see the inside of Kristen's restaurant?" I asked my niece.

She shrugged and kept tapping her small screen. "Not really."

"But the crème brûlée . . ."

"I get headaches, remember?" she snapped. "From the smell of cooking food?"

Ah, yes. The famed headaches, the reason Kate couldn't work any of the lucrative restaurant jobs. I'd called my sister-in-law about the mysterious malady, and she'd said it was news to her.

"Of course I remember," I said soothingly. Didn't really believe her, but I remembered. "The kitchen closes at eight, and it's five past. By the time we walk down there, there won't be a single scent of cooking in the place."

Kate heaved a huge sigh. "I don't suppose you'll go without me."

"Nope," I said cheerfully. "And you've met Kristen. It'll be fun."

My niece sighed again, stabbed at her tablet a few more times, then swung her feet to the floor. "Then let's get this over with."

Her upbeat attitude continued as we walked the wide waterfront sidewalk. She kept her head down the entire way, paying no attention to the bevy of boats on the water, to the eclectic mix of people playing in the adjacent park, or to the gorgeousness of the sun sliding down the edge of the sky, about to dip behind the long line of hills that separated Janay Lake from Lake Michigan.

With me in the lead, mainly because Kate continued to lag behind, we barged in the back door of Three Seasons. Once upon a time, the building had been a Chicago family's summer cottage, but they'd long ago abandoned it in favor of a larger place on the secluded and exclusive point. When Kristen renovated it to restaurant use, she'd magically kept the charm of the original structure, but the kitchen itself she'd gutted from top to bottom, enlarged, and made into a gleaming space of white and stainless steel.

Harvey, Kristen's devoted sous-chef, smiled without looking up from what he was doing. This was a good thing because he had a long, undoubtedly sharp knife in his hand and was slicing strawberries. "She's in her office," he said. "I'm almost done with the dessert."

After Kristen's engagement, I'd been a bit worried about Harvey's reaction, since for years I'd been convinced he was deeply in love with

Kristen and would fall into the depths of despair when he realized there was never any chance of romance between the two of them. She'd always waved off that opinion, and she was right, because Harvey was still happy as sous-chef and was now dating one of Kristen's cousins, who'd been a bridesmaid.

"Come on," I told Kate, who was still lagging.

"She doesn't like me," Kate whispered.

"What?" I stopped in the narrow hallway and turned. "What are you talking about?"

"Your friend. Kristen. She doesn't like me."

I stared. What on earth could have given the child that idea? "Of course she does."

"She's always yelling at me," Kate said.

"Always" was a stretch, since the two had met only a handful of times. "That's Kristen's default." I smiled and patted my niece on the shoulder. "It's not personal. She yells at everyone. You should hear her with Harvey."

Kate crossed her arms over her chest. "She doesn't like me," she repeated.

It would have been better if she'd mentioned this earlier, when I would have had time to straighten everything out. But we were now walking into Kristen's office and it was too late to do anything about Kate's misconception.

"About time you two got here." Kristen tossed a three-ring binder to the floor and picked up her desk phone's receiver. "Harvey, are they done

131

or not done? Not done, and you're fired." She slammed the receiver down. "Hard to get good help these days."

I grinned. If Kristen didn't fire Harvey at least three times a week, there was something wrong with the world. But his job was safe for the day, because almost before Kate and I sat, he was walking in the door with a folding stand and a tray of delectable dessert.

Harvey set up the stand and laid the tray atop. Kristen rolled her chair around, squinted at the ramekins of yumminess, and pronounced him hired until next time.

"Yes, your worship," Harvey said, backing out with a bow.

Kristen snorted and distributed spoons and linen napkins. "That boy is a trial, I tell you."

Kate looked at me, wide-eyed, and I sent her a reassuring smile. "How was your weekend?" I asked Kristen. "Good, I assume, with the Fourth just last week."

She tossed her long blond ponytail off her shoulder. "If by 'good,' you mean busy, then yeah, it was good. But have I mentioned how hard it is to find supplemental staff? My people are working themselves into the ground and there's no end in sight.

"And you," Kristen said, banging her spoon on her desk and glaring at Kate. "I hear you get headaches from the smell of cooking food. You must be the first in the history of the world. What's up with that?"

"I don't . . . I can't . . ." Kate leapt to her feet and ran out of the room. A few seconds later, the kitchen door slammed.

Kristen half stood, then sat back down. "I'm such an idiot. Sorry, Minnie. I'm used to being able to say whatever I want around you. I wasn't thinking."

"Don't worry about it." I gave my crème brûlée a longing glance, picked the strawberry off the top, popped it in my mouth, and went after my niece.

The next morning I wasn't scheduled to work until noon, so I made a Real Breakfast for Kate and me. Omelets—egg and cheese only because that's all there was—and fried potatoes. I didn't burn a thing, and Kate ate hers without a single complaint.

The night before, after I'd caught up with her halfway back to the boathouse, she'd agreed to return to Kristen's only after I convinced her that though Kristen was crusty on the outside, inside she had the proverbial heart of gold. Or if not gold, at least high-quality silver. Kate had dragged her feet all the way back, but once there, Kristen turned on the charm and had her laughing in minutes. She laughed the hardest at Kristen's stories of a young Minnie's attempts to play basketball, and I was so glad to see her laughing I didn't mind the ridicule a single bit.

Now, Kate finished her glass of orange juice and put her dirty dishes next to the sink. "I'm working late," she said. "Don't know when I'll be back."

"Are you at the toy store?" I asked, turning to look at the whiteboard, but it was blank. "Kate, you didn't write down—"

"Mrr," Eddie said, just as the door shut. I felt the deck of the houseboat shift as Kate jumped to the pier and was gone.

"What am I doing wrong?" I asked my cat as I washed the dishes.

He jumped down from the nest he'd made of Kate's sleeping bag and, purring, bumped my shin.

"This summer isn't anything like I imagined," I said, picking him up and giving him a good snuggle, one guaranteed to get Eddie hair all over my clothing.

"Mrr!" He squiggled out of my grasp, jumped to the floor, and pelted down the steps and into my bedroom.

Nice. Even my cat couldn't stand me. "Love you, too, pal," I called. I brushed off what feline hairs I could, grabbed my backpack, managed to drop it, picked it up again, and headed out into the sunshine. Rafe had left at oh-dark-thirty for a short fishing trip with some friends, but I looked at the house as I walked by, somehow hoping to catch a glimpse of him even though I knew he was gone.

"Silly," I murmured, shaking my head at myself. Had I really come to this? That a single day without him was too long to endure? Was this what love could do?

I decided to think about it later and turned my face to the morning sun, the better to enjoy my walk. The last few days, I'd been thinking about John and Nandi Jaquay and how Polly from the chamber of commerce had said they'd seemed intent on putting Rex out of business. Even though I'd passed that information on to Ash, I'd thought of a way that I, as a private and concerned citizen, could learn more about the Jaquays without raising anyone's suspicions. It could be that Kate's unhappiness with me was due to associating me with finding a murder victim, and if I could help find the killer, maybe she'd shift from angry adolescent to nice niece.

The alliteration was pleasing, but it wasn't quite right, so instead of going straight to the front door of the Tonedagana County Building, which was right in front of me at this point, I wandered a bit on the county's complicated system of sidewalks, thinking about other possibilities. Radiant relative? Kind kin? Friendly family?

"It's Minnie, right?"

I jumped at the gravelly voice. In the shade of

a large maple tree, a man was sitting on a picnic table bench. He was thin, with long, sun-streaked hair and was smiling at me over the innards of a lawn mower. One of Ash's friends, and last summer he'd helped teach me to water-ski. Sort of.

"Hey, Tank." I eyed his uniform of dark blue pants and a light blue short-sleeved shirt with a name embroidered on the left pocket. "Is your name really Cecil?"

"Yeah, and if you call me that, I'll never talk to you again." He smiled, wiping his greasy hands on a rag.

I laughed. "No worries. I didn't know you worked here."

"Maintenance for almost three years, did roofing before that. What brings you to the county building?" he asked.

It occurred to me that my plan of going up to the building department could be revised. I'd met the head of the building department last year and had hoped to expand our acquaintance this morning, but maybe Tank could help me. "Do you know John and Nandi Jaquay?"

Tank's easy smile faded fast. "Why do you ask?" His voice was wary.

And now was the time to trot out the not-quite-true story I'd dreamed up for the building department. "I have a friend who's thinking about doing some work for them, but I've heard—"

136

"If whatever you've heard is bad, then it's right." Tank pulled a screwdriver out of his pocket and leaned forward to replace the lawnmower's housing. "Those two are why I ended up here at the county. Things came out okay for me, but the roofer I worked for lost his business. Lost his house and his wife, too."

"That sounds horrible." I sat across from him. "Do you mind telling me what happened?"

He snorted. "We put a top-of-the-line standing seam metal roof on their house and never got paid because those two said our work was substandard." He said the word in almost a growl. "Substandard, my . . . my aunt Fanny. We did quality work, the best in the area, and because we finished a week late, they wouldn't pay."

"That can't be right."

"Yeah, tell me about it." Tank finished tightening and put the screwdriver in his pocket. "My boss took them to court, but it didn't do any good. The Jaquays had all these lies the judge believed and we didn't get a dime. Worse, those two spread the word that our roofing was crap, and before you knew it, business dried up and we were done."

I stared at him. "That's awful!"

He nodded. "So tell your friend to stay away." Standing, he said, "The only people I know to win against the Jaquays were Rex and Dawn Stuhler. They ran this huge social media blitz and got the Jaquays to back down. Of course, now Rex is dead." Tank shrugged. "You never know, do you?"

I thanked him for his information and time, and left as he pulled the lawnmower to life, but the engine's roar didn't drown out my thoughts.

The Jaquays were small-minded, grasping, and vindictive toward more than just ABK Pest Control. On the plus side, Rex and his wife had fought back and won against the Jaquays.

But had the fight cost Rex his life?

CHAPTER 8

There were still a couple of hours before I needed to show up at the library, so I did a Minnie-size U-turn and aimed myself downtown. If I could manage a few minutes with a detective or two, I'd save myself having to call or e-mail or text. Plus, if I showed up at their front door, it was harder for them to ignore me.

"Now that's an evil smile," Pam Fazio said. She was sitting on the front step of her store, which was one of the three places Kate was working. Pam was originally from Ohio, had retired early from a successful corporate career, and was now the successful proprietor of Older Than Dirt, with its eclectic collection of antiques, kitchenware, and shoes.

"Evil is in the eye of the beholder," I told her. "What does that say about you?"

She hoisted her coffee mug in my direction. "That I'm a remarkably good judge of character."

I laughed, and since it was a beautiful morning and I had time, I asked, "Any chance I can mooch a cup of that?" There was indeed, and two minutes later I was sitting in the sun next to Pam, sipping her outstanding brew. It had been Pam's post-retirement vow that she would, every morning, drink a cup of coffee outside in the fresh air, and to date she'd done so, if you counted her home's unheated glass porch as outside, which I did when the temperature was below freezing.

After chatting about this and that, I summoned the courage to ask the question for which I wasn't sure I wanted an honest answer. "How's it going with Kate?"

Pam's face had been buried in her mug, and when she came up for air, she was . . . smiling?

"It's only been a few days, but I can tell she's going to be outstanding," Pam said. "Shows up on time, stays late, works hard, bends over backward for customers. And she's funny."

No, she had to be talking about someone else. "Kate's funny?"

Pam laughed. "Haven't you ever heard her imitate—"

"Are you the owner of this place?"

Pam and I looked up at the couple standing in front of us. The male looked about fifty, she looked a few years younger, and they both looked cranky.

"That's me," Pam said, smiling. "And if I recall correctly, you're Nandi and John Jaquay. What can I do for you?"

I pricked up my ears. This was the couple who had given Rex Stuhler such a hard time? Interesting.

"We're returning all of this," John said, pointing with his chin at the bags they both held.

140

"None of it works in our house like you said, and we want a full refund."

"Okay." Pam eased to her feet. "Well, come on inside and I'll take a look."

"There's nothing to look at," Nandi said loudly. "Here's the receipt. Just give us our money back, cash is fine, and we won't report you."

"Oh?" Pam's eyebrows went up and she glanced in my direction. I gave her a quick wave and a nod good-bye. Pam had genius-level conflict management skills, so I had no doubt she'd come out of this situation with flying colors.

Thinking, I made my way to the sheriff's office, where a new deputy showed me into the dragon-less interview room and told me to make myself comfortable, because both Detective Inwood and Deputy Wolverson were in another meeting.

"No problem," I said, pulling a copy of Josephine Tey's *The Daughter of Time* from my backpack.

The deputy blinked, then she smiled. "That's right, you're the bookmobile librarian, aren't you? Brynn talks about you all the time."

"Brynn Wilbanks?" I let the book drop to my lap. "How do you know her? And how is she? We haven't seen her in months."

And I'd been concerned, because the seven-year-old Brynn was in remission from leukemia. At least I hoped she was. Brynn was the primary reason Eddie was a fixture on the bookmobile.

141

When Eddie had stowed away on the vehicle's maiden voyage, I'd initially vowed it would be a one-time deal. But Brynn had also discovered the bookmobile kitty. On the second Eddie-less trip, she'd been so disappointed at his absence that she'd dissolved into tears and that was that.

The deputy said Brynn's mom was her cousin, that Brynn was fine, and that the family had moved to Charlevoix.

"Next time you see them, tell them Eddie and I say hello." I sat back, smiling. Brynn wasn't sick; they'd just moved, and I hadn't heard the news. Easy explanation, nothing bad at all. Sometimes it happened.

"Hey," Ash said, sliding into the seat opposite. "Hal's in with the sheriff and it sounds like they're going to be there for a while. Hope you can live with the disappointment of not seeing him."

"If I die in the night, you'll know why." I smiled. "Thanks for making time for me. I was walking past and thought I'd pop in to see if there's anything new on Rex's murder."

Ash glanced out the open door and hitched his chair a little closer. "I can't see how it would hurt to tell you this. Remember Rex's wife, Fawn? We're back to considering her a suspect."

"How?" I frowned. "She had an alibi."

"Not all alibis are created equal," he said enigmatically. "And don't bother asking for details, because I'm not going to give any. But I'll say one more thing; the pest control business was in financial trouble."

Time ticked along, then my brain caught up. "You think she might have killed him for the insurance?"

Ash smiled and quoted Hal Inwood. "All avenues of investigation are being pursued."

I flapped my hand at him. "Whatever. But do you know why the business wasn't doing well?"

"Because they didn't have enough customers," he said promptly.

I sighed. "Yes, but *why* didn't they have enough customers?"

"Because they weren't good at getting rid of pests?"

"This," I told my imaginary audience, "is why I'm here." I put my elbows on the table and leaned in. "Have you ever heard of John and Nandi Jaquay?"

By the time I left the sheriff's office, the sky had clouded up something fierce. Lightning flashed, thunder crashed, and I was glad I'd worn sensible shoes because running in sandals never ends well for me.

I dashed inside the library just as the heavens opened up, and I stood in the entryway, chest heaving, until I caught my breath and could turn back into a calm and collected assistant director.

That coolheadedness stayed with me all the way through until the eight o'clock closing time, and persisted until I had to double back to the library to check that I'd turned off the coffeepot.

Which I had, but not being able to remember for sure was going to make me late for whatever Rafe was cooking for dinner at the house. Luckily, he and Kate had been playing a cutthroat game of double solitaire and hadn't noticed I was late.

After a quick dinner of grilled cheese sandwiches accompanied by the salad masterpiece of iceberg lettuce, one cherry tomato, and shredded cheddar cheese topped with ranch dressing, Kate retreated to the houseboat while Rafe and I sat on the front porch and watched the rain come down. It was a nice feeling, sitting there side by side and hand in hand, and I had a vision of us sitting the same way in front of the fireplace this winter.

"What's so funny?" Rafe asked, rubbing the back of my knuckles with his thumb.

"Nothing. I'm just happy."

"There's an easy way to fix that." He stood. "Let's go down to the basement. Now that we're getting a good rain, I want to make sure nothing is seeping in."

"So romantic," I murmured. But in a way, it was. Rafe was making sure the house was safe and sound, which meant we could be safe and sound, and what was more romantic than that?

It might have been the ranch dressing, the rain, or pure serendipity, but the next morning, I woke with an idea of how to come at a motive for murder from a different direction. Rex's obituary, finally available online, had said he was survived by his parents and that they lived in Chilson, so there was a possibility that either his mom or dad had spent time at the Lakeview Medical Care Facility. Many people did, either as a resident or in temporarily for a stint in long-term rehabilitation. Maybe they were even still there, and maybe I could talk to them and learn more about Rex and Fawn from a parental point of view.

Cade had spent time there after a stroke, and when visiting him, I'd come to know a number of residents and staff fairly well. I also regularly dropped off and picked up books, and there was no reason I couldn't stop by that very morning to see if there were other ways the library could help out.

I bounded out of bed—or more precisely, I slid carefully out from between the sheets in a way that didn't disturb a sleeping Eddie—and was ready to go in half an hour. At the houseboat's door, with a laden cat carrier in hand, I glanced at the sky. Still gray. "Kate," I asked, "do you want a ride to work?"

"Huh?" She was standing at the kitchen counter, a spoon in one hand as she ate a bowl of cold cereal, her cell phone in the other. "Oh. No. I'm good."

"If you're sure. See you for dinner."

The spoon and phone were lowered. "Who's cooking?"

I was tempted to say me, just to see the expression on her face, but I resisted temptation. "Aunt Frances. I think she's making fajitas."

She nodded. "Okay. I should be there just after six."

"Great. Have a good day."

My niece shrugged and the phone and spoon went back up.

"You are dismissed," I muttered as Eddie and I headed to my car. Had I treated my mom like that when I was Kate's age? Someday I'd have to ask. Although not now, because it was possible I wasn't ready for the answer.

At Lakeview, I parked in the shade, cracked the windows, and told Eddie I'd be back in ten minutes. "Mrr," he said, yawning, and rolled over. I eyed him. "It's great that you'll be okay, but sometimes it would be nice if you expressed a little concern for me in my absences."

His mouth opened and closed in a silent "Mrr," which made me laugh, and I was still smiling when I walked into the facility.

"It's Miss Minnie!" A white-haired man in a wheelchair, who had been pulled up to a table with a jigsaw puzzle spread across it, zipped over to me. "But what ho? You are bereft of books!" Max Compton made a display of peering at my empty hands. He looked up at me, his face contorted into an expression of horror. "You've come with bad news, haven't you? You're making a special stop to let me down gently. Just tell me now," he said, hanging his head. "Rip off the bandage."

Max was one of my best friends at Lakeview, and he was a huge fan of books by thriller writers, especially thrillers set in the Great Lakes region. Any day a large print John Sandford book was released was a day of celebration for Max, but it was also a day of fear, because Max was never certain he'd live long enough to finish reading the book.

"Are you sure?" I asked.

His thin chest rose and fell as he sighed. "Do it."

"Okay, then." I paused dramatically. "It's about Sandford's latest book. It's . . ." And because I have a teensy bit of a mean streak, I paused again. "It's almost eight hundred pages."

Max's eyes practically bugged out of his head. "Are you kidding?"

"Well, actually, yes. I am."

He slumped in his wheelchair and put his hand on his bony chest. "My heart . . . my heart . . . I think you've pushed me to the brink. The abyss is looming beneath my feet. The chasm is opening . . ."

Though I'd hurried toward him, as he kept talking, I eased back and said, "Max, no one having a heart attack could possibly talk as much as you do."

He looked at me, still slumped, still with his hand on his chest. "Maybe this is one of those asymptomatic heart attacks."

"You could be right," I said. "Just to be sure, let me call nine-one-one. We'll get an ambulance here in no time and—"

"And I'm suddenly feeling much better," he said, straightening, and looking for a second like the picture of a younger Max I'd seen in his room, in army uniform, standing with a group of fellow Korean Era soldiers. "The sight of you alone, Miss Minnie, is enough to give an old man palpitations. No wonder I got confused."

I laughed. "Nice try, Max. But I am sorry I didn't bring any books." Then, because he was clearly about to ask me why I was there, I added, "I'm looking for some information and was hoping to talk to Heather." She was an extremely competent certified nursing assistant and had a wealth of knowledge about Lakeview tucked up inside her head.

"Looking for dirt?" Max grinned and rubbed his hands together. "She's not going to tell you anything good, you know. All those rules."

I realized he was right. Privacy rules would no doubt prevent Heather from giving me any of the information I wanted. "Okay. I'll ask you. If you can keep a secret, that is."

Max, from his wheelchair, managed to look down his nose at me. "My dear young librarian. I am the soul of discretion. How could you doubt?"

I did doubt, because Max, as my grandfather had said, could talk the hind leg off a donkey, and who knew what he'd let slip? Still, it couldn't possibly matter that much; anything he knew was almost certainly common knowledge. "Did you know Rex Stuhler?"

"He who was murdered?" Max nodded. "His mother was here for a few weeks after she fell and broke her leg." He patted his thigh. "Pins and screws and rods all over the place. Rex was the only offspring still in Michigan, and he stopped by every day."

"Was he . . ." I hesitated, trying to find the right words. "My niece is the one who found Rex's body. She's having trouble dealing with it, and I'm hoping that if I can learn more about Rex . . ." I trailed off, since I wasn't about to tell Max that I was trying to find a killer.

"Looking for closure?" Max snorted. "Not sure what I can tell you. Courtney took Mary home and—"

"Hang on." I interrupted because sometimes that was the only way to get a word in edgewise with Max. "Mary is Rex's mom, but who is Courtney?"

"Home health aide," he said. "Courtney Drew. Skinny kid, long hair in a ponytail so tight she must have an eternal headache. Makes me wince to look at her. She comes in to help move people back home."

Max kept talking, and I tried to listen, but I was completely distracted by the knowledge that there was a connection between Courtney—she of the spilled pills—and Rex, that Courtney had taken care of Rex's mom. New information was good, but then there was the big question: Did it mean anything?

CHAPTER 9

Dinner ended up with girls on one side of the table and boys on the other. Kate, Aunt Frances, and Minnie facing Otto and Rafe. We were in the bucolic backyard of Otto and Aunt Frances's house. Birds twittering, water bubbling out of a fountain Otto had built, leaves sighing softly overhead, all that. It was a gorgeous summer evening. Peace and contentment reigned. Life was happy and good. All was well with the world.

Except it wasn't.

Things were a little bit off all the way around the table. Rafe was picking at his food, something so unusual I was afraid he was coming down with something. Kate was, as usual, trying to avoid me as much as possible, and even Aunt Frances seemed to be keeping her distance. Otto was the only one behaving normally, but it was hard for two people to carry a conversation for five.

I ground black pepper on my salad and thought about what to say. It was time to leap into the topic that my aunt had been avoiding the entire meal. I didn't want to upset her, but I also didn't want to ignore what was going on. One more bite of salad, I figured, might help, so I forked in a small pile of greens, carrot, cucumber, feta cheese, and unfortunately, an inordinate amount of pepper.

151

The moment the bite went in my mouth, I started coughing. Which is bad when you have a mouthful of food. I grabbed my napkin and held it to my lips as I hacked away.

Rafe looked up from his plate. "Are you okay?"

Coughing, I shook my head. Definitely not okay.

Aunt Frances turned. "Do you need the Heimlich?"

Tears streaming down my cheeks as I kept coughing, I shook my head again. Definitely did not need the Heimlich maneuver. I'd be fine in a minute; I just had to get that pepper out of my throat . . .

"Here." Kate reached in front of Aunt Frances and picked up my water glass. "Drink."

At that point I might have taken a drink from the River Styx if it had been put in front of me. I grabbed the glass and drank deep. And like magic, my cough disappeared.

"What was that all about?" Aunt Frances asked.

"Pepper," Kate and I said simultaneously. This struck me as hilarious, so I laughed, but since my throat was exhausted from the coughing jag, it was a soft and spasm-y sort of laugh.

My aunt looked from Kate to me. "Must be from your mother's side of the family."

And there was an excellent sequel opportunity! I thanked Kate for the water, and said, "Speaking of Mom, I talked to her the other day and she asked how Cousin Celeste was doing. You knew that Kate and I were over at the boardinghouse for breakfast the other day, right?"

"That's what you said you were going to do," Aunt Frances said, "so I assumed you did it. And I've been waiting patiently ever since to hear how it went." She sounded almost snarky, a completely un-Aunt-Frances-like tone.

I glanced at Otto. He caught my eye and shook his head the tiniest bit. I wasn't sure what he meant, but I added *Pull Otto aside* to my mental list of things to do before we left.

"Sorry," I told my aunt. "You're right, I should have called."

"Apology accepted. And I'm sorry I snapped at you. It's just . . ." She looked off into the dark green of the trees. "It's just different."

"Not as much as you might think," I said. "At least across the street. A pair of guests made Sunday breakfast and were going to try kiteboarding in the afternoon. Another pair was asking about scenic back roads, and the final pair was looking forward to having the house to themselves. So it looks like the old Saturday breakfast routine has shifted to Sunday."

I finished with a great big smile, but Aunt Frances just stared at me. "That's nice," she finally said. Then she must have heard how she sounded, because she added, "Really nice."

Rafe glanced from her to me, opened his mouth,

shut it without saying anything, then opened it again. "This chicken is great, Frances. What was in the marinade?"

Since he'd barely eaten two bites of chicken, I knew full well he was doing his best to change the subject. It was good timing, though, and I flashed him a grateful smile.

Afterward, I told my aunt that Otto and I would do the dishes. "You three play a game of croquet or something," I said to Rafe. "If you're feeling up to it. You looked a little funny earlier."

"Just thinking about some work stuff." He patted my head, something I didn't tolerate from anyone else. "I'm fine."

I frowned. "It's July. What work do you have?"

"Work on the house," he said. "It's July, silly. Why would I be thinking about school?"

I gave him a gentle push in the direction of the croquet set and carried a pile of dishes inside. Otto loaded the dishwasher and I put the food away in what I hoped were the right places.

"So earlier," I said, "I thought Aunt Frances would be glad. About Celeste running the boardinghouse the same as she did."

"Ah." Otto nodded. "She is. Or she will be. What she's dealing with now is, if my experience with retirement is any judge, a dislocation of sorts. The old way of living is gone, but the new way hasn't settled in yet."

That made sense. Sort of. I filed it away in my

head, hoping to remember it when the time came for me to retire, which was at least thirty years off, so remembering was unlikely. "How long will it take her to get used to the new way?"

"Everybody's different." Otto looked out the window, where Aunt Frances was relocating the croquet wickets Rafe had haphazardly stuck in the ground. "Could be weeks, could be months. Some people never truly adjust to retirement."

I must have made a noise, because he turned to me. "Don't worry, Minnie. She'll come around."

"What if she doesn't?"

"She will." He smiled. "I have a plan."

Otto's plan, it turned out, was to take Aunt Frances on a tour of northwest lower Michigan. That she'd lived there more than forty years didn't seem to bother him. And he was probably right, because when you live somewhere, you tend to get occupied by the work of living and don't get around to doing the fun stuff.

He rattled off Up North summer things she hadn't done in years. Ride the Ironton Ferry. Pick cherries. Sit on the patio at Legs and watch the sun go down over Lake Michigan. Kayak the Chain of Lakes. "And I don't want to limit us to the northern lower part of Michigan," Otto said. "We should tour the Soo Locks. Go up into Canada and take the Agawa Canyon train. Take the circle tour around Lake Superior."

Ideas gushed forth, and by the time the dishes were washed and put away, he'd described activities to last five summers and I was half convinced his plan would work.

The next morning, standing and watching coffee drip down into the carafe, I wasn't so sure.

"You look sad. What's the matter?" Holly had just come into the library's break room, carrying a small plate of her legendary brownies.

I hesitated, thinking about choices and consequences. Then, shushing the calorie-oriented part of my conscience, I reached for the closest brownie—which was also the biggest, but sometimes serendipity is a real thing—and said, "I'm suddenly feeling much better. What's the occasion?"

She put the plate on the table and smiled at it. "Brian wanted a care package to take with him. These are what's left after I boxed up his and the kids ate theirs."

"Well, thanks for bringing any at all." I ate a bite and closed my eyes, the better to enjoy the sensory rush. "These are so good."

"Yep." She poured herself a cup of coffee. "Sit down with me for a minute."

"Sure, what's up? Oh, hey, Mr. Goodwin. How are you this fine morning?"

The white-haired Mr. Goodwin, everyone's favorite library patron (not that we had favorites, of course), came into the room, sniffing the air.

"Does my nose deceive me? Ah, it does not!" He pointed at the brownies with his cane. "Fifty dollars to your favorite charity if I get the last one."

Holly laughed. "No charge for you, Mr. Goodwin."

"You sell yourself short, Holly Terpening." He shuffled to the table and took the smallest square. "Now, tell me that Kelsey brewed the coffee, and then life will be perfect."

"Sorry." I smiled. It had been because of Mr. Goodwin's self-diagnosis of caffeine deprivation that we'd opened the staff break room to the general public. It mostly worked out, except for the one time Mr. Goodwin set up the coffee. He made Kelsey's version look like tea.

The three of us chatted for a bit, then Mr. Goodwin returned to the reading room and Holly turned back to me. "First off, what's wrong? For a second you were looking like you did last winter when Fat Boys Pizza closed for a week."

"Just some family stuff. I'm sure it'll work out."

Holly looked at me. "You don't want to talk about it? No? Well, if you're sure . . . what I really want to ask about is"—she glanced at the door, which was still empty—"is about Stan's money for the library. Everyone has been saying what they want left and right, but you haven't said a word. So I'm wondering. Do you know something we don't?"

My response was immediate and one hundred percent truthful. "Nope."

"Really?" Holly's expression was disappointment mixed with a dash of disbelief and the tiniest sprinkle of hope.

"Really." I watched the hope vanish, the disbelief fade, and the disappointment swell. "Sorry, but I just don't. It's a board decision. Graydon seems as clueless as we are."

"Well, what do you think should be done with the money?" she asked. "You're assistant director. You were interim director and could have been director if you'd wanted. So you can't tell me you haven't thought about how the money should be spent."

Of course I had. And there was only one thing that made sense to me. "It's a board decision," I said weakly.

"Duh." Holly rolled her eyes. "But tell me what you think."

I smiled at the ceiling. "It would be great if they would put part of the money to buying a new bookmobile every five years."

The current vehicle had celebrated its second birthday in late May, but we were driving over twenty thousand miles a year and new ones cost the earth and the money I'd been putting aside wouldn't buy even a used one for roughly a hundred and ten years. I'd been told that Stan had wanted to create a foundation with enough capital to buy a new bookmobile every ten years, but I wasn't sure Stan had written his will so tightly that it couldn't be interpreted differently by an attorney whose clients had a different agenda.

"We all want something," I said, wiping the corners of my mouth with a napkin.

Holly nodded, and we sat there for a moment, just thinking.

Because we all did want something and there was no way all of us were going to get what we wanted. Some of us were going to end up disappointed.

Or even all of us.

After my library day ended, I walked back to the marina through downtown. I'd felt my feet moving to go around and had corrected myself. "No way," I told my feet, and reoriented them in the direction of the main drag. "You enjoy downtown. You like the people and the energy. You will not be afraid of getting pushed into the street again."

More than a week after I'd fallen, I'd come to the conclusion that whatever had happened had been sheer accident. No one had tried to kill me; that was silly. No one had tried to kill me since, right? If they'd been serious about the effort, there had been plenty of times when I'd been by myself and could have been picked off by various methods without too much trouble. Ergo, it had been an accident.

"It couldn't have been anything else," I murmured, and promptly walked straight into a large human being.

"Sorry!" I gasped, backing up and almost running into an elderly couple and their little dog. "Sorry," I said to them, then turned to face whoever it was I'd collided with.

He was big and tall and sturdy, and luckily, he was smiling. "Hey, Minnie," Mitchell Koyne said. "Funny running into you here." He laughed.

I sort of laughed back, because he clearly thought he'd made a joke. "Sorry," I said again. "My mind was elsewhere, I guess." We edged out of the way of foot traffic and stood next to the toy store, under the perky striped awning.

"Me too." Mitchell hefted a broom. "The beach is a quarter mile away but somehow sand gets tracked in all day long." He made a face. "Hate the feel of sand under my shoes."

I wasn't sure what was more surprising, that Mitchell knew exactly how far away the city beach was, that he was skilled in broom handling, or that he had an opinion on cleanliness. For the millionth time, I told myself not to underestimate Mitchell. All these years, he'd been hiding an upright and contributing member of society underneath an aw-shucks exterior. It had taken the love of a good woman to bring forth the butterfly from the caterpillar, and if, every so often, I missed the old Mitchell, then shame on me.

Mitchell leaned on his broom and looked down at me. That downward look was something I was used to, because most adults and many children on the planet looked down on me that way, but especially Mitchell, because he was more than a foot taller than I was. It made conversations with him a bit awkward, because if I stood a normal distance away, I risked a stiff neck, and if I inched far enough away to ease my neck pain, it looked like I was trying to escape.

"I keep meaning to talk to you about your niece."

"Oh?" I kept my tone light, but on the inside everything from my shoulders to my toes clenched tight. Kate was insubordinate. She didn't deal well with the customers. She was late, left early, took long breaks, and used her cell phone all day long. He needed to fire her and wanted to let me know first. "What's up?" I asked.

"Just wanted to say that she's a great kid."

I blinked. "She's . . . what?"

"Well, I figured she'd be a decent worker, being your niece and all, but she's really good."

"She . . . is?"

"You bet," he said, nodding. "If all of my employees worked as hard as she does, I'd be able to hire fewer people."

Kate was a hard worker? Pam had said much the same thing, but it was difficult to reconcile

Kate the Industrious Employee with the Kate who didn't bother to fold her clean laundry. "So things are working out?"

"Absolutely." He beamed. "So I wanted to thank you for sending her my way, that's all. I've already told her that if she wants to come back next year, she'll probably get bumped up to—"

My phone rang loudly. "Sorry," I said, fumbling to turn it off. But since it's almost impossible to turn off a ringing cell phone without looking to see who's calling, I looked and saw it was Ash.

"Um, Mitchell," I said, "it's great that you like Kate, and I'd love to talk more, but I need to take this call."

"Sure. See you later," he said, and went back to his sweeping task.

I poked at my still-ringing phone. "Hey," I said. "Any news on the investigation front? Or is this a social call?"

"Both," he said.

I sucked in a quick breath. His voice had been terse and grim. "What's the matter?"

"It's your niece. She's been hauled in by a deputy. You'd better get over here."

CHAPTER 10

I rushed down to the sheriff's office, and on the way called Aunt Frances, then Rafe. I started to call my brother, but stopped just before I pushed the button. No. I'd call after I knew more. Maybe this wasn't as bad as it sounded. Maybe there was just a misunderstanding.

I burst in the front door as Aunt Frances and Otto pulled into the parking lot. A deputy ushered us back to the interview room, where three people were already sitting; Kate, Ash, and Sheriff Kit Richardson.

The two law enforcement officers sat across the table from Kate, who was slouched in her chair, arms crossed and chin on her chest.

"Kate, are you okay?" I asked. She muttered something that could have been "I'm fine," and Aunt Frances and Otto and I pulled chairs up to the table. It was a tight fit for six, but we made it work.

"Sheriff," I said, nodding at Kit Richardson. Straight-backed and serious, she was an imposing figure, but I'd once seen her in an ancient bathrobe while cuddling Eddie, so I knew she had a human side.

"Ms. Hamilton," the sheriff said. "Good to see you, Ms. Pixley, or I suppose it's Ms. Bingham now?"

Aunt Frances smiled. "And it's always Frances. Have you met my husband?"

The sheriff shook hands with Otto. "Haven't had the pleasure. Good to have you in Chilson, sir."

Kate sighed, but not heavily. Which was good, because if she had she would've gotten a jab in the ribs from my elbow. The sheriff's interview room was not the place to display an attitude. I knew this from personal experience.

"What's going on, Kit?" my aunt asked. "Why is my great-niece here?"

The sheriff turned to Ash. "Do you want to explain, or shall we pull in Deputy Gardner?"

Ash looked at the sheriff, at the rest of us, then back at the sheriff. "If it's all right with you, ma'am, I can describe the incident."

She nodded. "Go ahead, Deputy."

"Yes, ma'am." He took a breath, and stared at the wall as he spoke. "We have learned that Ms. Katrina Hamilton, known as Kate, had taken cell phone photos of the Fourth of July crowd on her cell phone before her discovery of the body of Mr. Rex Stuhler."

Kate's relatives swiveled to gaze at her. Kate herself started sliding down in her chair.

Ash went on. "Since that day, Ms. Kate Hamilton has been taking the pictures into downtown businesses and asking staff and customers if they could name the people in

164

the photos. An hour ago, she walked into the Wood Shed bar. Deputy Gardner was inside the establishment, off-duty, and recognized Ms. Hamilton. Knowing that she was under age, the deputy approached and overheard her conversation with the bartender. He called Detective Inwood regarding the matter. Detective Inwood requested that Deputy Gardner bring Ms. Hamilton into the sheriff's office."

There was so much wrong here that I didn't know where to start being angry. But . . . the Wood Shed? Really? The dive-iest bar in Chilson? How did she have the courage to walk into a place like that at her age?

Sheriff Richardson stirred. "Ms. Hamilton," she said flatly. "Please explain two things. One. What on God's great earth did you think you were doing? Number two." The sheriff leaned forward, focusing her laser-like stare on my niece. "Get us those photos or I'll charge you with obstruction."

Kate looked up. "But—"

"Now!" the sheriff roared.

My niece flinched, then hurriedly pulled out her phone.

Sheriff Richardson glanced at Ash. "Give her your e-mail," she said, then pulled Aunt Frances and Otto and myself into her office, where she assured us Kate wasn't in any real trouble. "The girl has guts, I'll give her that," the sheriff said. "But she has to be safe and smart."

165

I liked that phrase: "safe and smart." So I used it when, half an hour later, Aunt Frances, Otto, Kate, and I sat in their kitchen with my cell phone on speaker, talking to my brother and sister-in-law.

"You did what?" Jennifer asked, her normally calm voice going shrill.

"It was no big deal, Mom," Kate said. "I didn't do anything wrong."

"Really? Then why were you hauled down to the sheriff's office?"

"I'm more concerned," Matt said, "that you didn't show those pictures to anyone. How could you not know that the police would want to see them?"

Jennifer sighed. "Katrina, I thought we could trust you, but this isn't working. You need to come home."

A pang of disappointment made me swallow, but I understood. "Sorry," I murmured. "This is my fault. I should have kept a better eye on her."

"She's old enough to know better," Jennifer said firmly. "Thanks for taking the blame, Minnie, but it's on her. When we talked about her going north this summer, she promised she was old enough to be trusted. It's not your fault."

Though it was nice my sister-in-law was letting me off the hook, I knew I shared in the responsibility for Kate's actions. I sighed. "I'll look up flights first thing tomorrow and let you know what time to pick her up."

My niece sat up straight, glared at me, then

glared at the phone. "What about my jobs? I have three. You want me to leave without telling them? Or give them what, an hour notice?" She snorted. "Isn't that what you're always complaining about, that kids today aren't being held accountable, that we don't have common courtesy, that we don't understand how our actions impact others?"

Matt sighed. "Honey, you can't pull out the responsibility card when it suits you."

"No, but she has a point," Aunt Frances said. "Summer help is hard for retailers to find, let alone good summer help."

I nodded at the phone. "And two of her employers have, without prompting, told me how happy they are to have her."

"Yes, but . . ." Jennifer's voice trailed off. She was clearly wavering.

"Mom, Dad, they need me." Kate's hands turned into fists. "No one has ever . . ." She stopped, then started again. "They really need me," she said quietly. "Please let me stay?"

And eventually, they did.

The next morning, my boss was in the break room ahead of me. "The sunset was gorgeous last night," Graydon said, as he poured coffee into his mug, and then into the travel mug I was clutching. "So many colors. I've never seen anything like it."

I stared at him through bleary eyes. The

bookmobile was ready to roll, parked temporarily just outside the door, with Julia and Eddie aboard, but I'd popped in to pull a book that had just been requested online and was making double use of the time by maximizing my caffeine possibilities.

"Didn't see it." I screwed down the mug's top. "I was . . . busy."

Which was almost certainly the understatement of the year. Graydon was stirring creamer into his coffee and eyeing me.

"Are you all right?" he asked. "You look a little tired."

Again with the understatement. I put on a smile. "Some family problems. Nothing I can't handle." I hoped.

Graydon smiled as he edged toward the doorway. "More niece issues?" Then, before I could say anything, he added, "Just remember that everything gets better eventually." He nodded, and was gone.

"Yeah," I muttered to myself, "but what kind of time frame are we talking about?" What did "eventually" mean? A week? A month? A year? Lots of years?

Sighing, I headed out to start the day, and immediately felt my spirits rise, because no matter what else was going on, everything was better on the bookmobile.

Julia squirmed around in her seat, rearranging herself and her seat belt so she could reach into the pocket of her shorts. "Hah!" she crowed. "Got one!"

I was about to ask "Got what?" when I saw that she was pulling back her long, loose strawberry blond hair and tying it up with a hair elastic. It was times like this—when Julia was so completely human—that I had a hard time reconciling the woman seated next to me with the pictures Aunt Frances had shown me of a younger Julia in the days of her Broadway success, cavorting with the rich and famous, and dazzling everyone with her smile.

"Do you miss it?" I asked. "Being an actor?"

She snorted. "Hardly. The backstage arguments, the hotels, the crappy food, the sheer hard work, the wondering if I'd ever get another role after the way I yelled at that bean counter for how he was messing with director's vision . . ." She paused. "Which was a lot of fun. Did I ever tell you about it?"

I grinned as I braked, because the pending story sounded excellent. And I'd ask for it specifically after the bookmobile stop. I turned into the parking lot of a convenience store and came to a halt in the shade of an even more convenient maple tree, because it was now afternoon and the temperature was very July-like.

We ran through the pre-stop routine of turning the driver's seat around to face a small desk, unlatching Eddie's carrier, releasing the rolling chair in the back, firing up the computers, and popping the roof vents. Julia did the vent thing, because she could do it through the simple act of reaching, while I would have had to use some kind of step, which we would have had to find, purchase, and then store somewhere, so it was handy to have a ride-along clerk who was tall.

"Come one, come all," Julia sang out as she opened the door.

A flurry of feet scurried up the stairs. When everyone was inside, I counted three children in the three-to-seven-year-old range, one female adult about my age, and one elderly male. I'd never seen any of them before, and neither had Julia, so introductions came first.

"And that's Eddie," I said, nodding at my cat, who had squished himself into the angle between the windshield and the dashboard. From the outside, it must have been an interesting sight.

"Mommy," one whispered, "can I pet the kitty cat?"

Mom smoothed her child's hair, smiling. "You'd have to ask Miss Minnie."

Big blue eyes looked up at me. "Miss Minnie, can I pretty please pet the kitty?"

"Of course you can. Wait right there." By this time, I'd managed to sort out the relationships of our new patrons: The two older children belonged to the woman and the youngest child was with her grandfather. Not one group as I'd assumed, but two. Silly Minnie, getting things wrong again.

I went forward, rotated a purring Eddie around to picking-up position, and took him back to the children's section, where his newest fan was sitting on the carpeted step. "Grace, this is Eddie. Eddie, this is Grace."

"Mrr," Eddie said.

Grace sucked in a deep breath, her eyes wide open. "He said hello!"

Sure he did. Just like he actually replied to the open-ended questions I routinely asked him. But before I could come up with a comment that was both true and free of sarcasm, there was a sudden tumbling noise from the back of the bus. It was a noise that was sadly familiar, that of books cascading to the floor, and was followed immediately by a child's frightened wail.

Julia was closest, and she hurried over. "Oh, honey, that scared you, didn't it?" She crouched down and started soothing the youngster with a smile and a calm voice, and the incident was over within seconds.

My life seemed to be filled with things falling to the floor. Books, those pills that Courtney dropped, my backpack, and . . .

Hmm, I thought. Courtney. I'd tucked away what I'd learned about Rex's mom into a back corner of my brain and hadn't taken the time to think about it. But now thoughts were ticking away. Could there be a tie between Courtney and Rex? If so, how could I find out what it was? And could it possibly have led to murder?

The rest of the bookmobile stop passed quietly, and when we were tidying up, I said to Julia, "I need to make a phone call. Is this the parking lot where you can get three bars?"

She pointed at the store. "Stand between the ice machine and the Dumpster."

As soon as my feet touched gravel, I was scrolling through my contacts, looking for Ann Marie and Rupert Wiley. By the time I found the sweet spot Julia had described, I was pushing the Call button. "Hey, Ann Marie. This is Minnie Hamilton, from the bookmobile."

"It's so nice to hear a voice that isn't Rupert's!" She laughed. "What can I do for you this morning?"

"First I wanted to make sure Rupert had enough reading material to last until our next scheduled stop. If he's running low, I could drop by with some reserves."

"Oh, aren't you the sweetest," Ann Marie said. "But the old bugger is fine. He's getting out and about a little more and isn't even half through that pile."

"That's great!" The getting-better thing, not the not-reading thing, but I wasn't going to say that out loud. "My second question is about the first seven days of July. Some of my records are incomplete and I'm trying to get everything straight." Which was true. Sort of. "What might help my memory was if you could tell me what days your home health aide, Courtney, was at your house that week. I didn't meet her until the other day, so if I knew what days she was there . . ." I heard myself starting to babble, so I stopped talking.

"Easy enough," Ann Marie said. "All I have to do is turn around and look at the calendar. Let's see . . . that week Courtney was here Thursday, Saturday, and Monday. And Saturday she was here until dark, because Rupert was having some difficulties and she was kind enough to stay late. Does that help?"

It certainly did. I thanked her, asked her to say hello to Rupert for me, and ended the call.

So Courtney had worked until dark on the night of the Fourth. No way could she have driven to Chilson and killed Rex; there just wasn't time.

I looked up at the bookmobile and saw that Eddie was again on the dashboard, only this time he was staring straight at me and yelling his furry head off. At least I assumed he was yelling, because although his mouth was opening and closing, I couldn't hear him through the windshield.

"What's with him?" I asked Julia as I settled into the driver's seat.

"He was worried about you," she said, shutting

173

the cat carrier door as Eddie slinked inside. "He watched you the whole time and started howling right there at the end."

I started the engine and looked at Eddie, who was glaring up at me with the intensity of ten thousand suns. If his problem was separation anxiety, you'd have thought there'd be a happier expression on his fuzzy face. "What's the matter, my little friend?" I asked. "Talk to me. I'm sure we can work something out."

"Mrr!"

Julia leaned forward against her seat belt and patted the carrier's top. "Now, now, Mr. Edward. She didn't mean to sound condescending. It's just that she doesn't always understand what you're saying. It's her fault, not yours."

I laughed. "Let me guess. You're fluent in Eddie speech and you're going to tell me exactly what he was trying to get across to dumb old me."

"Moi?" Julia arranged her face into an expression of shock. "While I occasionally grasp a fleeting thought out of our feline friend, I do not have the gift for translating ninety-nine percent of what he's trying to communicate. Only you, dear Minnie, could do that. You're his chosen life partner, after all."

"Such an honor," I murmured. Most of the time I had an excellent idea of what was going on in Eddie's head, and his thoughts fell into one of three categories: sleep, food, or entertainment. If it was sleep, he'd be thinking about where next to curl up and spread his Eddie hairs around. If it was food, he'd be wondering when I'd offer him another treat, or maybe when I'd rearrange his dry cat food into the rounded pile he preferred. If it was entertainment, he'd be testing whatever object was closest to him to see if it could be a suitable cat toy. Curtains could do the trick, as did paper towels, toilet paper, newspapers, pencils, and shoelaces.

There was also a fourth category, one I hesitated to use under any circumstances—the dreaded miscellaneous. This was a dangerous thing, because I'd learned that if a miscellaneous folder existed, half the world could get stuffed in there. Far better to have many accurately labeled folders than a massive pile of—

"Mrr!"

I flinched. In the half mile of roadway we'd just driven, I'd gone deep into my thoughts, and Eddie's sharp cry startled me. "What's the matter, pal?"

He didn't reply. I glanced over and couldn't see anything inside the carrier except the pink of his blanket smashed up against the wire door. He'd never done that before, and I didn't like not being able to see him.

"Julia, he's managed to cover the door with his blanket. Can you fix that? Who knows what he'll get into when he's hidden from view."

"Eddie, my good sir," Julia said in an upper-crust English accent. "Will you give me permission to rearrange your bedchamber?" She opened the wire door. "While your renovations with the blanket, sir, are attractive, they pose a—hey!"

My cat bolted out of his carrier, scrambled over the console, and galloped to the back of the bookmobile, howling all the way. "Mrrr! MrrrRRR!"

"Egad," Julia said, still English. She turned around to watch him. "The cat is something possessed."

In the rearview mirror, I caught glimpses of his black-and-white self running from front to back, running from side to side, then jumping from floor to desktop and down again. "He's something, that's for sure." The noises and antics went on and on and showed no sign of stopping.

I was torn between concern for my furry little friend and annoyance that he was being so weird. Surely if he was sick, he'd be lying in a pathetic heap inside the carrier and whining, not bouncing off the walls. But with cats—or at least with Eddies—it was hard to tell illness from normal.

"We're going to make a quick stop," I said to Julia. "To make sure he's all right and get him back in his carrier." I thought I heard her mutter, "Better you than me," but she said much louder, "Good idea."

Up ahead was a small lakeside park where we

occasionally pulled in to eat lunch if the parking lot was empty of trucks and boat trailers. Happily, the only vehicle in the gravel parking area today was a small sedan in a back corner and we were able to slide into the shady side of the lot.

I turned off the engine and stood up. "Okay, Eddie, it's time to . . . hang on. Where did he go?"

"What do you mean?" Julia stood and looked over my shoulder. "Did he get up behind the paperbacks again?"

Eddie had done that numerous times, but I'd finally come up with the bright idea of placing empty cardboard boxes behind the books. This kept Eddie away and kept the books from sliding around during travel. "He can't anymore, remember?"

But we peered behind the paperbacks anyway. No Eddie. "He has to be somewhere," Julia said. "Cats don't just disappear."

I opened a cabinet door and retrieved the canister of cat treats. "This will get him. Here, Eddie Eddie Eddie," I called, shaking the canister up and down, making a soft maraca type of noise, which was Eddie's favorite noise in the whole wide world.

But he didn't come running. Fear clutched at my heart and a thousand scenarios ran through my head. I pushed them all away as impossible, but . . . where was he?

"Mrr," came a soft noise.

My tight throat released itself. Worry vanished and was immediately replaced by irritation. "What are you doing down there?" I asked, because the noise had come from the doorway. Steps led from the door up into the bookmobile, and as I drew near, I saw that Eddie had compressed himself into the corner of the bottom step, leaving only his dark fur visible to the naked eye, which was why we hadn't noticed him down there.

"Come on up, buddy," I said encouragingly, but he didn't move a muscle. Didn't even look up at me. "Are you okay?" Still nothing. I moved down a step. "Say something. Anything would be fine." He didn't say a word. Concern wormed its way into my heart, but I summoned my inner Aunt Frances—she of "why worry?"—and banished my fear. Or most of it.

"Eddie," I murmured, moving down another step. "Talk to me. Do I need to take you to Doctor Joe? If you're sick, I'll take care of you, you know I will. I'll hold your kitty head if you need to . . . you know. I'll figure out a way to give you pills"—something that had been problematic in the past, but Rafe would help—"and I'll buy whatever expensive cat food you need. Just talk to me."

"Mrr," he said, but it was the weakest "Mrr" I'd ever heard from him.

"Maybe he needs some fresh air," Julia said. "Maybe in the carrier he was breathing exhaust fumes and they got to him."

The bookmobile had a far more stringent maintenance schedule than my personal vehicle did, so Julia's suggestion was unlikely. But it was also possible, and since I didn't have any better ideas, I unlatched the outside door, and pushed it outward.

Before the door was open three inches, Eddie had hurled himself outside, zooming like a black-and-white arrow.

"Eddie!" I yelled, but he paid absolutely no attention to me and continued straight ahead, toward the lake.

"He'll be fine," Julia said, laughing. "See? He did just need some fresh air."

I sighed and we both jogged after my cat. There had been one or two occasions in the past when Eddie had escaped, but lately he'd been content to stay in the bookmobile. "Stupid cat," I muttered.

"Au contraire," Julia said. "It's a beautiful day. Look at that sky, those clouds, and this adorable little lake, whose name escapes me. Mr. Ed has given us this moment, so let's give ourselves permission to enjoy the opportunity."

I glanced at the sky. It was pretty, a gorgeous blue, with fluffy white clouds so perfect they could have been painted on the set of a theater's stage.

"Mrr!" Eddie yelled, and I ran ahead of Julia.

"Where are you, buddy?" The park had a small boat launch and a beach area, but Eddie wasn't on either the dock or the sand. He was off to the left, rustling around in the shrubbery.

If he'd been about to hack up a hairball, I was just as glad he'd chosen the great outdoors, but his behavior wasn't of the about-to-get-sick variety.

"Mrr!"

With Julia right behind, I elbowed my way through a jungle of shrubbery, following the direction of his voice, which had advanced to an insistent "Mrr! Mrr! Mrr!"

"We're coming, Eddie," I called. "Hang on, bud, we're almost there, okay?" Where "there" was, I had no idea, but we were getting closer. "Just a few more 'mrrs' and we'll be with you, and—"

I stopped so fast that Julia bumped into me.

"What?" she asked. "Why did you stop?"

But I couldn't answer her. Instead, I pointed to what Eddie had found, half in and half out of the water. Or more accurately, who he'd found. Because Eddie was sitting next to the unmoving body of a woman in a one-piece bathing suit, a redheaded woman about forty years old, a woman we knew.

Julia gasped a huge breath. "Oh, no . . . oh, no. It's Nicole. What should we do?"

I was already fumbling for my phone to call 911, but there was nothing anyone could do, because she was dead.

CHAPTER 11

A few hours later, Rafe held me tight, murmuring soft words of love, support, and calm. When I thought I would be able to stand up on my own, I took a deep breath and pulled away from his warmth. This should have been okay, because the weather had taken a hard turn toward the hot and humid, but even though my skin was pleased to be a teensy bit cooler, the rest of me missed him very much.

As Julia and I had waited for the EMT and law enforcement to show up, I'd texted Rafe that I'd be late for dinner because there'd been a horrible accident, that a woman had died, and that I knew her.

Now I sighed. "It was Nicole Price," I said.

"How did you know her?" Rafe took my hand and led me to a nearby chair, a wicker one on the porch, since the front porch was as far as I'd made it before I'd started crying into his shoulder. "The name isn't familiar," he said.

"No, it wouldn't be." I sat, making the wicker creak. "She was summer only, a high school teacher from downstate. Her family owns a hunting cabin near that little lake"—whose name neither Julia nor I could remember but had been told by an EMT it was Stump Lake—"and Nicole spent her summers up here. I only knew her from the bookmobile."

Rafe pulled a chair up close to mine. "Was she married? Kids?"

"Married," I said. "Her husband's name is . . ." I looked at the ceiling, which was painted a slightly greenish blue, and tried to remember. "Dominic. Dom, she called him. He comes up most weekends."

"Kids?"

I shook my head. "No." At least I didn't think so, because never once in any of her trips to the bookmobile had Nicole ever mentioned any offspring.

Rafe hitched his chair closer and held my hand. "What was she like?"

"She was . . ." I let the sentence wander off as I thought about the question. Nicole hadn't been chatty. She hadn't talked much about anything, and hardly at all about herself. Even still, a few things had leaked out. "She loved it up here. One of her favorite things was to swim in the lake."

I closed my eyes against the memory of Nicole's long hair spread over her shoulders like a dark red fan, but the image didn't go away. Then I remembered Eddie bumping up against my shin as I called 911, and remembered his purring, and the sharp pain eased to a dull ache.

"Nicole," I said, thinking back to the few conversations we'd shared, "liked coffee and ice cream. She was left-handed. She loved a good thunderstorm. She liked quirky novels. *The Hitchhiker's Guide to the Galaxy* was her favorite, but she was a big fan of *A Gentleman in Moscow* and anything by Alexander McCall Smith. And I introduced her to Jodi Taylor's books." I smiled, remembering. She'd loved the Chronicles of St. Mary's so much that she'd sent me a Christmas card last year.

"So that was where she used to swim?" Rafe asked. "At that little park? You don't have to answer," he added quickly, "if you don't want to talk about it."

"No, it's okay." And, I discovered a second later, it actually was. "Yes, that was her usual swimming spot. Although I thought her normal time was first thing in the morning. And I do mean first thing. She said she liked being out alone, before anyone else messed up the water."

I frowned, thinking about that. Nicole always went for morning swims. Always. So why had she been out there in the afternoon? And . . . I suddenly felt a shiver at the back of my brain. Both Rex and Nicole had been on the bookmobile that Thursday before the Fourth of July, and now they were both dead. Tragic coincidence? Or could Nicole's death be related to Rex's murder?

Rafe reached around and opened a small cooler. He poured me a glass of wine, then popped a can of beer and held it up in toasting position, waiting.

"To Nicole," I said, then stopped, because I had no idea what else to say.

Rafe tapped his beer can to my glass. "To Nicole. To live in hearts we leave behind is not to die."

And so we drank to her memory.

The next day, Saturday, I spent the morning with my niece. Well, to be more specific, we were both on the same houseboat at the same time, and while I spent our quality together time cleaning the bathroom, kitchen, and outside deck, Kate whiled away the morning either poking at her tablet, checking her phone, or commenting on the spots I'd missed.

When I replied back that she could, you know, help, she'd heaved a heavy teenage sigh and flounced off. Since the houseboat was small, her flouncing only lasted as long as it took for her to get out to the deck, but I gave her points for quality.

At half past eleven, she bolted up from one of the deck's two chaises and ran past me into the bathroom, wailing, "I'm going to be late to work! Why didn't you tell me how late it was?"

She was showered, dressed, and out the door in ten minutes, which gave her more than enough time to walk up to Benton's, but from the glare I got as I handed her a brown bag of peanut butter and jelly, chips, and an apple for her dinner, you'd have thought I was responsible for the air's high humidity, unrest in the Middle East, and the declining population of honeybees.

The next day wasn't much better, and I breathed an invisible sigh of relief when she declined my invitation to go up to Three Seasons for Sunday night dessert.

"You know what your problem is?" Kristen pointed her custard-laden spoon at me.

"Friends who think they have the answers to my problems?"

Leese Lacombe started to laugh, but changed it into a very fake cough when Kristen pointed the spoon in her direction.

"I'll get to you later," she said, then closed her eyes as she ate the custard. "A bit more vanilla," she murmured. As per always, I thought the crème brûlée was perfect, but I also knew better than to disagree with Kristen on food, especially when we were in her own restaurant eating food she'd prepared herself.

"Right." Kristen opened her eyes. "So what's new?" She sent me a meaningful glance.

I focused on getting the perfect ratios of strawberry, custard, and sugar on my spoon. It was a difficult job, but worth doing. "I was hoping to hear when you and Scruffy were scheduling some quality married time."

"Next week," she said, "and no changing the subject."

Leese looked from Kristen to me and back again. "What's up? Because there's unspoken subtext going on between you two so loud I can almost hear it."

Kristen smacked the back of her spoon against the dessert's thin hard layer of sugar, making a loud cracking noise. "She's not talking to me," she said to Leese, tipping her head in my direction. "Is it because I got married? He's not even in the state, for crying out loud. Why is she holding back?"

"Holding back what?" Leese asked, frowning.

"She's gotten involved with another death!" Kristen waved her arms about. "Every time somebody in this county dies who isn't old as the hills, it's on her doorstep."

"Well," I said, "doorstep is a little strong."

My best friend seared me with an Eddie-quality glare. "You know perfectly well I was using a metaphor and it was a darn good one, if you ask me."

Leese put down her spoon. "Who died?"

Bowing to the inevitable, I told them about Nicole Price. About her job downstate, her family cabin, and how she'd drowned while swimming. And about how we'd found her.

"You poor thing," Leese said sympathetically. "But I see Kristen's point. You do have a tendency to find dead bodies."

186

"See?" Kristen gripped her spoon and thumped the table with its handle. "What is it with you?"

I looked from one friend to the other. Though Leese's concern was obvious, Kristen's was manifesting itself as annoyance, irritation, and anger. She had a long history of reacting this way and I was used to it.

Well, almost.

My chin went up. "It's not like I'm trying to find dead people. What am I supposed to do, walk away?"

"Of course not," Leese said gently. "We just want you to be careful."

Kristen made a rude noise. "She's careful enough when she wants to be. It's just she doesn't think things through before jumping in."

I glared at her. "When I want my mother's advice, I'll call her and ask."

"Maybe you—"

Leese cut into the burgeoning argument. "Minnie. It's just . . . we don't want you to be next."

"Next?" I had no idea what she meant. "Next what?" Then it sank in. They didn't want me to be next to die. I laughed, because the idea of dying was ridiculous, especially in Kristen's office on a summer Sunday with dessert in front of me. "Don't be ridiculous."

Then my brain snapped back to that day downtown, that day when I'd tumbled to the street, the day I may or may not have been pushed.

But I didn't say a word.

My thoughts were bouncing all over the place as I walked back to the houseboat through the dusky light. I thought about Nicole and her husband, Dom. Then I wondered what kind of mood Kate would be in when I returned. Which led me to thinking about Rex Stuhler. About Fawn Stuhler. About Barry Vannett. About John and Nandi Jaquay. And about everyone else who might possibly be involved with Rex's death, which included everyone who'd been at the fireworks that night, which got me wondering what kind of progress Hal and Ash had made with Kate's photos, which led me . . .

Nowhere.

I tried to enjoy the warm quiet of the evening and was hoping for a talk with my niece, but when I arrived at the houseboat, Kate was already tucked into her sleeping bag, earbuds in and tablet on, playing an episode of *That '70s Show*.

"Hey," I said softly.

She muttered something unintelligible, rolled over, and was lightly snoring half a second later. Smiling, I removed her earbuds, shut down the tablet, and went to snuggle with Eddie and a book.

"Mrr," he said as I slid into bed, disturbing him not even a fraction of an inch.

"I love you, too, pal." I kissed the top of his head and stared at the pages of *The Trouble with Goats and Sheep* while I thought about Rex Stuhler and creativity. The next morning, before I did the hard work of hauling out two bowls and two spoons for our breakfast, I asked Kate if she wanted cereal.

"Huh?" She popped her head out of the sleeping bag and blinked at me. "Do I what?"

"Breakfast. Cereal." I hefted the bowl up. "You?" For weeks, in obedience to her mother's wishes, I'd done my best to make sure Kate left the houseboat with a full stomach.

"Oh. No." She yawned and stretched. "I have to be up to Benton's early. I'd rather get a bagel from Tom's."

Yet not that long ago, I'd brought down a bag of bagels and she'd ignored them completely. "Sounds good," I said. "See you tonight at the house. Rafe said he'd grill."

My loving niece grunted a response that could have meant anything from "Can't wait" to "Wild horses couldn't drag me there." I had a suspicion it was more the horse thing than the other, but decided not to pursue an interpretation. Some things you're just better off leaving open.

The walk to downtown under a blue sky decorated with wisps of long clouds cleared my head of niece thoughts (mostly) and I found myself smiling. It was summer in northwest lower Michigan and I wasn't going to spoil this fantastic time of year by wallowing in worry.

"Have to tell Aunt Frances," I said out loud. My aunt was forever reminding me that worrying never helped a thing, that it mostly made things worse. Some days her advice was easy to take, other days not so much. But if I could push away the notion that Kate couldn't stand living with me and that she was secretly plotting to get back to Florida as soon as possible, maybe I was making progress in the non-worrying department.

My phone rang. It was Ash. "Morning!" I said. "What's up?"

"Make a right turn, please."

I blinked and looked to my right. I was almost in front of the sheriff's office, and Ash was standing at the door, waving at me. He thumbed off his phone and said, "Do you have a minute? Hal and I need to talk to you."

Seconds later, I was sitting in the interview room across the table from Deputy Ash Wolverson and Detective Hal Inwood. "Before you say anything," I said, "last night I was thinking about Rex Stuhler's death, and maybe we need to get really creative about—"

Hal cut across my words. "This isn't about Mr. Stuhler."

"Oh." I sat back a little. *Please,* I thought, *don't let it be about Kate again.* "This, um, doesn't have to do with my niece, does it?"

190

Ash half smiled. "After her talk with the sheriff, I don't think that kid will so much as break the speed limit until she's thirty."

Though I didn't agree, his opinion was good to hear. "What's the matter, then?" Because from the looks on both of their faces, something was clearly not right. It wasn't as easy to tell with Hal, because his long face had a permanently morose cast, but Ash's default expression hadn't yet hardened into cop mode and I could tell he wasn't happy.

"We have received," Hal said, "the preliminary autopsy on Nicole Price."

Since I didn't know how to respond to that, I kept quiet, because there was obviously more coming.

"Ms. Price was murdered."

I stared at Hal. "No, she wasn't. She drowned. It's sad, but it happens. There are all sorts of reasons she could have drowned. Tell your medical examiner to look again." I could hear my voice going high and shrill, so I took a short breath. "Look again," I said calmly. "There has to be a mistake."

But both Hal and Ash were shaking their heads. "She double and triple checked," Ash said. "She said there's no doubt whatsoever. I'm sorry, Minnie, but someone strangled Nicole."

Hal droned on about the particulars of Nicole's death, citing all sorts of medical evidence that I understood sort of, but not really. I made a mental note to brush up on my basic knowledge of human physiology, and after he finished talking about the cellular level of something I'd never heard of before, I asked the obvious question. "Do you know who killed her?"

Ash glanced at Hal, who remained impassive. "We're looking at all possible suspects," Hal said.

I knew the drill. All avenues of investigation will be pursued, blah blah blah. They'd leave no stone unturned as they went down the avenues of investigation, the roads of investigation, and the streets of—

Streets. I sighed. It was time to tell them about my own street-side experience. "There's something I should tell you."

The two men waited.

"It's possible that . . . I mean it might be . . ." I took a breath and came out with it. "I think someone tried to kill me."

CHAPTER 12

Staffing the reference desk was, right after the bookmobile, the best part of working at the library. Yes, people came to me with the everyday questions, starting with "What's the library's Wi-Fi password?" and the whispered "Where are the bathrooms?" But there were also the fun quests, like "Is there any book that could turn my nine-year-old son into a reader?" and "When did the first fudge shop in Chilson open?" and the search was on. I practically lived for moments like that, and seeing a patron's face light up when we found the answer was worth every dollar of the student loans I still owed.

Today, however, the building seemed to be empty of everyone except staff and there was little to distract me from my final moments in the sheriff's office.

"You what?" Ash had sat up straighter, something I wouldn't have thought possible because he always had better posture than I'd ever been able to achieve with a book on my head.

"Um, fell into traffic. I wasn't hurt," I added hastily. Because scrapes couldn't possibly count as a real injury to anyone except my mother, and since I hadn't told her about the incident, and since the scrape on my shoulder had healed days ago, the memory of the whole thing was getting a bit fuzzy.

"But someone pushed you," Hal said. And I knew I was in trouble because he took a notebook out of his shirt pocket.

I often walked along without paying too much attention to where I was and where I was going, but it was a stretch from that to falling into traffic. "I didn't fall sideways into the street of my own volition," I said. "Someone pushed me. But what I don't know is whether or not it was intentional."

"You're telling us now? Almost two weeks later?" Ash asked, his voice a little too loud for the small room. "Minnie, why on earth didn't you mention this earlier?"

I shrugged. "And you would have done what? It was the week of the Fourth, the sidewalks were packed with people, and I didn't see who pushed me. All you or the city police would have done was file some sort of pointless report, and you had better things to do with your time."

Hal and Ash exchanged a glance at my "pointless report" comment, and I knew I'd hit a nerve. "So instead of a long report that would have taken hours," I said, "all you have to do now is make a note in Rex Stuhler's murder file. Way easier. And . . ." I looked at them beseechingly. "I'd appreciate it if you didn't mention my falling to anyone outside this office."

"Like your aunt Frances?" Hal asked.

Ash eyed me. "Like Rafe, Kristen, or anyone at the library?"

Yes, and yes, and now that I was at the library, and my mind was full of Nicole Price, I wouldn't have minded a distraction and wished fervently for someone—anyone—to ask me any question whatsoever.

Just then, Denise Slade appeared in front of me, feet wide, hands on her hips, scowl in place.

I quickly revised my fervent wish, but it was too late. She was here and would stay until I listened to what she had to say.

Denise had been, once again, voted president of the Friends of the Library, and it was, once again, my job to get along with her. To be agreeable. Some days this was easy, as Denise was smart, capable, and efficient. She also had a personality that would be better suited to foreman of a demolition crew.

"Do you want to know what the Friends think the Board should do with Stan's money?" she demanded.

In my heart of hearts, I wanted to make a flippant reply. Like the money should pay for a giant statue of Stan (something he would have found appalling) or that it should perpetually fund monthly Big Name author events. Or that it should pay for uniforms that the Friends would wear.

"Of course I want to know," I said, smiling at

the style of uniform I'd already selected. Not everyone would look attractive in horizontal stripes, but Stan had favored bold patterns, so my imaginary design only made sense.

The fifty-ish and fireplug-shaped Denise dragged a chair away from a nearby table, slid it next to my desk, and plopped down. "Well, it's not an official vote." She glanced around. "But I'm sure everyone agrees with me."

"I'd like to hear it," I said, nodding and doing a mental fist pump for saying something that didn't overtly agree with Denise yet gave the appearance of congeniality and cooperation.

"What I think—what the Friends think—Stan Larabee's money should do is build an addition."

I blinked. "Addition to what?"

"To the library, of course." She waved her arms. "I told them from the beginning that having our space upstairs was ridiculous, but did they listen to me? No, they didn't. If the Friends are going to be truly successful, we need to have our book sale room on the main floor, and Stan's money is exactly what we need to get there."

"Um." There were so many things wrong with her idea, I didn't know where to start. But it also occurred to me that it wasn't my job to break that particular piece of news to her, so I just asked, "Have you talked to the board about this?"

She harrumphed. "I'm on the agenda for their next meeting, for all the good it will do."

"You never know," I said. "And if you don't get the idea in front of them, they'll definitely never consider it."

She muttered agreement, stood, and stomped off. Well, technically she just walked away, but there was something about the way Denise carried herself that made her gait come across as an angry thumping.

I got up to put her chair away and thought about the differences in the two conversations I'd had that morning. I'd told the sheriff's office about my street-side accident, but didn't want anyone else to know. Denise had told me about her addition fantasy, and wanted everyone to know.

And then it occurred to me that, though I'd asked Hal and Ash to keep quiet about my not-so-near-death experience, neither one had actually agreed to do so.

"Fish?" Kate wrinkled her nose, which in person is not nearly as attractive as it sounds. A true nose-wrinkling isn't just the nose, but includes the entire face and, if you're really skilled, the neck, jaw, and hairline. Though Kate's attempt scored a solid seven, she had a long way to go before she could achieve the classic Minnie face my brother had recorded for posterity with his camera the day I'd tried jalapeño peppers for the first time after being told by that same brother that they were "kind of like pickles." I'd been six years old and still didn't care for jalapeños.

"It's walleye," Rafe said. "Fresh. You'll like it, trust me."

I'd kept quiet during this little interchange, as I'd reluctantly come to the conclusion that Kate was more likely to try something if it wasn't me who was encouraging the attempt.

We were on the front porch, all of our knees knocking against each other as we sat at the small table Rafe had conjured up out of nowhere. Rafe had grown up in Chilson, as had his parents, grandparents, great-grandparents, all the way back to the days of homesteading. His connections in the area were broad and bone deep, and given his twin tendencies of laid-back-ness and a willingness to lend a hand to anyone in need, he could call in favors like no one else I'd met in my life.

"What's this stuff on it?" Kate poked at the fish with her fork.

Rafe reached back into the cooler and handed out sodas. "Bread crumbs and Parmesan cheese."

"I like cheese." It was a grudging admission, but an admission nonetheless, which put it into the Win column.

The two legal adults at the table surreptitiously held their collective breaths as the adolescent deigned to try the food hunted, gathered, cooked, and plated for her. She chewed, swallowed . . . and then went back for another bite. "This isn't too horrible," she said.

Not wanting to startle the girl out of her newfound liking for fresh fish—Rafe and a friend had been out on the lake that morning—we kept quiet, but underneath the table, Rafe and I bumped knuckles.

When the fish and accompanying grilled potatoes and red peppers were mostly gone, I realized I'd become so successful at keeping my mind off the events at the sheriff's office that morning that I hadn't told Rafe any of it. And Kate should probably hear about it from me instead of hearing it second or third or fourth hand.

"This morning," I said, "Ash asked me to stop at the sheriff's office."

"Oh?" Rafe asked. "Why's that?"

His tone was casual, but Kate looked at me straight on. "Do they know who killed Mr. Stuhler? Did they arrest someone?"

I shook my head. "Not yet."

She shrank back inside herself a bit, and my heart ached for her. She needed some good news, but what I was about to say was anything but. "Ash and Hal wanted to tell me about Nicole Price, that drowning victim we found on Stump Lake."

Rafe and Kate looked up from their plates. "What about her?" Rafe asked.

I did not want to tell them about this; I really truly did not. "Nicole didn't drown." I sighed and

199

said the words echoing in my head out loud. "She was murdered."

"What?" Rafe sat back. "You're kidding."

"Don't I wish. They said the preliminary report from the medical examiner was conclusive."

"That's . . ." He frowned. "Well, hard to believe, first off. The two of you make quite the team for coming across murder victims."

I looked at Kate, but she was still working on her fish. "Can I pull Eddie into this conversation?" I asked. "We would have driven right past Stump Lake if he hadn't gone into that bizarre howling fit."

"When all else fails, blame the cat," Rafe said. "Doesn't seem fair."

Clearly, he did not yet understand what living with a cat was like. The man had so much to learn. "No, you blame the cat from the beginning. Especially when the cat is Eddie."

Kate pushed her plate away. "Was she married?"

"Nicole? Yes," I said. "Dominic is her husband's name."

"What if . . ." My niece pleated her paper napkin. "What if this Dominic and Mr. Stuhler's wife were having an affair? What if they killed their spouses so they could marry each other? It would be a lot cheaper to do that than to get divorced. That costs a lot and you lose half your stuff."

Soap opera drama at its finest. I did not look at Rafe. Did not even think about looking at him, because if I did, I might start laughing, and if that happened, Kate would retreat from me even further and—

My thoughts came to an abrupt halt. I'd gone through that same murder-instead-of-divorce thought process not so very long ago. A different scenario altogether, but I shouldn't laugh at her for having the same idea I'd had. Especially since, if I remembered correctly, when I'd presented my theory to law enforcement, they'd basically laughed at the notion.

I didn't want Kate to suffer that, so I thought a moment and said, "That possibility wasn't mentioned this morning. It might be a little melodramatic, but I'll pass it along to Ash."

Kate looked up. "You will? Really?"

"Absolutely." Maybe not right away, and maybe not as a serious theory, but I absolutely would. Someday.

"Cool," she said, and smiled at me.

Early the next morning while crunching my cereal as quietly as possible because Kate was still in her sleeping bag, snoring gently, I spent a few minutes in a text exchange with Deputy Ash Wolverson. Early on, it became clear that he did not want to drag Detective Hal Inwood into another meeting with Ms. Minnie Hamilton, even

201

if it did mean fresh baked goods from Cookie Tom's.

Ash: *Anyway, Hal's wife wants him to drop 20 pounds.*

Minnie: *One doughnut isn't going to make that much difference.*

Ash: *Try telling Mrs. Inwood that.*

Minnie: *Isn't she downstate this week with grandkids?*

Ash: *She has spies. Don't do it.*

I smiled at that, but the spy thing was probably true, and I would have bet it was the sheriff herself who tattled on Hal. Women in an overly male environment tend to stick together, especially when the health of the men in their lives is involved.

Minnie: *OK, but I still want to stop by on the way to the library.*

Ash: *Hal won't like it.*

Minnie: *Didn't figure he would.*

Ash: *Do you have something new for the investigation?*

Minnie (after a pause): *A theory.*

But not Kate's soap opera theory, although it was possible the wispy thoughts I'd woken up with had their roots in her ideas. Then again, it might have been Eddie's cat food breath in my face half the night. One never knew.

Ash (after an even longer pause): *Fine.*

I could almost hear the sigh as he typed. Before

I could thank him, the dots indicating that he was still typing popped up. Then: *I can get you 10 minutes, right when he gets here.*

Minnie: *When's that?*

Ash: *8, straight up.*

Minnie: *You're . . .*

I glanced at the clock. It was all of five minutes to eight. I finished the text with: *getting as bad as Hal*, sent it off, slung a sleepy Eddie off the houseboat's dashboard and into his carrier, and hurried to my car.

Up at the sheriff's office, I parked in the shade and jogged into the reception area. Ash was waiting for me, arms crossed. "As bad as Hal?" he asked.

I colored a bit. He hadn't deserved the comment. "What I meant to say was 'getting as good as.' Detective Inwood is a highly competent law enforcement officer, and if you're like him, that means you're also highly competent."

Ash, since he knew me well, ignored all that and led me into the interview room, where Hal Inwood was already seated and sipping a mug of coffee. "Ms. Hamilton, to what do I owe the pleasure?"

I sat in my chair. "Did you notice I asked for an appointment?"

Hal eyed me over the top of his mug. "I'm not sure that texting Ash five minutes ago counts as asking."

Once again we would have to agree to disagree. But I didn't want to start our conversation with more disagreeableness than necessary, so I gave him a tiny nod. "What I wanted to talk about was the relationship between the murder of Rex Stuhler"—I took a deep breath, because this was the tricky part—"and the murder of Nicole Price."

There was no movement from Hal. Or from Ash, either, which could only mean he was getting very close to being an official certified detective. A year ago, there was no way he would have kept a blank face after I'd said something like that.

Finally, Hal slid his small notebook from his shirt pocket. His shoulders rose and fell just once as he flipped pages. "You have reason to believe there is a relationship."

He didn't exactly phrase it as a question, but I decided it was close enough and nodded again, more decisively this time. "I'm glad you asked," I said brightly. Which was pretty much a flat-out lie and I was pretty sure that a lie inside the sheriff's office was worse than most lies. "No," I said, sighing. "I'm not glad. I kind of wish you hadn't. How about if we pretend—"

"Five minutes," Ash said. I shot him a glance, but he just shrugged. "We have a Region 7 meeting in Gaylord at ten and reports to finish first."

204

"I'm not trying to waste your time," I said, a bit tensely. "But I want to make sure you're considering the possibility that the two murders are linked."

"In what way?" Hal asked.

This was the next tricky part, because I had no idea how the murder of a local pest control guy by handgun had anything to do with the strangulation of a downstate teacher. So I gave them what I had: my gut feeling. "One unsolved murder is rare in a county this size. That there could be two unsolved and unrelated murders seems beyond the scope of possibility."

"Yet here we are," Hal said, tapping his notebook with the tip of his unopened pen.

Ash glanced at his supervisor, then at me. "Coincidences happen all the time, Minnie. You know they do. This is probably just a really sad one."

The more they disagreed with me, the more I became convinced I was right and they were wrong. "And what if it's not a coincidence?" I put my fists on the table. "What if these murders are connected? What if there's someone running around out there that has already killed twice?"

Finally, Hal clicked his pen on and made a mark in his notebook. "Ms. Hamilton, if you're concerned that you might be in danger, you should file a report."

"Me?" I blinked. What was he talking about?

"Yesterday," Hal said patiently, "you told us you'd been pushed into the path of an oncoming car."

"Oh." Right. I'd forgotten already. "That's not what—"

"Then we're done here, yes?" Hal stood without waiting for an answer. "Deputy Wolverson, better get on that paperwork if we're going to leave on time. You know how I feel about being late."

Ash nodded. "I'll get right on it. See you later, Minnie."

"Ms. Hamilton?" Hal ushered me out of the room and in seconds I was outside, staring at the closing door with my mouth opening and closing like a gasping fish.

The bookmobile day passed quickly, but it was overshadowed by the knowledge of what I needed to tell Julia. More than once I started to, but every time I opened my mouth to say something, the words disappeared, or someone came into the bookmobile, or Eddie needed attention. All of which would be summed up into one explanation: I chickened out.

But it had to be done, so as I closed the cat carrier's wire door on a snoring Eddie, and as Julia finished tidying after the day's last stop, I told her we needed to talk.

She eyed me over the top of the reading glasses she'd recently taken to wearing. Since she'd never once squinted at the text of a book or held it out at arm's length, I was pretty sure the glasses were a new prop she was trying on to see how they fit her Bookmobile Lady persona.

"What's up?" she asked. "You're not firing me, are you?"

I shook my head, took a deep breath, and started. "A couple of weeks ago . . ." Once I got going, the story of my near-death fall into traffic didn't take long to tell. Julia showed dismay and concern, and when I got to the end, she gave me a hug.

"That's horrible, but you're fine and all's well that ends well, yes?"

"Yes, but . . ."

She frowned. "But what?"

I sat on the bookmobile's carpeted step and motioned for her to do the same. "It's Nicole Price. She didn't drown."

Julia's frown deepened. "Of course she did. She was in the water. What else . . . oh, no." Her eyes closed. "You're saying—"

"Yes. She was murdered. The sheriff's office says there's no doubt."

We sat there for a moment. The door was open and sounds of summer drifted in. A breeze, stirring the leaves of a nearby tree. A distant lawnmower. A chirping bird.

" 'O villain, villain, smiling, damned villain!' " Julia murmured, quoting what I was pretty sure was *Hamlet*.

"And there's more," I said. "I think all of these things are connected. Rex Stuhler's murder. Me being pushed into the street. Nicole's murder. It just seems too unlikely that all these things could happen without some link between them."

Julia smiled. "Unlikely things happen all the time. Just ask any lottery winner."

"Listen to me," I said, pounding my fists on my knees. "I need you to take this seriously."

She looked at me blankly. "Why?"

"Because you were here, too. You found Nicole, just like I did. I was pushed into traffic. And so . . . you might be in danger, too."

A beat of silence tapped past, then Julia asked seriously and deliberately, "Have you been watching too much television?"

She knew perfectly well that was an impossibility, since my television watching was limited to what I could watch at the boardinghouse due to the marina's very slow Internet connection. I felt my spine straighten and my chin go up. "I wanted to warn you."

"Sorry, Minnie. I just think it's pretty far-fetched."

I stood. "We need to get going," I said stiffly.

"Don't be angry," Julia said, springing up and pulling me into a hug. "And it's kind of you to be concerned. Thank you."

I returned the hug, murmuring that I wasn't mad. Because I wasn't, not really.

But I was worried.

CHAPTER 13

Julia's disbelief had been a bit wounding, so on the way home I vowed to be kinder and more patient with my niece.

"Have I forgotten what it's like to be a teenager?" I asked Eddie as we made the short drive from the library to the marina. "Can't be. It wasn't that long ago."

"Mrr?" he asked.

"Well . . ." I did the subtraction and came to the stunning realization that it had been sixteen years since I'd been a teenager. How could that be? I did the math backward, adding instead of subtracting, and came up with the same number. "Okay, it was a while ago," I said lamely, "but it doesn't feel like it."

In fact, some days it took very little to summon the self-consciousness that had plagued me all through middle school and most of high school. And if I was going to be completely honest, hadn't yet faded away to memory.

"Mrr."

"Thanks, pal," I said. "I love you just the way you are, too. Although I wouldn't mind if you kept your hairs to yourself a little more, and—"

"Mrr!"

Smiling, I parked in my reserved spot and

carried Eddie inside, all set to have a nice long sympathetic chat with my niece. "Kate, what do you think about . . ."

But I was talking to an empty room. I glanced up at the whiteboard, and lo and behold, she'd written something up there.

Closing at Benton's tonight. Back by ten.

"Well, there you go," I told Eddie as I let him out of his carrier. He leapt up to the dashboard and ignored me in favor of watching a flock of seagulls.

He remained on the dashboard while I changed into shorts and a T-shirt, was there when I left to go up to the house to work with Rafe on painting stairway risers, was there when I got back as the sun was setting, was there when Kate got home, and was still there when I left in the morning.

I patted him on the head as I left. "Are you stuck?" I asked softly, because Kate was still sleeping.

"Mrr," he said quietly, which I took to mean, "Don't be ridiculous. I just happen to like it here for the time being."

"You are so weird," I told him, and headed up to the library with Eddie's heavy gaze tracking me up the dock. "Well, he is," I said to the world in general, in case it happened to be listening. Eddie's weirdness was a solid fact, but maybe broadcasting it wasn't the way a loyal cat companion should behave. A quality cat caretaker would probably also provide better treats. And brush him twice a day. And never trim his claws.

"Fat chance," I said, drawing a curious look from Cookie Tom, because by this time I was halfway through downtown.

He was, as always this time of morning, out sweeping the sidewalk in front of his bakery. He cocked his head at my comment and stopped, mid-sweep. "Anything I want to know about?"

I slowed, but didn't stop. "It's our new phone system. There's a glitch with the connection between the VOIP messaging and the ISP—"

"Have a nice day, Minnie," Tom said, and went back to his sweeping.

Grinning, I walked on. At some point Tom would catch on that I didn't have a clue what I was talking about when I babbled tech-speak, but for now it was kind of fun.

But what wasn't much fun was that I also didn't have a clue how to find a connection between the deaths of Rex and Nicole. I sat at my desk and woke up my computer, wishing I could wake up my brain.

While I was waiting for the computer, I spun around in my chair and looked at the wall calendar I'd purchased from a local nonprofit. Each month had a different photograph of the region, and this month's was of Chilson's fireworks from the previous year.

I sighed, remembering what had happened this

Fourth of July, then sat up straight. Maybe if I studied the books Nicole and Rex had checked out that last time they'd both been on the bookmobile, I'd see something . . .

But that didn't make any sense. I slumped back. How could the book checkouts possibly mean a thing? Still, I didn't have any other ideas, so I launched the software and, elbow on the desk and chin in hand, started looking backward in time to see if the two had any books in common.

They didn't, of course. Rex had read nonfiction almost exclusively, while Nicole read a wide variety of fiction, including a smattering of legal thrillers.

I sorted their choices by date, Dewey decimal, copyright, and everything else I could think of, but saw nothing that meant anything, at least not to me. Though I hadn't expected to find anything, I was still disappointed that nothing had turned up, and—

"Hang on," I murmured. Because there was more to review than book choices. I could also look at who else had checked out books the last time Rex and Nicole had been on the bookmobile together. Maybe there was another bookmobile patron who had crossed paths with both Rex and Nicole. Yes, I tended to think all bookmobilers were fine and upstanding citizens, but maybe there was an outlier, an anomaly, someone who wasn't honorable, and maybe there was . . . something.

Knowing it was a long shot, I pulled up the day and stop. And sat back in my chair, staring at the screen.

I'd forgotten all about Violet Mullaly.

The first time I'd met the indomitable and irrepressible Violet had been early spring, and I'd just driven the bookmobile through ten miles of sloggy mess of rain and snow and slush. Which was no excuse for anything, but might explain why, when Violet completely rejected every single one of the books I suggested she might like, I formed an opinion of her personality and character I had yet to revise.

It wasn't fair, of course, and I was still trying to find a way to like the irascible forty-ish woman—we had many things in common, or at least we were the same height, which should have been a special bond—but every time I saw Violet striding down the road to the bookmobile stop, I made every attempt to be busy when she came aboard.

Julia found the situation amusing, and had no problem saying so every time Violet left. "It's nothing personal; she's horrible to everyone. Think of her as a character in a play," she said, turning her palms upward in a stage gesture of openness. "A minor character who wreaks havoc in the lives of everyone else. Or think of her as a foil to display the fine qualities of the other characters."

"I'd rather not think of her at all," I said later that afternoon as I drove out of Chilson. Though the day had started out with blue sky, a thick bank of clouds had been creeping across from west to east, and now rain was starting to splatter on my windshield.

When I'd remembered that Violet and Nicole and Rex had been on the bookmobile at the same time, I'd spent some time trying to think of reasons for Violet to commit murder. I hadn't come up with anything I could take to Detective Inwood, or even Ash, but that didn't mean there couldn't be something.

Maybe there was some long-running Hatfield and McCoy thing between the three families and Violet was carrying out her grandfather's dying wish. Maybe she was a wannabe poet, and Rex and Nicole had seen her copying something out of a book that she was trying to get published as original work. Or maybe Kate had been on the right track with the hired killer idea, and Violet was the hiree.

Because Violet as the killer had a certain appeal. And maybe she had a darker personality than I'd ever suspected. Maybe her angry nature rippled out to widespread anger against humanity, and maybe that day on the bookmobile had tipped her over the edge.

But even as I mentally played with the concept of a murdering Violet, I was ashamed of myself.

Bad Minnie, to think someone I didn't get along with could more easily be a murderer than someone I liked. And an even worse Minnie to *want* to think of someone who rejected every book I recommended as a killer.

"I'm a horrible person," I said, glancing over at Eddie.

But Eddie wasn't there. He was back at the houseboat, probably still on the dashboard. And Kate was hanging out with one of our nearest marina neighbors, Louisa Axford. Louisa and her husband, Ted, were in their early sixties and spent a large chunk of most summers in Chilson on their boat.

Though we hadn't seen much of them the previous year due to the birth of a grandchild, this summer the Axfords had convinced their daughter and son-in-law that they wouldn't let the toddler drown and had brought the child north for her first Chilson summer. Kate, in what I'm pretty sure was an effort to avoid spending time with me, had volunteered to help entertain the youngster, and seemed to be happy learning the ins and outs of caring for a tiny human.

"Better her than me," I murmured to the absent Eddie. Cleaning litter boxes was as much caretaking as I wanted to deal with at this point in my life. What I wanted to do most right now was find a connection between Rex Stuhler and Nicole Price, something that would prove to

Detective I'm-so-smart-and-you-aren't that they should be looking for one killer and not two.

"There has to be a link," I said, mentally inking Violet onto the list of suspects and vowing to learn more about her later.

During lunch, I'd availed myself of the opportunities provided by the good taxpayers and commissioners of Tonedagana County and used their online Geographic Information System to find the location of the cabin owned by Nicole Price's family. Luckily, she'd once mentioned her maiden name—Rodriguez—and joked that she'd married Dominic because his last name was short and sweet. "Just like him," she'd said.

I swallowed down tears at the memory, and concentrated on traffic. Which was a total of one pickup truck at that point, but you never knew when someone might drop their cell phone and swerve. This focus kept me from dropping into heaving sobs, and I thanked every vehicle on the road between there and the gas station/convenience store that was my final destination.

It was one of those classic Up North places, clean but worn at the edges, all the coolers full of beer and soda, all the shelves only one product deep. It was also halfway between Rex and Nicole's houses and stood an excellent chance of being a point of contact for the two of them.

The kid behind the counter made brief eye contact and said something that, if I'd been

216

required to spell the word, would have been "Uhnh," but which I decided to interpret as a sprightly, "Good evening, how can I help you?"

"Hi," I said, smiling and ready to trot out the story I'd concocted on the drive. "My name is Minnie. I drive the bookmobile."

The kid just looked at me. My smile got a bit fixed, but I kept going.

"Anyway, I'm sure you know that two of your customers recently died. They were also bookmobile patrons, and I was wondering if anyone was putting together a fund for flowers, or a contribution."

But he was shaking his head. "I just started working here. This is, like, my second day. I don't know anyone that's dead."

Not a situation I'd anticipated. "Well, who's the person who worked here the longest? And when would she or he be working next?"

"Dunno. Like I said, I just started here." He shrugged. Then, when I kept looking at him expectantly, he sighed. "Guess I could leave a note."

"That would be great," I said, beaming. "Thanks so much."

"Yeah. Sure. Uh, have a good night."

I drove away, pleased with myself, but when I reached the Chilson city limits, I realized something. The kid hadn't actually reached out a hand to find a pen and paper. Sighing, I guessed the odds that he'd write anything down as unlikely at best. I parked the car and headed to the houseboat, where I could see that Eddie was indeed still on the dashboard.

"It's hard to find good help," I told him through the window.

"Mrr," he said. "Mrr."

I went inside, dropped my small purse on the counter, wrote *At the house* on the whiteboard, and headed up to spend the rest of the evening with Rafe. As I hurried down the dock and onto the sidewalk, I heard something I hadn't ever heard before—giggling noises coming from my niece.

"Huh," I said, slowing down to walk on my tiptoes, which was the only way I could see over the edge of the Axfords' boat and onto the deck. Yep, there was Kate and the kid, playing what I vaguely remembered as patty cake.

The sight made me happy and sad at the same time. Happy Kate was enjoying herself, but sad that she never seemed that happy around me.

"What am I doing wrong?" I asked Rafe.

My beloved was in the downstairs half bath, standing on a ladder with his back to me and his attention fully on the ceiling. He had a small hand-held light in his hand and was peering at the trim he'd recently installed. "You want a list?" he asked.

I should have been ready for that response. It was the same one I'd given the other day when

Rafe had watched Eddie bounce from one piece of furniture to another for no apparent reason and asked, "What is wrong with that cat?"

So, yes, I should have been prepared, but somehow I wasn't, and felt as if I'd been slapped. Down in the base of my throat I could feel tears forming and I whirled around. I had to get away, find a dark quiet spot where I could—

Rafe, who magically managed to get down the ladder, across the room, and to the door before I did, put a gentle hand on my shoulder. "Minnie, please talk to me. What's wrong?"

My hand was on the doorknob. I stood there for a moment, swallowing down silent sobs. When I thought I could speak without my voice quavering, I said, "Honestly? Nothing." Though this was technically true, it was also completely wrong. I sighed. "But really . . . everything. It's all messed up, from top to bottom."

To Rafe's great credit, he didn't make fun of me for my mixed messages.

"Come here," he said, and pulled me close. "First off, we'll do this hugging thing. And if that doesn't help—though I feel sure a quality hug will knock the edge off—we'll move to the next step."

"What's that?" I asked, my voice muffled against the front of his paint-spattered T-shirt, a shirt commemorating the 1998 Chilson High School regional champion football team.

"All in good time, my little pretty. All in good time."

Rafe was competent at many things and highly skilled at even more, but he did horrible imitations, and his rendition of the Wicked Witch of the West was downright awful—nasal and screechy.

I giggled, which was no doubt his intention. "That was horrible," I said, pulling away.

He pulled me back. "Not done yet," he murmured at the top of my head.

It was a long and calm moment, standing there. I felt the beat of his heart, the warmth of his skin, and the stirring of my hair as his breath rustled my curls. "Thank you," I whispered, holding him as tight as I could.

"All part of the service." He leaned down to kiss me. "Do you want to talk?"

"You know what? I can think of something else I'd rather do," I said, tipping my head back for a longer, deeper kiss.

"What's the matter with you?" Julia asked.

I was in the middle of a huge yawn, and before I could finish it and reply, she added, "I've been counting, and that's the three thousand and forty-second time you've yawned this morning and it's only ten. Are you getting sick?"

I smiled. "Nope. I was just . . . out late, that's all."

Julia studied me over the top of her reading glasses. "Why, you little minx."

"Minx?" I rolled my eyes. "Don't tell me you're on a P. G. Wodehouse kick again."

"There are worse things," she said. "But this weather isn't one of them." She opened the door, letting in the smell of sunshine and summer, and breathed deep. "Would we love summer so much without winter?"

"Mrr." Eddie jumped from the console to the top of the front desk to a shelf of Young Adults, to the ground, and to the parallelogram of sunshine by the door. "Mrr," he said, flopping down and managing to keep every one of his appendages— including his tail—in the sunlight.

Julia and I watched him arrange himself. "A cat of many talents," she said. "But what is he like when he's angry?"

"A lot like this, only noisier." But Julia's question reminded me of yesterday's research. "Question for you. What do you remember about the bookmobile stops before the Fourth? Specifically, the one by the detour."

"Rex and Nicole's last visit," Julia said, her voice sad and slow. "We already talked about this and didn't come up with anything."

"Let's try and think about it differently. Yesterday, I looked up the checkouts from that day. Rex, Nicole, and Violet Mullaly all took out books. I remember they were all here, and that

Nicole stayed the entire time, and didn't seem to want to go when we told her we had to leave, but I took Eddie out for a kitty rest stop. When we were outside, did anything happen?"

Julia pushed the toe of her flip-flop against one of Eddie's back feet. He ignored her. "That's right, you were both gone. You missed the whole thing."

"Missed what?"

"Violet being Violet." Julia stood and, using her muscles and some acting magic, became someone else completely. Not quite Violet, but a very reasonable facsimile.

"How can they both be gone?" she queried in a high tone. "I specifically wanted to borrow those books!"

Julia relaxed, turning into herself again. "I'm sorry, Violet, but they've both been checked out. If you'd like, I can put your name on the wait list."

Back in Violet-shape, she said, "I don't want to wait! I want to read them this weekend! Who checked them out? I bet I can talk them into letting me have my books for a few days." Julia-Violet glanced around. "You! You have my book!"

Julia shook her head and returned to herself. "It went downhill from there."

"So who had the books?" I asked.

"Rex had the new Malcolm Gladwell book."

Julia grinned. "He ignored her completely, which drove her nuts. And I never looked to see who had the other one."

"Do you remember what book it was?" I walked to the front computer.

"One of the Tana French titles."

I typed the author's name into the computer and the list popped up in front of me. Most were still on the shelf, but two were checked out. "Why didn't you tell me this before?"

Julia shrugged. "We got busy and I forgot. Plus I know she's not your favorite patron and I didn't want to make her more of an unfavorite. Why fan the flames?"

Why indeed? But when I clicked to see who'd checked out the Tana French book, I got a chill. The name was Nicole Price.

Word had oozed out that Nicole's death was murder, not a sad drowning accident, and I spent too much time the next morning with people who thought they were being funny when they asked if I was the one who'd killed her.

Well, it was one person, but Denise Slade could make you feel as if you'd given a presentation to a large and unforgiving audience.

"Really? Another one?" Denise shook her head and chuckled. "You'd think we were living in Cabot Cove."

Though I wasn't sure I'd been born when the

old television show *Murder, She Wrote* had aired, the reference wasn't lost on me. I managed to smile at Denise. "You could suggest a name change at the next city council meeting."

She snorted. "That bunch of old fogies won't change anything unless they're forced to. But you." She pointed at me, her stubby index finger ending six inches from my collarbone. "I'm starting to wonder about you. What better killer than the mild-mannered bookmobile librarian?"

I gave her what I hoped was a sly and wolfish grin. "Then you'd better be careful. You never know when I'll snap."

Denise threw her head back and laughed. "That will be the day. I hope I'm around to see it." Still laughing, she moseyed off in the direction of the Friends of the Library book sale room.

I tried to squash my unprofessional impulse to make a face at her back, but I must not have been successful, because behind me I heard the quiet giggles of a woman in her early seventies. I turned around and faced Donna, who was at the front desk and had heard every word. "Why," I asked, "does being called mild-mannered irritate me?"

She smiled. "You wouldn't have been if I'd said it. Or Holly. Or Josh. Or anyone else other than Denise. It's a reaction to the speaker of the words, not the words themselves."

This made me feel better, so as a sort of reward,

I asked for her opinion on an issue I really didn't want to talk about. "You're about the only one," I said, "who hasn't told me what you think should be done with Stan Larabee's money."

"There's a reason for that." Donna pointed at the ceiling. "My opinion won't make a spit of difference when the board decides. So why bother talking about it?"

She was right, but that wasn't keeping anyone else on the staff, including me, from dreaming. I wished the board had asked for staff opinions, but they hadn't, so there wasn't much point in forcing them to listen to us. "Still," I said. "You must have a preference."

"Well, if you insist . . ." Donna pursed her lips and gazed off into space. "Did you realize," she said, "that Tonedagana County's most populous demographic is people over the age of fifty? And that it's our only age group increasing in population?" Her face lost its faraway look and she fastened her gaze on me. "Wouldn't it be great to have the biggest, best, most recent collection of large print books in the area? Even the entire state?"

"Um, sure." I didn't know where we'd put it, but the idea was attractive.

"Think of it, Minnie." Excitement colored her voice. "Think of what a draw that would be. Yes, I know, e-readers let you bump up type sizes, but lots of the elderly prefer print, and I even know

225

kids your age who like to read large print books while on the gym's treadmills."

"Really?" The concept of going to a gym was foreign to me, but if I could read while I was working out, maybe there was a reason to go. I told Donna I'd present her idea to the board if I got an opportunity—unlikely, but you never knew—and headed to my office, where a multitude of tasks awaited me.

"E-mails to answer before I sleep," I said, smiling at my reworking of the Robert Frost poem. It didn't quite scan, but it wasn't bad.

The door to the stairway opened and Graydon came through, coffee mug in hand. "Good morning," I said. "Guess what, I have another staff idea for Stan's money."

"Oh?" Graydon slowed.

"I'm making a list," I said. "Just in case the board asks."

He nodded. "Excellent plan."

Which didn't sound like he'd be willing to take the list to the board, but at least he knew the list existed. "Say, when you have a minute, could I talk to you?"

"Sure," he said. "Just come on up. My door is always open for you."

"Well, it's something personal." I inched closer. "My niece. Kate. I've mentioned her before and I could really use some advice on—"

He snapped his fingers. "Minnie, I am so sorry,

but I forgot. There's a phone call I have to make." One quick U-turn, then he was back through the door, and his footsteps headed up the stairs.

"That was weird," I said to the empty air. But weird bosses were something I was used to, so I shrugged and went to my office. To answer e-mails.

My most fun task for the day was Reading Hour up at Lakeview. The Medical Care Facility had a list of volunteers that read out loud to a group of residents, and I'd long ago signed up to be part of the rotation.

Since difficulties with short-term memory were an issue for many of the residents, the books were read as quickly as possible, and I started compiling a list of shorter books for the group to choose from. Max, of course, always voted for anything by John Sandford, but to date he'd been outvoted every time. Though he tended to grouse that he was being discriminated against, he always showed up to listen, no matter what book was chosen, a habit of which I tended to remind him every time he complained.

"Tell me," he said as we entered the living room–style space where the group met, "what book would you want read to you?"

"Today? Or when I'm your age?"

He looked up at me and squinted. "Hmm. You will be a very hot-looking old lady, Miss Minnie."

Since I'd never been high on the "hot" scale ever in my life, I didn't see going higher as I aged. Not that I cared. Well, mostly. "How do you figure?"

"Because as you get older, your character gets more and more visible." He made a horrible face. "Remember when your mother said not to make faces because someday it'll freeze that way? She was right. Oh, sure, you laugh at me now, but look around. You'll see what I mean."

"Okay, I promise to look. But I don't remember seeing any twisted-up faces. Certainly not in the book group."

By this time we were entering the room where the group assembled, and Max suddenly started coughing. Hard. Concerned, I turned to look at him, and saw that he was holding his hand to his mouth, but was also using his index finger to point.

"Face," he gasped out between what I now understood to be a completely fake cough. "Her."

I patted him on the back. "Wow, Max, that's quite a cough. Maybe I should call the nurse. She'll probably take you back to your room and you'll miss Reading Hour, though."

Max gave one final guttural cough. "I'm feeling much better, thank you," he said, glaring at me. "How about you, Doris?" he asked the woman to whom he'd been pointing. "How are you feeling today?"

Doris, white-haired and thin, with a crocheted blanket across her wheelchaired lap, frowned. "How could I be anything but awful? I'm in here, aren't I? Imprisoned by my ungrateful children who are far too busy to stop in and see their mother."

During my visits to the facility, I often crossed paths with other visitors and it was easy to fall into conversation with folks you saw more than once, so I happened to know that Doris's two sons came by weekly and her daughter stopped in two or three times a week. Plus, Doris had multiple medical issues that made home care difficult, and, her youngest son had said, "This was what Mom wanted. Didn't want to be a burden on any of us, she said. And now . . ." He'd shrugged.

Max waggled his eyebrows at me and tapped the corner of his mouth. I looked at Doris and, now that she'd stopped talking, saw what he meant. The down-curved lines she'd made in her face when talking were still there when she wasn't. Her face had indeed frozen that way.

Shaking my head, I settled myself into a chair and pulled the current book out of my backpack; Karen Thompson Walker's *The Dreamers*. We had a few minutes to go before it was time to start reading, and people were still trickling into the room. Some walked with the aid of canes or walkers, some pushed their own wheelchairs, and some were pushed by CNAs. The chatter grew in volume, but most of it involved food and medications until I heard someone say, "Did everyone hear about that woman who was murdered?"

I looked up quickly. The speaker was Clella, a woman in her mid-eighties, who'd had a decades-long career as Chilson's postmistress. Sadly, I'd never known the post office under her control, but I'd heard a story about the diminutive Clella facing down a giant of a man who shouted that if he didn't get the package that was supposed to be delivered that day, he'd hurt someone. In the end, she had reduced him to apologetic tears.

"What woman?" the man rolling in the door asked. Lowell, the CNA steering the wheelchair, parked the man next to Clella and came around to lock the brakes and flip up the foot plates. I'd met Lowell a few months earlier and had fallen in love with his last name of Kokotovich. He'd laughed at my delight and said it wasn't so much fun when learning how to spell it at age five.

"Summer folk," Clella said. "Her family had a place up here since God was in short pants. Used to have mail come general delivery, back in the days when people did that."

"What was the name?" he asked.

I almost said it, but Clella was talking again. "Her family name was Rodriguez, but she married a man named . . . oh, let me think." Clella drummed her polished fingernails on her wheel-chair's arm.

"Well, where was she from?"

"Detroit area," Clella said absently, the pink fingernails continuing to tap out a rhythm. "She was a high school teacher, school name is the same as the town, starts with an M. Macomb, Madison Heights, Melvindale, Milan, Milford . . ."

I smiled at her alphabetic recitation. A woman after my own heart.

"Monroe!" she announced. "Nicole. From Monroe. Don't remember her married name, though."

Lowell, who had started to stand, froze in place. "Price," he said. "Her last name is Price."

Everyone turned to look at him. He flushed. "I used to live there. A long time ago." He gave a brief nod and hurried out.

I watched him go. A long time ago, he'd said. But Lowell was in his mid-twenties, so how long ago could it have been? And how long had Nicole been in Monroe? Though Monroe was a big city by Up North standards, it was a small town for downstate. Was there a connection between Lowell and Nicole?

It certainly seemed as if there could be.

And it was up to me to find out.

CHAPTER 14

Kate stared at me. "You want to do what?"

I kept my smile affixed to my face. Maybe if I kept it up, I'd look like Clella when I was in my mid-eighties, and not Doris. "I want us to make supper together. And it'll be something that doesn't smell much, so you won't get a headache."

"But you don't cook. Not really."

My smile became a tad rigid. "Just because I don't, doesn't mean I can't." At least in theory. "Anyone with a fifth grade education should be able to follow a recipe." I flourished the small pile of printouts I'd made at the library during lunchtime, five cents a page into petty cash, thank you. "Pick one. Any ingredient we don't have, we can walk over to the grocery store and buy. It's Friday night, after all. We can make cooking our entertainment for the evening."

"It's not like it's a real Friday," Kate said, rolling her eyes. "I have to work at the toy store tomorrow morning, you know."

I had not known. How could I have? For me to know what was going on in her life would have required that she talk to me. "Then I promise we won't make anything that will take longer than ten hours."

Kate sighed. "You're going to make me do this, aren't you?"

"Absolutely," I said brightly. Or as brightly as I could through teeth that were starting to clench tight. "It'll be fun."

"Fun?" Kate's eyes narrowed. "How?"

I had no idea. But then inspiration struck. Though my niece didn't listen to me, she did listen to pretty much everyone else. "Kristen says there's nothing in the entire world better than cooking a good meal."

"Yeah? She really says that?" Kate glanced at the houseboat's kitchen-like area.

"Here." I held out my phone. "Go ahead. Ask her."

Kate ignored my phone and, instead, took the stack of recipes. This relieved me mightily, because what Kristen had actually said was, "There's nothing better than coming up with a new recipe that my peeps are willing to shell out thirty bucks a pop to eat." She might have given me a pass on the translation, but now I had a chance to prep her for the question. And if I told her approval would result in Minnie Hamilton cooking a full dinner from start to finish, she would probably have paid admission to attend.

"Some of these don't look too horrible," Kate said. "Can I pick?"

"Absolutely," I said rashly, which was why we ended up in the grocery store, filling a cart with a multitude of items to make shrimp pad Thai, a recipe that happened to be on the same page as the far simpler shrimp stir fry, the dish I'd had my eye on when I'd hit the Print button.

After I'd handed over my credit card for an amount that was more expensive than going out would have been and we'd hauled everything back to the houseboat, we read over the recipe and I divvied up tasks. Kate on the sauce, me on the slicing and dicing.

But after she'd watched me almost slice my fingertips off, she forced a switch.

"Have you ever used a knife in your life?" she demanded.

"Sure," I said, carefully dividing oil into two tiny dishes usually reserved for Eddie's morning milk. "It's just that I'm often thinking about something else, and that something else is almost always a lot more interesting than cutting pretty much anything."

"I can't believe you have a master's," she muttered.

Clearly she had not yet learned that advanced degrees were an inaccurate indicator of life success, but that was something she'd have to figure out for herself.

When I was in the middle of spooning out rice vinegar, I felt Kate shoot me a quick glance. "Have you talked to Deputy Wolverson about what I was saying the other day?"

"About . . . ?" Since my thoughts had been focused on what Rafe had been murmuring into my ear the previous evening, I blinked at her question.

She paused, mid-chop. "You've forgotten about it, haven't you?"

"Of course not," I said automatically as I tried to remember what she was so sure I couldn't remember. A bit wildly, I looked around for a clue. Eddie, who was trying to wedge himself into the tiny crack between the dining bench and the wall, was no help. "It's just I, um, haven't had time."

"Really?" The knife dropped onto the counter and she put her hands on her hips. "It was days ago you said you'd talk to Deputy Wolverson about my theory, that maybe Mrs. Price's husband and Mr. Stuhler's wife were having an affair, and they killed their spouses so they could be together without paying for a divorce."

Ah. That. "Yes, but—"

"But what?" She was almost yelling now. "You were never going to tell him, were you? You don't take me seriously. You never have and you never will." She lurched away from my outstretched hand. "Leave me alone, okay? Just leave me alone." She ran out the door, bobbing the houseboat as she jumped off.

I hurried after her, keeping her in sight as she ran down the length of the dock and took a hard right, and then another right a few yards later.

Sighing, I slowed. She was headed to Louisa and Ted Axford's. I watched as she climbed aboard the sleek boat and lingered until I heard Louisa's calm and reassuring voice.

"Now what?" I asked Eddie as I returned to the houseboat.

"Mrr," he said. And he said it in a very critical way. Before I'd taken up residence with a cat, I hadn't understood how judgmental they could be.

"Thanks so much." I sighed. "I know I screwed up. You don't have to beat me over the head with it." I flopped on top of Kate's sleeping bag. Then squirmed around a bit. "You know what? This is actually very comfortable. No wonder she likes sleeping on this."

"Mrr."

"Well, sure, you knew that a long time ago, didn't you? And you were just waiting for me to acknowledge the combined wisdom of an Eddie and a seventeen-year-old." The yellow eyes swiveled my way and I quickly added, "Sorry, that came out a little snarky, didn't it? I apologize. I should never doubt your capabilities."

His little kitty shoulders went up and down in a sigh, looking for all the world like an aggrieved parent who knew their offspring was lying through their teeth.

In the name of distraction, I said, "But you never answered my question. What do I do now? Is she going to talk to me anytime soon? And by 'soon,' what I mean is within the next decade?"

Eddie, who had been sitting on the dashboard, jumped to the floor and stalked past me.

"Okay, you're right. What I should do is what I told her I'd do: talk to Ash about her theory that Fawn Stuhler and Dominic Price had a thing going and killed their spouses to clear the way for mutual eternal bliss. After their reception of my one-killer theory, I doubt they'll welcome anything like that." But I'd have to talk to them eventually, since I'd promised.

Sliding down, getting close to horizontal, I tried to consider Kate's theory as realistic. I'd never met Fawn, but Rex had been in his late forties, so odds were reasonably good that Fawn was roughly the same age. Nicole had turned forty last winter—I remembered her talking about the surprise party her husband had given her—so Dominic was probably about that, too.

"Not that you have to be the same age to fall in love with each other," I told Eddie. "There are lots of couples out there who are years and years apart in age."

I started counting on my fingers. Donna's husband hadn't retired since he was holding out for maximum social security benefits, so he had to be at least five years younger. And I was pretty sure Uncle Everett, Aunt Frances's first husband, had been significantly older.

"Okay, that's only two couples, but I'm sure

237

I could come up with more if—" I stopped, frowning. Underneath me there were sounds of a cat getting into something he shouldn't. "Eddie, what are you doing?"

The unexplained noise continued unabated.

I slid over the edge of the bench seat and oozed onto the floor. "Please don't tell me you've crawled into Kate's luggage again," I said, peering underneath the lowered table. "You know she hates it when you get your white hairs on her black T-shirts and your black hairs on her white T-shirts."

A single piece of popcorn rolled out and came to a rest next to my right knee.

"Nice." I wondered how long it had been there and decided not to think about it. "You could have eaten that and saved—"

A second piece of popcorn rolled out and stopped by my left knee. "Double nice. Thanks for your commentary on my housekeeping—"

"Mrr!"

"I said thank you. What more do you want?"

"MRR!" Eddie crawled out from the darkness, gave me a Look, and stalked off.

"Some days," I said, watching his tail end, "it just doesn't pay to get out of bed."

"Mrr."

When Kate eventually returned, I was sitting on a front deck chaise, reading, with Eddie flopped across my legs. She stepped aboard, muttered an apology for leaving without telling me where she was going, and slunk inside.

"Not sure that counts as talking," I said to Eddie. "What do you think?"

He purred, which was the exact response I'd hoped for.

I'd been texting Louisa on and off since Kate had fled for the Axfords' greener pastures and the fun of playing with a toddler, and when Louisa had asked if I wanted Kate to apologize, I'd responded: *In a perfect world, sure. But though Chilson may be paradise, it's not perfect.*

Louisa: *Shouldn't we be trying to make the world more perfect?*

I'd returned with: *But who gets to decide the definition of perfection? Not sure I want that job* and an emoji of a yellow face sticking its tongue out.

After sitting a few minutes longer, I picked up Eddie and my book—because it was way too dark to read, even for me—and headed inside. As I passed Kate, who'd already brushed her teeth, changed into pajamas, slid into her sleeping bag, and started up a video game on her tablet, I said, "See you in the morning."

She made a grunt-like noise in return, and I went to bed with a calm heart. She might not be talking-talking to me, but I wasn't getting the silent treatment.

"What do you think about that?" I whispered to Eddie, who was curled up between my right hip and the outer wall.

Once again, his only answer was a purr.

The next morning, Rafe and I had arranged to meet for breakfast at the Round Table. We hadn't shared our Friday night because he and some buddies had tickets to a concert at the flat-out gorgeous Great Lakes Center for the Arts, and I wasn't invited.

He looked at me over the coffee Sabrina had just poured. "You could have gone, you know."

I hesitated, then reached out for the cream. It was definitely a cream kind of day. Then again, if I could justify the calories, most days were cream kinds of days. "Really? Me and all of your stinky guy friends, hanging out before at Knot Just a Bar, going to hear some band whose music I've never cared for, and then going back to Knot Just a Bar afterward to talk about how great the music was?"

"You'd have fit right in," he said, toasting me with his mug.

It probably would have been fun, if I'd brought along earplugs. His friends were good guys, and they were always willing to expand their circle to include anyone who laughed at their jokes. Still, I liked that the two of us had slightly different sets of friends. I figured it was probably good for our relationship. That is, if the article I'd read in the women's magazine at the beauty salon last time I was getting my hair cut had any truth behind it.

"How did it go with Kate last night?" he asked.

Grimacing, I said, "Not now, please. I don't want to ruin my breakfast."

"That bad?"

"It wasn't good."

We sat there, sipping coffee while we waited for our food, and as the caffeine started to work its happy way into my body, my outlook started to improve. "But it ended up okay. And on my way out this morning, I said, 'Have a good day,' and she said, 'You too,' so I'm going to count that as a win."

"Speaking of wins . . ."

Rafe let the sentence trail off, and I took the bait. "What did you win?" I asked, looking around. "Don't see any big stuffed animals." I craned my head and neck around to see out the window. "A car? Did you win that Lamborghini I see sitting out there?" Not that I could recognize a Lamborghini from any kind of ghini, but that wasn't the point.

"Better. And just so you know, I was very clever about this." He beamed.

"Given," I said, nodding.

"It's about Dominic Price."

My coffee cup stopped halfway up. "Nicole's husband?"

"The very one."

"What did you learn?" I put the cup down. "Is it something I should tell the sheriff's office? Who did you learn it from?"

Rafe crossed his arms and glared at me. "Are you going to let me tell the story or not?"

"Is there time?" I flipped my phone over and thumbed the Home button to wake it up. Rafe Stories were rated by his friends by the number of beers they consumed while he talked. Amounts ranged from one short draft beer for the shortest tale to three tall beers for the stupendously long but immensely entertaining Appendix Story. "Okay, I don't have anything going until tonight. I should be good."

He frowned. "I could have sworn it was my turn to be the funny one."

"Not until noon."

"Oh. Well, okay then." He looked around, and started. "Late yesterday morning, just before lunch, I ran out of finishing nails."

This I could believe, because I'd watched him install trim, and I was pretty sure the house would end up with more weight in nails than in any other item.

"So I went up to the hardware store." He walked his fingers across the table top. "It only took me a second to get the box of nails"—also easy to believe, since he'd practically worn a groove in the concrete sidewalk making nail

242

trips—"so I got in line. The guy in line ahead of me looked familiar, but I couldn't quite place him until someone called him Father."

That seemed overly formal. "Not Dad?"

"Nope. Father as in Father David, the Catholic priest at that little stone church, you know, the one near Dooley, over on the other side of the county."

I did indeed know that church. The bookmobile and crew drove past it once a week. Made of fieldstone, with a beautiful bell tower and oak double front doors, it recently celebrated its hundred and twenty-fifth anniversary.

"Anyway," he went on, "some guy I didn't know asked Father David how Don was doing." Rafe paused and gave me a meaningful look. "At least that's what I thought he said."

I rolled my hand in a move-along gesture.

"You are the worst audience ever. Father David said he was suffering, but would make it through with faith and God's grace. And then . . ." Rafe drew the word out long. "The guy asked Father David how the congregation was dealing with the murder of one of its members."

My breath sucked in and I almost choked on my coffee. "Dom. Not Don, but Dom."

"Exactly. But I had to make sure, so I inched forward and said how my girlfriend had known Nicole, and how sorry you were. And that you'd never met Dom, but would like to give him your condolences."

243

True enough. I waited, because the story was surely not over.

"Father David said Dom would be fine, because even though he—that's Father David—only saw Dom during the summer, he knew Dom was faithful, loyal to the church, and very devout. That Dom was raised with the old ways, and followed them himself."

Huh. Interesting.

"Clever, huh?" Rafe did the one eyebrow thing. It was. "Yes, and you know what this means?"

"Yeah. It means Dom most likely doesn't believe in divorce, so Kate's wacky theory might be right. When are you going to tell her?"

An excellent question. "I don't suppose 'never' is the right answer."

"Nope."

"Then I'll say . . . later."

Rafe eyed me. "You sure about that?"

Not a chance. "Absolutely."

I wasn't due at the library until afternoon, so I used the opportunity to drive out to the gas station–slash–convenience store I had visited so fruitlessly a few days earlier.

When I'd mentioned to Rafe that I was doing so, he'd given me a look I didn't recognize at first. Only when I studied it for a moment did I clue in.

"You," I said, narrowing my eyes, "are looking at me askance."

244

"As what?"

"Don't play dumb with me, mister," I said mock-severely. "You know I'll win that game every time."

Rafe laughed, and the inside of my heart swelled with happiness. *Love,* I thought. *This was what love can do to you.*

"I think there are better ways you could be spending your time, that's all," he said.

"Because I could be doing . . ." I raised my eyebrows. "Oh, hang on. I know. I could be sanding. Or painting. Or sanding. Or painting."

"Well." He shrugged. "Yeah. The sooner the house gets done, the sooner you can move in."

Once again, I toyed with the idea of moving before the renovation work was done. And once again, I instantly rejected the idea. Living with dust, noise, and general constant disruption of construction was not conducive to quality reading time.

More important than my preferences, however, were Eddie's, and Eddie definitely wouldn't like it. Plus, the whole place was filled with cat toys. Painting tarps would turn into cat caves. Electrical cords for the power tools would be chewed. Wood trim that was cut, finished, and ready to install would be tested for clawing capacity. And it didn't do to think what he might do with sandpaper.

I'd shuddered. "Tomorrow," I'd told Rafe. "I'll work hard tomorrow, I promise."

Rafe had wished me good luck with my convenience store mission, and I'd spent much of the journey crossing my fingers and toes that the trip would be productive. Not that I had to be right and Rafe wrong, but I certainly wouldn't mind it.

I entered the store and looked around for my little friend.

"Good morning."

The guy behind the counter spoke in a friendly manner, and even had a smile on his face. He had the same long hair and same skinny build as my friend, but was a few years older and miles different in demeanor. This was a guy who might actually engage in a conversation.

"Morning," I said, smiling back. After introducing myself, and learning that his name was Mason, I said, "I stopped by a few days ago and talked to a young man about leaving a note. I'm looking for the person who has worked here the longest."

"A note?" He frowned. "I haven't seen any note. Who told you—" He stopped, sighing. "Was it a guy who kind of looked like me, only younger?" I nodded, and he said, "My cousin. I told my uncle I'd . . ." His expression segued into something that wasn't exactly a smile. "Well, never mind. I'm the one who has worked here the longest. What can I do for you?"

I blinked. The longest? Mason might have been

thirty years old, but couldn't be much older than that.

He laughed. "I grew up just down that road and started working here when I was maybe thirteen, shoveling the sidewalk for two dollars cash, no questions asked. A couple of years ago, the owner wanted to retire. I was working downstate, but when I saw this place listed, I started working the numbers."

It was a familiar story. Lots of young people who grew up in the region left for downstate jobs after high school or college, and after a few years many of them started looking for ways to move back. "And we all lived happily ever after?" I asked, smiling. It had worked for Kristen.

"Hoping so," Mason said. "We'll see what my accountant says at the end of this year. But what was it you wanted?"

I repeated what I'd told his cousin, that two people who didn't live that far away had died unexpectedly, that they were loyal bookmobile patrons, that I figured they were customers of his, too, and that I was wondering if anyone was putting together a fund for flowers or a donation.

Mason was shaking his head. "I was out of town for a few days for a family wedding and I'm still catching up. Who died?"

"Rex Stuhler, who owned a pest control company with his wife, and a summer resident, Nicole Price. Did you know them?"

Mason looked at his hands. At the counter. At the rolls of scratcher lottery tickets. "I guess. Sort of."

Until now, Mason had been a friendly and talkative guy. Now, suddenly, after mentioning Rex and Nicole, he was acting like his cousin. Hmm. "Did they come in here often?" I asked. "If I remember right, Rex's house is only a mile or two south of here, and Nicole's family cabin is just a few miles over—"

"I didn't know them," Mason snapped. "Okay? And I'm sorry, but I have to get back to work." He hurried to the end of the counter, opened a door that revealed a tiny office, and entered, shutting the door behind him.

"That was weird," I said out loud.

And also very suspicious. Which meant I was right and Rafe was wrong about this trip being a waste of time.

But though I did feel a fractional ounce of happiness about that little fun fact, most of me felt sad. For Rex. And Fawn and Nicole and Dominic, and all the other people who were touched by murder. Then again, even if Fawn had an alibi the night her husband had been killed, it was still possible that she'd been involved. And could she and Dom really have been having an affair?

I sighed, cast one last look at the firmly closed door, and left.

• • •

"Minnie, is that you?"

Since I'd answered my desk phone as "This is Minnie, how may I help you?" the question seemed unnecessary, but since I was pretty sure the caller was Max Compton, I decided to give him some slack.

"Max, is that you?"

He chuckled. "Bright as a shiny new penny, that's what you are."

"Pennies can be shiny and old at the same time," I said. "And that's what you are."

"Is this the first meeting of Chilson's Mutual Admiration Society?"

I laughed. "Let's call it a pre-meeting meeting. What can I do for you, Max?"

"It's my—" He moaned. "It's my heart," he said, gasping.

"That's too bad." I patted my desk for the pen I knew was underneath one of the piles of paper. "I could call nine-one-one if you'd like. Or should I get Heather on the phone?" Ah, there it was. I unearthed the pen and clicked it open so I could start the draft agenda for the next staff meeting. Graydon usually did this, but he'd asked me to do it this time around.

"Not sure I can make it that long," he wheezed.

"That's too bad. Is there anything I can do to help you in your last moments on this earth?"

"I might . . ." He coughed. "I might make it

249

a little longer if you brought me a large print copy of *The Runaway Jury*. You know, that John Grisham book? It might be the only thing that gets me through this week."

Which was why, an hour and a half later, when I should have been going over to the house to start sanding the study's baseboard, I was instead walking into Lakeview Medical Care Facility with Max's book in my hand. He was waiting for me, rolling his wheelchair forward three inches, back three inches, forward, back.

"You made it!" he almost shouted, beaming.

I handed over the book. "And you seem to have made a miraculous recovery."

"Eh?" He peered up at me and gave a fake cough. "Oh, yes. Much better."

"Why are you coughing? I thought it was your heart this time."

"All connected," Max said vaguely, turning to the first chapter, and I lost any chance at conversation with him.

"You do realize that the next bookmobile librarian won't be nearly as accommodating when it comes to personal deliveries, don't you?"

"The next one?" He sat up straight. "Minerva Hamilton, what are you saying? You're not leaving Chilson, are you?"

"Just wanted to make sure you were paying attention."

He let out a huge breath. "Don't do that to an old man. I'm not sure my heart can take it."

"You told me last winter that your heart was as healthy as a fit seventy-year-old."

"Things can change," he said, going back to the book. "You never know."

Which was true enough, but I didn't want to think of Lakeview without Max, so I shoved the reminder of his advanced age into the back of my brain, murmured a good-bye, and turned to leave. But before I took a single step toward the entrance, I pivoted and headed down an interior hallway. A few rooms down I saw the CNA I knew best.

"Hey, Minnie," Heather said. "What are you doing here on a Saturday?"

I inched closer. "Don't tell anyone, but Max has me wrapped around his pinkie. I made a delivery just for him."

Heather laughed. "Sounds like Max."

"Say, would Lowell Kokotovich happen to be working today? I met him at the reading hour the other day and wanted to talk to him about something."

"Um, I think so." Heather glanced down the hallway at a white light just outside a resident's room that was blinking. "I have to go," she said, hurrying off. "Lowell's probably in Otter Lane."

I called a thank-you and made my way around Lakeview's big square. Eventually, I found Otter

Lane and Lowell Kokotovich, who was standing at a cart outside a resident's room, poking at a computer screen with a stylus.

"Hi," I said, approaching. "I don't know if you remember me, but—"

"Sure. From the library." He nodded, then frowned. "It's Saturday, isn't it? There's not a reading hour today, right?"

I refrained from saying that every hour was reading hour as far as I was concerned. He didn't seem the type to appreciate the joke. "No. I wanted to talk to you about something else. You said you'd lived in the same town as Nicole Price. She was a regular bookmobile patron. Some of us were thinking about putting together a donation in her name, and I wondered if you'd be interested."

"Oh. Uh." He looked at me, looked at his computer, looked at me, then back at the computer. "I, um . . . oh, look, there's a call light I have to answer. Sorry."

And he hurried off, just like Heather. But the white light above the room he entered wasn't blinking.

Hmm, I thought as he closed the door.

Very, very hmmm.

Late that night, I was dead to the world when a *scratch*-ing noise woke me from a dreamless sleep. Kate had abandoned me for the attractions of Aunt Frances and Uncle Otto, and Rafe was helping a buddy move, so I'd had no one to tell me that spending four hours on my hands and knees sanding, sanding, and sanding some more was Too Much for someone who normally spent her time either behind a desk or behind a steering wheel.

Around nine, Rafe had hauled me to my feet, fed me pizza, walked me home, and helped me tumble into bed. "Sleep tight," he'd said, kissing my forehead. "Don't let the bedbugs bite."

Even if they had, I probably wouldn't have woken unless they'd bit me down to the bone. However, my ears had become sensitive to noises related to Eddie getting into things he shouldn't and I was wide awake in an instant.

I sat bolt upright. "What are you doing?" I called.

Scritch-scritch-scritch.

Throwing back the sheet, which was my only cover on such a muggy night, I put my feet on the floor and stood up. "Where are you?"

"Mrr."

His response had come from the kitchen, but the noise had stopped. I padded back to bed, flopped down, and was almost asleep when the noise started all over again.

Scritch-scritch.

"Eddie!" I yelled. "Cut it out!"

Scritch-scritch-scritch.

I flung back the sheet, stomped up the stairs to the main cabin, and fumbled for the light switch. Brightness exploded into the room, and like the proverbial deer in the headlights, Eddie stopped what he was doing and stared up at me. But defiantly, which wasn't at all deerlike.

"For crying out loud," I muttered.

Because my furry little friend had managed to extract a Tonedagana County map from my backpack and unfold it. His right front paw was poised over the northeast part of the county, and his claws were extended and about to rip right into Bowyer Township.

"Nice try," I said. "But no way am I letting you plot the next bookmobile route."

"Mrr!"

"Because I said so." I took the map away from him, folded it in a way no mapmaker would ever recommend, and shoved it into the backpack, which I zipped shut and shoved under Kate's sleeping bag.

"Mrr," he said in a manner that could only be called a sulk.

I rolled my eyes and went back to bed.

Cats.

CHAPTER 15

Julia folded her hands and laid them across the computer keyboard. "No one is coming," she pronounced.

She was probably right. It was one of those triple H days: hot, hazy, and humid. Days like this did not lend themselves to high bookmobile usage. You never knew, of course, because it wasn't outside the realm of possibility that half a dozen cars would suddenly converge on our shady parking spot, all packed with occupants intent on checking out an armload of books for use on screened porches. But it seemed unlikely.

"Too hot." The door was open and I was sitting on the steps, fanning myself with the February copy of *Traverse Magazine*, hoping for a breeze to flutter by.

"Mrr," Eddie said.

"How goes it with the niece?" Julia asked.

"Eh." I shrugged. Or I would have, but the movement might have caused me to overheat, so I mostly just moved my eyebrows. "She spent most of the weekend up at Aunt Frances and Otto's place, hanging out in their air-conditioning."

"Is she still on about her love quadrangle theory?"

"Far as I know." And I still hadn't talked to Ash

about it, so perhaps it was just as well she was up the hill with a superior role model.

Julia languidly tapped at the keyboard. "Who else checked out books that last day Rex and Nicole were here? Other than Violet Mullaly."

"There weren't any others at that stop, remember? And . . ." I sighed. "I haven't done anything about looking into Violet." Which was something I really needed to do.

"Hmm." Julia did some focused typing. "Let's look at a broader list."

"Of what?"

"People who checked out books in this part of the county. Just looking at the names might jog something in our memories. Turning over all stones, yes?" She entered the specifics into the system, then turned the laptop so we both could see. "We've stopped out here four times since Memorial Day. Here's a side-by-side comparison."

Though I was pretty sure it was going to be a wasted effort, I expended the energy to get up and study the list. Eddie, who was sleeping pancake-flat on the dashboard, ignored it.

After a few minutes, I shook my head. "There are some anomalies, but we know the why of most of them."

Julia nodded. "Darla Holton and John Currie didn't show up for the first July stop because they both had family in from all over the country and didn't have time."

"Mrs. Karden showed up in July but not in June because of her husband's surgery."

"Bob Balogh was only here in June because he and his wife are taking a road trip up the Alaska Highway."

"And Mary Santos was only here this last time because she's been working double shifts at the brewing company but finally got a day off." I was once again reminded of how much we knew about our patrons, information that came easily on the bookmobile but would never have happened in the bricks and mortar library. It was just different out here.

"There are a couple of others," Julia said. "But they're all absences, not presences, if you know what I mean."

Somehow, I did. "And it's hard to see how an absence could have anything to do with a motive for murder."

"Really?" Julia did the one-eyebrow thing. "I can see all sorts of reasons. A husband promising to pick up a book, but forgetting." She tsk'ed. "A regular patron, instead of coming here, instead dallied with the mail carrier and the spouse caught them."

I could tell she was winding up for a long litany of murder motives that she'd read or imagined or acted in. "Yes, fine, there are probably an infinite number of possibilities, but knowing our regular bookmobile patrons, and of who is missing, can you think of any realistic ones?"

"Well," she said, "if you're going to insist on reality, boring as it is, then no. I can't think of anything."

My brain circled around lazily. "So we have Violet, who was angry at both Rex and Nicole for checking out books she wanted, and . . ." I stopped. It was starting to feel like a story problem in algebra class. "So," I said slowly, "could something possibly have happened when Nicole and Rex were here on the bookmobile that led to their murders?"

"Seems far-fetched." Julia yawned. "Because wouldn't Violet be dead, too? And the two of us? Oh, I know, you think we're in danger, but I haven't seen hide nor hair of a killer in the last three weeks, so I feel pretty safe."

I wished I did.

That evening I deposited Eddie back onto the houseboat and checked the whiteboard for Kate's whereabouts. She'd written, *Working late at Pam's, sleeping up the hill at Aunt Frances and Otto's if that's okay*, followed by a stick figure with beads of sweat pouring off that, if you used a lot of imagination, could have looked like Kate.

I stood there, staring at the board. So there was hope. Hope that I wasn't the worst aunt in the history of the universe. Hope that the two of us would eventually grow into a happy and comfortable niece-aunt relationship. Hope things would all work out.

Smiling to myself, smiling at the world in general, I headed back outside, where it had grown even hotter and more humid though I wouldn't have thought it possible.

"How do people in Florida stand it?" I asked.

Louisa Axford, who was starting charcoal in one of the marina's grills installed for the boaters, looked up. "Stand what?" she asked.

"This weather." I took the neck of my T-shirt and fluffed it up and down, trying to get some air movement. "Hot. Humid. Bleah."

"You have the question all wrong," Louisa said, glancing up at the hazy sky. "It's not how do people in Florida stand the heat, it's how do people Up North stand the winters?" She shivered, and I wasn't sure it was fake. "Cold and snowy for weeks at a time, with maybe a single day of sunshine a month to tide you over? No thank you."

I'd long ago stopped trying to convince Louisa of the joys of winter—that the transformations a fresh snowfall wrought were wondrous, that the one sunny day was so gorgeously brilliant it made all the cloudy ones fade from memory, and that venturing out into winter's sharp cold made you feel brave and adventurous, even when you weren't—and we'd agreed to disagree about what climate was best for human habitation.

Louisa dribbled the charcoal with lighter fluid and lit it with a match. She eyed the conflagration, poked at the pile of bricks with tongs, and nodded with satisfaction. "Steak should be done in forty-five minutes. Do you and Kate want to come over? We have extra."

I explained Kate's whereabouts. "And I need to get to the house. Rafe promised to pick up dinner."

"Sub sandwiches?" She laughed. "Veggie with extra cheese for you?"

"When you have a good rut going, it's best to stay in it," I said.

"Unless you're tired of your nice, comfy rut," Louisa said. "I hear it happens."

"I'll let you know." I sketched a wave and walked off, stopping at the front steps of the house. There was a law enforcement officer on the porch, slouched in a chair with his feet up on the railing, paging through what looked like a recent copy of *Field & Stream*. "Are you here to help or hinder?" I asked.

Ash looked up. "Can't I do both?"

"Sure," I said, climbing the wood stairs and pulling a chair around to match Ash's arrangement, which looked so comfortable I couldn't believe I hadn't tried it myself. "Just not at the same time. Where's Rafe?"

"Hunting and gathering."

"Are you staying? Please say yes. We need to

install upper cabinets in the master bath, and my height efficiency isn't exactly a help in this case."

He nodded. "That's why Rafe's getting three subs plus loaded potato skins."

"Perfect." I sat and put my feet up on the railing. It was a stretch for me, but still comfortable, and I gave a sigh of contentment. "What would be nice out here is a ceiling fan."

Ash eyed me. "What, for the six days a year it gets this hot?"

"Do you have a problem with that?" I asked, closing my eyes.

He turned a page. "Not really. But I'm guessing it's not going to be at the top of Rafe's punch list."

Though I figured a ceiling fan was more a change order than a punch list item, Ash was probably right. "Speaking of murders," I said, and ignored Ash's heavy sigh. And then before he could object that I was making him work when he was off duty, I went on. "First off, I have to tell you about Kate."

"How's she doing?" Ash asked. "She was pretty upset after the fireworks, and I get it. Stumbling across a dead body on TV or the movies isn't anything like it is in real life."

No, it wasn't. On the screen there was no indication that the sounds, tastes, and smells that accompanied such a traumatic experience would forever remind you of what had happened. I figured that, the rest of my life, whenever I heard Beyoncé's "Crazy in Love," I'd think about Nicole, because that song was playing on the radio as we drove home that awful afternoon. And I wasn't exactly looking forward to the fireworks next July. So if it was this bad for me, who was reasonably close to a fully functional adult, how must the adolescent Kate be feeling?

"She's doing okay," I finally said. "She hasn't had a nightmare in almost a week." As far as I knew. "But she's come up with a theory I promised to share with you."

He settled a bit farther down in his chair and crossed his ankles. "I had no idea that messing around with murder investigations had a genetic component."

"The theory," I said, ignoring his comment, "is that Fawn, Rex's wife, and Dominic, Nicole's husband, have been having an affair. And to avoid lengthy and costly divorce proceedings, which Dominic didn't believe in anyway because he's a really devout Catholic, Dominic killed Rex and Fawn killed Nicole. Which was why they had alibis for the murder of their spouses." I was embellishing a bit, but now that I was saying it out loud, I was warming to the idea.

Ash, however, did not look convinced. "One question." He yawned. "Do you have any evidence that Fawn and Dominic knew each other? E-mails, letters, witnesses."

Of course not. "I think it's a possibility that's worth looking into."

"Sure," he said. "I'll get on that, right after I work through those other theories you've tossed into my lap. How many were there for Rex Stuhler? There's Fawn, naturally. And John and Nandi Jaquay, plus Barry Vannett. And who have you come up with for Nicole Price?"

I refrained from pointing out that Fawn had been their own first suspect. "I have some thoughts."

"Of course you do," he murmured.

"Hark!" I said, holding my hand to my ear. "Do I hear the echo of Detective Hal Inwood?"

Ash clutched his chest. "Ooo, that hurt. Stop it, already."

"If you promise to listen to me, sure."

"Since it's way too hot to move, and it's pretty comfortable here, I don't have much choice."

"That's what I like in law enforcement," I said. "A captive audience."

And I proceeded to tell him about what I'd discovered in the last week or so. That Violet Mullaly had expressed deep anger about the library books Rex and Nicole each had just before Rex was killed. That Lowell grew up in the same town where Nicole taught, and had acted oddly when I'd casually asked him about it. That Mason at the convenience store had been friendly up until I'd started talking about Nicole and Rex. The only possibility I didn't mention was Courtney Drew, the home health aide, who'd

263

worked with Rex's mom, because that didn't seem like enough, even for me.

"Violet Mullaly, Lowell Kokotovich, and Mason Hiller." Ash pulled a large cell phone out of his front pocket. He tapped away without saying anything.

Finally, I couldn't take it any longer. "What are you doing?"

"Oh, just looking," he said idly. "How do you spell 'Mullaly'? Okay, thanks, that's . . . huh."

He stared at the screen.

"What?" I asked. "Something about Violet? What is it?"

Ash shook his head and slid the phone back into his pocket. "Looks like dinner is coming up the sidewalk," he said, standing. "Want anything out of Rafe's fridge?"

I shook my head and let him go without pressing for answers. Clearly, he'd learned something about Violet, and he'd tell me when he could. And if I couldn't wait that long, I could always drop by the sheriff's office and not go away until they shared.

"You look happy," Rafe said, dropping the bags of food on the porch table.

I smiled up at his handsome self. "That's because I am."

The next morning I embarked on a new outreach venture. Instead of trying to combine bookmobile trips with dropping off books to shut-ins, I'd decided to try using my own vehicle to do the drop-offs.

"Only in the summer," I'd told Eddie as I was leaving. My fuzzy-headed buddy was sitting on top of his cat carrier and clearly ready to head out for a day of bookmobiling.

"Mrr?" He looked at me in a questioning manner.

"Because in the summer there are a lot more people around," I explained patiently. "Word has spread that people who qualify as shut-ins can have books picked up and dropped off, and it's getting too hard to mesh their needs with the bookmobile's route and schedule. It's cheaper for the library to pay me mileage than it is to drive the bookmobile to all these people's houses."

Eddie stood and scratched at the carrier with his front feet, then his back feet.

I watched him for a moment. "If you're trying to bury that, it's not working."

"Mrr!"

"No, you're not coming. You wouldn't like it, honest. It's going to be mostly driving and you'd never get out of the carrier. Remember the last time I took you downstate?"

We'd driven to Dearborn to stay with my parents over Christmas, and I'd taken Eddie because everyone I might have left him with was either out of town or coming along. My dad's allergies meant that Eddie had to live, work, and play in my bedroom, but that wasn't the hard part.

It had turned out that Eddie didn't care for car rides when the car was driving faster than sixty miles an hour. And when Eddie didn't like something, everyone knew about it. Aunt Frances, Otto, and I had endured four hours of nonstop howling on the way down and another four hours on the way back up. The three humans had made a shuddering vow never to do that again, and so far we'd kept our promise.

Of course, a trip around Tonedagana County wasn't likely to provide many opportunities for driving that fast, but there were a couple of straight stretches of county highway on the east side, so it might happen.

"See you tonight," I said, leaning down to kiss the top of his furry head.

But he collapsed himself, missing my gesture of endearment by an inch, then jumped down and ran off with thumping feet.

"Have a good day," I called. "I'll miss you!"

Though he called back—"Mrr!!"—I was pretty sure he wasn't returning my sentiment.

Four hours later, by the time I arrived at the home of Rupert and Ann Marie Wiley, I'd decided I was never again going to do a book run.

"Not like this anyway," I said, gratefully taking the chair they offered me on their front porch.

"What do you mean?" Ann Marie asked. "No, wait. Let me get you something. I just made some lemonade, this heat simply calls for it, and I made some brownies this morning before it got hot because I knew you were coming, and—" She saw my expression of dismay. "But you like brownies. Don't you?"

"Used to," I muttered.

Ann Marie frowned, but Rupert had already caught on. Nodding, he said, "Bet you've been offered brownies, cookies, pie, or coffee cake at every place you stopped this morning."

"You forgot the bagels and doughnuts. And everyone's so nice, how could I say no?"

Ann Marie laughed. "You're going to have to learn fast; otherwise you'll get too big to fit in the bookmobile."

I patted my stomach, then winced, which made her laugh all the harder. "So kind of you to laugh at my misfortune."

"It's what she does," her loving husband said. "You should hear her when I'm trying to put on my socks."

"Now *that's* funny." Ann Marie pointed at Rupert. "Plumber's cracks are nothing compared to—"

"Come to think of it," I said, interrupting before I got an image in my head I'd never be able to erase. "A glass of your lemonade would taste great."

Rupert watched her go, then he turned to me and rubbed his hands. "Now. What did you bring me?"

I handed the books over. "Have you finished all the others I dropped off?"

"Waiting for you inside." He touched his chest. "I should be able to drive soon," he said quietly. "I'm sorry to make this extra work for you, but Ann Marie's medications . . . well, let's just say that getting behind a wheel wouldn't be good for her. We hope she has a lot of years left, but . . ." He shook his head.

"It's not extra work," I said quickly. "I'm happy to do this." As I watched him open Jane Smiley's *Some Luck*, I thought about what I'd learned so many times over: that you could never really know what was going on in people's lives, and that you rarely knew what burdens people were carrying. All I'd known regarding Rupert's request for a book stop was that for six weeks, no one in the house would be able to drive. I'd had no idea that Ann Marie had serious medical issues, and the knowledge that she did was deeply saddening.

"Happy to," I said again, this time more firmly.

"And at least you keep your car in decent repair." Rupert shot a look at my modest sedan. "That Courtney's dripped oil all over the driveway. I swear she parked in a different spot every time she came here."

"Noisy, too," Ann Marie said as she came through the front door, laden with a tray. "No, you sit down, Minnie. I can do all this. Rupert would just get to nodding off in his chair and up that girl would drive. Don't know if she even had a muffler on that thing. Or if she ever washed it. And those bumper stickers, my goodness. They're nice and colorful, but the things they say aren't anything I'd want our preacher to see."

Something in my head went "click." The last time I'd stopped at Ann Marie and Rupert's house, Courtney, their home health aide, had been there, and I'd seen her car, but not the rear bumper. Could it have been the same car that had driven past the bookmobile on the day Rex and Nicole had been on the bookmobile for the last time?

"Those bumper stickers," I said slowly. "Are they bright pink?"

Ann Marie handed me a glass of lemonade. "They certainly are. Shocking pink, they used to call it. Now I don't think anything shocks anyone."

So Courtney had indeed driven down Brown's Road that day.

But what did it mean? Everything . . . or nothing?

CHAPTER 16

My niece stared at me over her half-empty plate. "You want me to do what?"

The heat had abated somewhat from the previous few days, and she'd come back to the marina early that morning. Partly because she'd run out of clean clothes and partly because Louisa had texted her, asking for babysitting services until she had to get to work, which would enable Louisa and Ted to run errands approximately ten thousand times faster than if they had a toddler in tow.

Kate had, apparently, been happy to do so, and when she'd returned after a few hours at Pam Fazio's Older Than Dirt, I'd surprised her with a home-cooked dinner. Okay, it was spaghetti from a box with sauce from a jar, but Kristen had snobbed me up enough, food-wise, to want fresh Parmesan cheese instead of dried, and grating cheese counted as cooking to me.

We'd been eating on the front deck, with Eddie up on the roof keeping an eye on everything. Once upon a time I'd been worried when he'd jumped up there, but I'd laid those worries to rest long ago. He was fine up there. I even joined him, every once in a while, just to get a different view.

I smiled at Kate. "We," I said, "are going over to visit Barb and Russ McCade tonight. They're great people and they're looking forward to meeting you."

"Why?" she asked, frowning.

"Because they're friends of mine and . . ." I stopped, because I didn't have an answer for her. Not one that would make sense to a seventeen-year-old. Because how many high school kids could understand how rare true friendship was? And that the opportunity to grow that circle of friendship was a chance to grab on to? I was mixing metaphors in my head, which was never a good sign for comprehensible conversation, so I simply repeated myself. "They're friends of mine and they want to meet you."

Kate grumbled a bit, but after enticing Eddie off the roof by rattling the treat can, she got into my car without further complaint. And when I turned down the long and twisty driveway, she started to look interested in her surroundings.

"This goes to their house?" she asked.

"All the way down to the lake," I said. "Did it in the bookmobile once."

"Yeah?" Kate, for once, sounded impressed with her aunt. And when we stopped in front of the McCades' lovely home, her eyes went wide. "Wow," she said softly, staring at the fieldstone, the massive timbers, and the wooden front door with the rounded top. "This place is—"

The front door opened. "Minnie Hamilton!" Cade bellowed. "Get over here this minute!"

"Let me guess," I said as Kate and I approached. "You and your lovely wife are fighting over whether or not a word is appropriate and you need me to referee. No, don't tell me whose side is whose. Just give me the setup and the word."

Despite the twenty-some-year differences in our ages, the McCades and I had bonded for life in a hospital room when I entered wholeheartedly into their word game. Rules had shifted over time, but it went something like this: The game started organically (part of the game) through each of them accidentally saying a word starting with the same letter. The winner was the last one to use a word that fit the situation and the loser had to acknowledge this gracefully.

"The letter is G," Cade pronounced. "The word under consideration is 'gracious,' which was preceded by 'go gargle,' 'great galoots,' and 'good gravy.' "

"Well," I said. "Those are all double G words, so 'gracious' would have to be paired with another G word, but you can't use anything that's already been used. So unless someone comes up with something fast to go in front of 'gracious,' I'd say 'good gravy' is the winner."

Cade gave me a smacking kiss on the forehead. "Hah! Did you hear that, Barb?"

"Of course I heard. Everyone within half a mile

heard you. You were right and I was wrong. Now let me get a look at the niece." Barb elbowed her way past her husband and smiled as she pulled her shoulder-length brownish-gray hair into a ponytail. "Kate, it's nice to meet you."

The two of them beamed at us. Well, Barb beamed. Cade did what he did, which was inspect the face of any new person he met as if he were selecting paint colors. He peered at Kate, his craggy features and cleft chin deepening in thought and his bushy eyebrows bushing. His hair was now more gray than brown and he was in dire need of a haircut, which usually meant one thing: He was painting, and Barb hadn't been able to tear him away from his studio long enough to take a pair of scissors to him.

"Kate," I said, "these are my friends Barb and Russell McCade."

"Call me Cade, my dear." He bowed, then took her hand and lifted it to his lips. "Any niece of Minerva's," he said, bestowing a gentle kiss on her knuckles, "is a Godsend to the world."

Kate's wide eyes stared at him and she snatched her hand back as soon as he let go. "But . . . you're . . ." she stammered. "You're that painter."

"Ah, yes, the price of fame." Cade smiled. "Yes, I'm that painter."

"My art teacher?" Kate crossed her arms. "He says you sold out years ago." I stepped close to her, whispering to mind her manners, but she sidestepped me and kept going. "He says there's nothing you wouldn't paint to make a buck."

"Is that so?" Cade tipped his head back and half closed his eyes. "He could be right. Barb, my darling, shall we go through? We have dessert to serve, yes?"

He moved into the oak-floored foyer. After a moment Kate followed, but I held Barb back.

"I am so sorry," I said. "This was supposed to be a nice surprise for her. I didn't know . . ." But what could I say that would make up for hurtful words from someone who should have been a friend?

Barb patted my arm. "He's heard worse, don't worry about him."

" 'Sentimental schlock'?" I quoted a famous art critic.

" 'But quality schlock,' " Barb quoted back, citing another famous critic.

We laughed and went inside. But I made a vow to have a firm chat with Kate on the way home.

The chat, of course, didn't go well. As soon as we got back to the marina, Kate hurled herself out of my car and stormed off.

"Where are you going?" I called. It was getting dark and I didn't want her wandering around by herself.

"Someplace where people don't think I'm a complete screwup," she yelled.

I watched as she stomped down the sidewalk and up to the railing of the Axfords' boat. "Works for me," I muttered, and immediately felt like the worst aunt, and possibly the worst person, in the world. Sighing, I pulled out my phone. Louisa and I exchanged a short flurry of text messages, during which she indicated that Kate was always welcome and that she (Kate) would be sent home to the houseboat no later than ten thirty, which was the time that my brother and sister-in-law had laid down as Kate's weekday curfew.

"Well." I stood in the middle of the marina parking lot and surveyed my options. Go for a walk? Too hot. Go back to the houseboat? Possible, but the undone dinner dishes would be there waiting for me and I was very disinclined to put my hands in hot soapy water until it cooled down a bit. I sent up a short prayer that my mother never learn of my lapse in housekeeping, and walked over to the house, which was where I'd wanted to go all along.

Rafe, sitting on the porch with a sweating can of what I recognized as Keweenaw Brewing Company's Widow Maker, saw me approach on the sidewalk. "Hey there, honey bunch. How did your night go?"

I climbed the steps and flopped into the chair next to him. "Don't want to talk about it. But . . . really? 'Honey bunch'? Where did that come from?"

"No idea." He leaned over to give me a kiss and, simultaneously, opened the small cooler behind my chair. "Would you like an adult beverage?"

I wasn't much of a drinker, but every once in a while it was just the ticket. "Do you have a tiny bottle of white wine in there?" Because something cool and light sounded perfect.

"Your wish is my command." He flourished a small plastic bottle and wrenched the screw top off. "And look, I even have a glass." Grinning, he poured the pale liquid into a plastic cup of questionable origin. When he handed it over, however, I didn't see anything floating, and the rim looked clean.

"Did you bring this out here for me?" I asked.

"Sure. Let's go with that."

I gave him a look, which he ignored. This meant I could either pursue the issue and learn how the cup had really ended up on the porch, or I could let it go and, for the rest of my life, wonder about the possibilities.

Settling deeper into the chair, I sipped the crisp liquid and listened as he described the progress he'd made with the house. Due to the heat and humidity and the fact that not only did the house lack air-conditioning, we also hadn't installed any ceiling fans, the progress was limited.

"Is this house ever going to get done?" I asked.

"Don't be silly," he said. "Of course it won't. That's part of the fun. I thought you knew."

I snorted. "You and I have vastly different ideas of what constitutes fun."

"Yes, but I have high hopes that someday you'll come around and see how funny the bloop joke really is."

That would never happen, because the bloop joke was horrible. However, I didn't like to destroy a man's dreams, so I changed the subject. "I learned something today."

"Then it's a good day." Rafe tapped his beer bottle to my plastic cup. The resultant noise was an odd, soft, and ultimately unsatisfying *clunk*.

"Yes, but I'm not sure this is useful."

"Does it have to be?" My beloved yawned.

"If we're going to help solve these murders, it would be nice."

At the word "murder," his yawn snapped shut. "Tell me," he said, suddenly all ears. "Maybe talking about it will help."

So I told him about stopping at Rupert and Ann Marie's house, about how I'd met Courtney there before, and about how I'd realized Courtney was in one of the two vehicles that had driven past the day both Rex and Nicole had been at the bookmobile.

"Not exactly," Rafe said. "We don't know for sure it was Courtney. What we know is that someone was driving her car. It might not have been her."

I drank the last of my wine. He was right, but somehow I couldn't see anyone else voluntarily

277

getting into that rattletrap. "But I don't see how it matters anyway," I said. "Courtney was working the Fourth of July. She couldn't have killed Rex."

"Well, even if we're figuring the two murders are connected," Rafe said, "there could still be two killers. Isn't that how the love quadrangle theory would play out?"

Though I wasn't truly buying the quadrangle thing, he was right about the two-killer concept. But if Courtney was one of the killers, who was her partner? Fawn? Dominic? Barry Vannett? Lowell? Violet? Mason? One of the Jaquays? Both of them? And how was anyone on that list connected to Courtney?

Rafe reached over and took my hand. "Don't worry," he said. "We'll figure it out."

I nodded, appreciating his confidence, and loving him for it.

But I wasn't sure we were anywhere close to finding the answers.

Josh poured coffee into my mug. "How much sleep did you get last night?" he asked. "You look like crap."

"Geez, Josh." Holly came into the break room, shaking her head. "Hasn't dating that cute-as-pie Mia taught you anything about women? Hearing we look like crap is the last thing we want to be told, but it's even worse to say that first thing in the morning."

"Whatever." He shrugged. "Minnie doesn't look too upset about it."

Mainly because I knew he was accurate. When I'd looked at myself in the mirror that morning, I'd immediately looked away. "If those are brownies in there," I said, gesturing at the container Holly had just put on the table, "I might be able to forget about my lack of sleep." My stomach had recovered from the outreach trip, which was good for brownie eating, but not so good for calorie counting. Happily, I wasn't doing that today.

"Is everything all right?" Holly, who was rattling through the utensil drawer, looked over her shoulder. "You're not sick, are you?"

"Sick and tired of this heat," I said. Josh and I hovered as Holly extracted a knife and used it to slice big brownies into the smaller brownies that would equal the number of library employees. "I can't believe you baked last night."

"Me either, but the kids were begging, and Bad Mom that I am, I caved."

"Wish my mom had been as bad as you." Josh reached for a brownie and yelped when Holly slapped his hand. "Hey!"

"Ladies first," she said. "And quit that face. Minnie's a lady, even if you're too dumb to see it."

I could see that the conversation was about to devolve into a bickering session, so I tossed up a diversion. "Do either of you know Courtney Drew?"

"The name isn't familiar. Is she from here?" Josh asked.

Now that was an excellent question. But given her relative youth, I figured the odds were good. "I think so. She's about ten years younger than us." I described her, but their faces remained blank.

"There are some Drews over in Dooley," Holly said. "Could be related. Why are you asking?"

I thanked them, saying that I'd met her out at Rupert and Ann Marie's. But I was disappointed, because what I'd wanted was firsthand knowledge of the young woman, an assessment of her character, that kind of thing. Also, an estimate as to how likely she was to commit murder.

"How's Kate doing?" Holly asked.

"Fine," I said automatically, then took my allocated brownie and fled, because I didn't feel up to talking about my niece.

But after getting a cup of coffee and Holly's brownie into me, it turned out I actually did want to talk, because when I went up to Graydon's office to review the new health insurance rates and saw his family photo on his desk, I asked, "When your kids were teenagers, were you and your wife always worn out?"

Graydon focused on the pile of papers he'd been shuffling through. "Um . . ."

"Because I'm exhausted. How does anyone do this? If you're not worrying about where they are, you're worrying about what they're doing. Or what they're thinking. Or what they might think or do tomorrow."

"It was hot last night," Graydon said. "I'm sure that had a lot to do with it. Now, about this—"

"No, really. How does any parent survive? And there's something else I don't get. Every time I talk to Kate, she ends up stomping off like a two-year-old, yet her three bosses are telling me she's a fantastic worker, and they wish all their employees were that well mannered and capable."

Graydon nodded. "It's a conundrum. So these rates. What do you think about—"

"And how on earth can anyone sleep that much? Some days I think I need to take her into urgent care to check for signs of life," I said, scowling and crossing my arms. "I love her dearly, but I'm not sure I can take much more of this."

My boss leaned back in his chair. "Minnie, if you have concerns about your niece, you should talk to her parents."

This was excellent advice and I knew he was right. "But I don't have any huge concerns, not really. She's home every night at the time she says"—close enough anyway—"and my aunt says she's fine. It's just . . ." What was the problem, at its heart? I swallowed. "It's just I don't know how to talk to her."

"And you want to." Graydon didn't make it a question.

"Of course! So . . . what should I do?"

"Minnie, you need to know one thing."

"What's that?" I perked up and prepared myself for life-changing advice.

"I don't give advice on parenting."

"But—"

He shook his head. "Or aunting, which is close enough. If I give advice and it doesn't work, you'll hate me. If I give advice and it does work, you'll come back to me for more until I give advice that doesn't work, and then you'll hate me. It's a vicious circle and we're not getting on that particular hamster wheel. Now, let's talk about something fun, like health insurance."

"You won't give me any help?" I asked in a small voice. "At all?"

He laughed. "Okay, but only this once, and only because I like you. Open your high school yearbook. Look at your picture, read what your friends wrote, remember what it felt like to be that age."

And then we talked about insurance.

My dreams that night were a jumble of what was on my mind. The bookmobile was towing Kate, who was in a canoe with Eddie, and we were being chased by a mob led by Violet Mullaly. Courtney Drew and my sister-in-law were close behind, followed by the unusual trio of a college roommate I hadn't seen in years, Mitchell Koyne, and Reva Shomin, who was asking why I hadn't stopped by the deli lately. Holly was at the rear of the group, brandishing a plate of brownies and yelling that she'd cut them all to the same size so there was no need for everyone to buy rulers.

I surfaced out of slumber partly because the dream was so stupid, and partly because Eddie was lying on my chest and putting his front paw on my nose.

"And good morning to you, too." I patted his head, which he appeared to enjoy about as much as I'd enjoyed his paw on my face. "That is what you were saying, yes? That it's a beautiful day in northwest lower Michigan and you're thrilled that you get to live here with me?"

"Mrr-rr."

"Exactly," I said, putting my feet on the floor, which was when I realized the outside temperature must have dropped, because the thought of putting my own self into a hot shower didn't make me cringe inside. "Did you notice?" I asked Eddie.

"Mrr-rr," he said.

"What is it with you and the double meow this morning? Did a frog get in your little kitty throat?" I eyed him, but decided against peering inside. "It almost sounds like you're trying to say something. Mrr-aculous? No, too many syllables.

283

Mirror? Mister? Monster? Mon—" And then I remembered something. Clella, up at Lakeview, had said Nicole taught school in Monroe, Michigan.

"And Monroe," I said, snapping my fingers, "is where Lauren lives!"

"Mrr!"

"Sorry, you don't know Lauren, do you? We were roommates my first two years of college, until she decided to go to massage school instead." And from what I saw on Facebook, she was doing well. "A business, a husband, two children, three dogs. Yeah, sorry about that, buddy, she's a definite dog person. But she's nice, honest."

Eddie rubbed his face against my elbow, so apparently he forgave Lauren her erroneous ways.

I reached for my phone, scrolled through my contacts, and sent her a quick text: *Hey there! Have a question. Can I call you later? What time?*

Lauren: *In five minutes.*

Minnie: *Awesome! Thx!*

Accordingly, right after I finished brushing my teeth, I picked up the phone and called.

"Minnie Hamilton, as I live and breathe," Lauren said. "What's the occasion? Life in paradise getting to be too much for you? If you need to come down here and slum a little, we can put you up. Well, if you don't mind dirt, disorder, and dogs, not necessarily in that order."

I laughed, delighted at her use of D words. "Why is it we don't talk more often?"

"Stupid, I guess."

This was undoubtedly true. But our friendship was the kind that, no matter how long it had been since we'd met, we were back into the rhythm instantly, as if we'd never been apart. It was like that with Kristen, too. And my brother and sister-in-law, come to think of it.

"So what's up?" Lauren asked. "I'm happy to chat all morning long, or at least until my youngest wakes up, but you said you have a question."

"Did you know Nicole Price?"

"Nicole . . ." Her voice drifted off, then sharpened. "Hang on, she's that teacher. The one who was killed somewhere Up North. Did you know her?"

I blew out a breath and admitted that not only was she a bookmobile patron, but that I'd been there to discover her body.

"Oh, Minnie." Lauren's voice was full of empathy. "I'm so sorry. Sorry for Nicole and her family, too, of course, but finding someone you know who was murdered must have been horrible."

I shook away the memory and got to the point of the call. "The weird thing is, a guy I ran into at the local nursing home is also from Monroe, and he acted all weird when I asked him about Nicole."

"Who's that?"

"Lowell Kokotovich."

"Hmm. The last name is familiar, but I can't place him. How old is he? Mid-twenties, you say?" The phone muffled for a moment and all I heard was Mom comments along the line of "Put that down right now! Do you want me to start counting? One . . . two . . ." She came back. "Sorry about that. My oldest likes to pretend she knows how to use the clothes steamer. Where were we?"

"Kokotovich," I said, laughing.

"Right. I happen to be having lunch today with my yoga group, which includes the former high school secretary. I can ask her if you'd like."

I did like, and said so, accompanied by my deep thanks.

When my cell rang just before one that afternoon, I snatched it up. "Lauren, thanks for calling me back."

"Had to," she said soberly. "There's quite a story, and it's not pretty."

I clutched the phone tight. "Tell me."

"Back in the day, Lowell was an excellent all-around athlete, not a star, but good enough to get an athletic scholarship to a small college. He probably figured he was all set."

Something bad was coming, I could feel it. "Until?"

"Until the last semester of his senior year. He was taking a government class, but wasn't taking it seriously, if you know what I mean, and he flunked. But it was a required class, so it kept him from graduating on time, and kept him from going to college on that scholarship."

"Nicole taught the class?"

"You were always the smart one," Lauren said. "The ugly part is that when Lowell found out he'd flunked—at that school the seniors get their grades before the underclassmen finish up—he barged into Nicole's classroom and screamed that she'd ruined his life. On his way out, he slammed the door so hard it bounced open again. Nicole had been headed toward the door by that time and it caught her on the shoulder. She hadn't been ready for it, of course, and fell and hurt her back."

"Oh, no," I breathed.

"Yeah, it was a real mess. Nicole ended up with horrible back pain, and, as you can imagine, lots of lawyers got involved."

I thanked her again, and we chatted a bit longer, vowing to talk more. Afterward, I sat quietly, thinking about what I'd learned. Nicole had a chronic back injury. No wonder she swam for exercise. No wonder she'd so often looked unhappy. She hadn't been innately cranky; she'd been suffering.

It was indeed an ugly story. And one I needed to pass on to Detective Hal Inwood.

I'd worked through lunch with my cell phone turned up on my desk so I wouldn't miss Lauren's call, and now I felt a sudden need to get out into the sunshine. Every library day I tried to get outside right after lunch, and there was no time like the present. As I breezed past the front desk, I nodded to Donna. "Headed out for my walk, but I'll be back soon."

"That's what you say now," Donna said, nodding gravely. "But with that nasty humidity gone, I'd take advantage. It's supposed to heat up again this weekend."

"Oh, ew." I made a face. "Then don't worry if I don't come back until tomorrow."

Donna laughed. "Don't worry, I'll cover up your dirty little secret."

My steps, which had heretofore been brisk, slowed a bit. Did everyone have a secret they wanted to hide? Possibly. Even probably. And some people surely had more than one. But how serious were the secrets? How desperate might someone be to cover theirs up?

I wondered all that as I walked through the lobby. Breathing in the fresh clean air and feeling a warm-but-not-blistering sun on my face made me feel a little better, but as I started my new favorite walking loop, the one that went past the renovation of an old hotel about the same age as Rafe's house, my thoughts returned to the hypothesis that everyone had secrets.

This, of course, brought up an obvious question. What were my secrets? I'd led a mild, librarian-like life. Never knowingly broken a law if you excepted speed limits, which I did. Never hit anyone other than my brother, which didn't count because he was nine years older than me and I'd never stood a chance of hurting him, and even at the time I'd only been eleven. Never cheated on my taxes, never—

"Oh." I stopped in the middle of the sidewalk. Because there it was, the memory I'd shoved to the back of my brain for years, the knowledge of that ill-fated ninth grade geometry quiz. The one whose questions made no sense at all to me, so I'd leaned over to look at what Jayne Smithson, the class math whiz, was writing down. The geometry teacher had, naturally, seen what I was doing, which I hadn't known until the quizzes were returned and I'd seen my 0 grade and a stern *See me after class*.

That was indeed a secret I wouldn't want the town to talk about. Sure, cheating on a quiz twenty years ago wasn't in the same category as burglary or embezzlement or grand theft auto, but—

Creak!!

I frowned and slowed, wondering at the loud,

and oddly metallic, sound. Where on earth had it come from? I was in front of the hotel, but there weren't any workers in sight. To the left, there was nothing out of the ordinary. To the right, there was nothing.

Creak!!

I suddenly had the sense to look up.

And saw a large object tumbling end over end, going down, down, down . . . getting bigger and bigger and bigger . . .

I bolted, running as hard as I could as fast as I could. The air whooshed, and behind me, something hit the ground with a huge *thump!!*

I stopped, mainly because I wasn't sure I could run any farther, and bent over, hands on my knees. The only noises on the entire street were of me panting and of my heart thudding.

When I could stand upright and breathe like an average human, I turned around and walked back. Lying on the ground, shattered into a zillion pieces, were the remnants of what looked like an old air conditioner.

I looked up. All of the tall double-hung windows had been replaced a few weeks ago, and all were closed.

Except for one.

After a short eternity, I pulled my cell out of my pocket and dialed. "Um, Detective Inwood? This is Minnie Hamilton. Sorry to bother you, but there's something you need to see."

CHAPTER 17

Ash arrived with Hal Inwood, and after one look at my face, he put his arm around my shoulders and ushered me into the front passenger seat of their unmarked police vehicle.

"You're going to sit here until I come back for you," he said in a gentle but firm voice. "If you get up before then, I'll handcuff you and put you in the back seat."

I laughed. Or at least, I tried to laugh, but it came out more like a sob. Which, since I wasn't given to crying in front of police officers in general and Detective Inwood in particular, showed me Ash was right and that I should sit down. "Then I guess I'll stay."

He settled me down, gave my shoulder a squeeze, and hurried off. I closed my eyes and put my head back. Ash had left the door open, and a soft breeze was curling around my ankles. A small patch of sunshine inched its way across my lap; birds twittered.

I felt myself relaxing and was, quite possibly, asleep when a knock on the car roof made me jump.

"Awake," I said. "I'm awake."

"That's obvious," Hal Inwood said dryly. "We've cleared the building. No one's here."

I climbed out of the car. No way was I going to enter into a conversation with Hal at an exaggerated vertical disadvantage. Given my tidy and efficient height, I'd long ago grown used to being almost a foot shorter than most men, but unnecessary height discrepancies weren't to be borne.

"What did you find out?" I asked, glancing at the bits of metal that had almost killed me.

Hal pulled his notebook out of his shirt pocket and flipped through pages. "The general contractor for the renovation project said no one was scheduled to work today, as they're waiting for the furnace installer to get back from vacation. I contacted all the subcontractors, and none of them had any worker stop at the site for any reason today."

A funny feeling formed in my stomach. "And the air conditioner?"

Hal shut the notebook and looked up. "It was an old one, one of the window units used when this was still functioning as a hotel. There are a pile of them stacked up in a corner, waiting for someone to take them away."

"So someone . . ." I didn't want to finish the sentence.

"Yes." Hal nodded. "Someone picked up that air conditioner and intentionally pushed it out the window. The contractor said he'd unlocked the back door this morning as he'd hoped for an early delivery of plumbing fixtures, which did not happen." He tapped the notebook with his pen. "Do you often walk past this building?"

Predictable Minnie. "This summer, when I'm at the library, I've walked this way almost every day, right after lunch. I like to see the construction."

He reopened the notebook and made new notes. "And the bookmobile schedule is posted on the library's website, correct?"

"Well, sure." Even to my own ears, I sounded defensive. "Why wouldn't we?"

Hal tucked his notebook into his shirt pocket. "Ms. Hamilton, it seems clear that this was a direct attempt on your life. I urge you to take steps to ensure your safety."

I looked at the heap of metal. Looked at him. "What do you suggest, exactly? Hide out for the rest of my life?"

"You should tell everyone who cares about you. The more people who know, the safer you'll be."

But I didn't see it that way. "The more people I tell, the faster word will spread and whoever did this will hear about it and try even harder to . . . to do whatever."

"At least tell Mr. Niswander," he said.

I wavered on that one. "I'll think about it."

And I did. Over and over. Most of me shrank from the idea, but by the end of the day I'd decided Hal was right, that I should tell Rafe. If our positions had been reversed, I'd certainly want to know. And I'd be furious if he didn't tell me.

"You win, Detective," I said out loud to an invisible Hal Inwood as I left the library that evening. "I'll tell Rafe tonight."

Since I was mostly thinking about how to frame the story, my feet went in the same direction they always did and I ended up walking past the old hotel. By now someone had been by to clear away the scattered bits of former air conditioner. The only thing indicating I'd almost died was a hand-size chip out of the sidewalk.

Dragging my toe over the chip, I eyed the windows—all now closed—and wondered about the whos and whys.

Was I really a target?

Who would do such a thing?

If so, why?

I kicked away a tiny piece of former sidewalk and then saw I'd managed to get my shoe covered with concrete dust. "Bad as being at the house," I muttered. "Construction can be murder." The common phrase caught at me, and I wished I hadn't said it out loud. Or even thought it. But suddenly, the jumble of ideas circling around in my brain coalesced into something new.

My feet started moving, then moved faster and faster. Because what I suddenly needed, what I wanted more than anything else in the world, was to talk to Rafe.

• • •

"I can't believe we're doing this," I said.

"In what way?" Rafe unscrewed the cap from a water bottle and offered it to me. "Can't believe we're being so proactive?" he asked. "Can't believe we abandoned our plans to paint the upstairs bathroom? Or you can't believe we're doing something so incredibly cool?"

I squinted at him. "How is sitting in your truck doing nothing a cool thing?"

"Clearly, you have no idea what's cool and what isn't."

This was true, and had always been. My career choice alone made that obvious, but there was also significant backup evidence: my preferred entertainment (reading), preferred beverage (lemonade made by my aunt), and preferred method of travel (tie between a bookmobile and walking).

"Let me guess," I said. "You are the arbiter of coolness in Chilson."

"No, but I'm good friends with who is. And so are you."

Ah. Kristen. He was right, she was very cool. "Should I text her and ask her to rate our current activity?"

"No, no," Rafe said, yawning. "I'm confident she'd agree with me."

I made a mental note to ask next time I saw her. But I hadn't seen much of her this summer due to her restaurant's surging success, and I wasn't sure I'd remember to ask in September, when things would slow down. Then again, Rafe was probably counting on that, so I pulled out my phone and added a reminder to my calendar.

"Are you really texting Kristen?" Rafe asked, leaning over.

"Nope." I saved the reminder and tucked the phone away. "Do you really think we're going to learn anything doing this?"

Two hours earlier, after I'd gone back to the houseboat, given Eddie a snuggle and a treat, and read on the whiteboard that Kate was working until close at Benton's and would be going out afterward to eat at Fat Boys with the store's staff, I'd headed up to the house and told Rafe the air conditioner story. And how my dusty toe had led me to, if not direct dot connection, the coalescing of old facts into new arrangements. Pink bumper stickers. Courtney Drew. Home health aide. Access to medications. Nicole's back pain.

He'd hugged me tight, then called Ash. "Hey, buddy. I hear Minnie almost got squished by an AC unit."

I started to sputter indignantly, saying that if he didn't believe me he could just say so instead of calling the cops, but he rolled his eyes and slung his free arm around my shoulders and kissed the top of my head. "Shh," he whispered, and said into the phone, "What's the deal?"

Due to having one ear against Rafe's chest and the other ear covered by his arm, I couldn't hear Ash, and heard Rafe's voice mostly as a deep rumbling vibration. What I could hear, though, was along the lines of "Any idea who did it?" and "Any chance of catching whoever it was?" and "Don't worry. I'll keep her safe."

I burrowed deeper into his warmth. Not that I needed to be any warmer, really, but being so close to him felt good. Discounting the winter months I spent with Aunt Frances, I'd lived more or less on my own since college. I'd grown accustomed to it. Had even enjoyed the solitude and the time spent learning to be myself. But now it seemed I was entering another phase in my life, one including that I would, every so often, be taken care of by a man named Rafe Niswander.

And it was turning out that I didn't mind the feeling. As long as he didn't get too carried away.

"Safe," I'd murmured into Rafe's shoulder. "You really think you can do that?"

"Yes." He'd kissed the top of my head and I'd closed my eyes against a rush of emotions that made my throat swell.

"It'd be easier, though," he'd added, "if you'd be okay with being encased from head to toe with bubble wrap."

I hadn't been, of course, and now the two of us were whiling away the evening sitting in his truck and watching the front door of an apartment building from half a block away. More specifically, the apartment building where Courtney Drew lived.

We'd been parked on the street outside Chilson's take-out Chinese restaurant for more than an hour, watching cars drive past, watching cars pull into the building's parking lot, watching people walk up to the building, watching people walk out of the building. It was remarkably boring.

"Let's do a list," I said.

Rafe squinted at me. "A bucket list, you mean? Number one is all the pro football fields in the country. We'd start with the current ones, but to do it right, we'd need to visit the sites of the previous fields, too. And while we're at it, we should visit all the major league baseball fields and hockey arenas. Maybe that's where we'd start, with the original six national hockey league teams. Yeah, I like that a lot."

He would go on for hours if I didn't stop him, so when he took a breath, I cut in. "A list of murder suspects."

"Excellent idea," he said, stretching and yawning. "The husband. The wife."

I pulled out my phone and started typing into the Notes app. "Dominic Price. Fawn Stuhler."

In short order, we had what we figured was a full list. In addition to Dominic and Fawn, we had Barry Vannett, Lowell Kokotovich, Violet

Mullaly, Courtney Drew, Mason Hiller, and John and Nandi Jaquay.

"That's eight," I said. "Nine if you count the Jaquays separately."

Rafe leaned over and looked at my phone. "Let's rank them."

"Do what?"

"A one-to-ten scale. One for not very likely to be the killer, ten for very likely."

"What if we don't agree?"

"We'll add the points and do an average."

It sounded reasonable, and we started with the spouses. We both gave them sixes and I tapped the numbers into my phone. "Next is Barry Vannett. His motive is murky, but I think he should be a six, too. He disappeared right before the fireworks on a beer run when they already had plenty of beer. So he had time to kill Rex." I couldn't remember if I'd mentioned this to Rafe earlier, but better late than never.

"Hang on," Rafe said, frowning. "You want to give the guy a six because he wanted more beer?"

"There was plenty in the cooler."

My beloved shook his head and pulled out his phone.

"Who are you texting?" I asked.

"Jon, my buddy who runs the party store down by the Vannett cottage. He was working the night of the Fourth, and he's one of those guys who knows the names of all his regular customers."

He pushed the Send button. "Just asked him if Barry was there that night, and if he knew the time."

"You really expect him to remember?"

Rafe shrugged. "Jon has a great memory. Birthdays are his favorite."

Before I could point out that recalling when a particular customer came into your party store on the busiest night of the summer was nothing like remembering a birthday, Rafe's phone dinged with an incoming text.

He read it out loud. *Vannett here that night to get six of Short's Bellaire Brown for BIL. Had to get it from the back, so I remember.*

I puzzled out the acronym as brother-in-law. "Okay, then I guess Barry's down to pretty much a zero. Lowell's next."

"Not enough information," Rafe said.

It was the same with Violet, Courtney, Mason, and the Jaquays. We simply didn't know enough. I slumped down. "The only person we've eliminated is Barry Vannett."

Rafe studied my phone. "Any progress is still progress. And maybe we'll learn more tonight." He nodded at the apartment, which was absent of human activity.

I sighed. "Are you sure this is where Courtney lives?"

"According to her old neighbor's sister, who is dating my cousin Jim, yeah. Though who knows if the information is good. I usually figure Jim's girlfriends have to be a little off to date him in the first place."

"Kristen and I said that for years about your girlfriends." I wriggled around to get more comfortable. No exterior or interior of any pickup truck had been designed for a person of my size, not ever.

"And you were right." He yawned again.

"So what does that say about me?"

"That you have excellent—" He stopped. "Is that her?"

Through the windshield, I watched as a young woman climbed out of a pickup that had just pulled into the apartment's parking lot. "Can't tell," I said, squinting and leaning forward, because surely that extra fourteen inches would make the difference. "If she'd turn . . . ah." I sat back. "It's Courtney." Even from this distance I could see the tight ponytail and square forehead. Plus she was dressed in scrubs, which had been a clue right off the bat, but I hadn't wanted to rely on that alone.

"Is that the other vehicle you saw?" Rafe gestured at the silver-colored truck.

"Could be," I said. "But you know me and vehicles. All I remember is . . . hang on, isn't that what's-his-name? From the hardware store?"

"Luke," Rafe said. "Luke Cagan. It certainly is."

We watched as Luke shut the driver's door of the truck and came around to the front, where Courtney was waiting. Hand in hand, they walked to the apartment's front door and went inside.

Rafe looked at me and I looked at him.

"Huh," he said.

I nodded. "Exactly what I was thinking."

"What else are you thinking? Because I know the wheels up here are churning." He tapped my forehead.

"I'm thinking that the vehicle I'd seen on the second of July could indeed have been Luke's. But why would Courtney and Luke have been out there, pretty much in the middle of absolute nowhere?"

We turned to study Luke's truck.

"No idea," Rafe said. "How about you?"

I sighed. "None."

"That means our next step is obvious."

It certainly was.

At the library the next morning, I wandered into the break room right about the time everyone else was wandering into the building.

"How long have you been here?" Kelsey asked, deftly scooting in front of me and putting her hand on the coffeepot before my preoccupied brain could order myself to get ahead of her. "Because you have that look," she said over her shoulder. "The one that means you got here hours ago, long before most people hit their alarms for the first time."

She was right, but hearing her say it out loud like that made me sound like a ladder-climbing overachiever, which didn't feel like a good match with my chosen lifestyle here in the laid-back Up North.

"I had stuff to do," I murmured, watching her fill the coffeepot's bin to the overflowing point. Kelsey had an amazing ability to maximize the bin's contents without making a huge freaking wet coffee-grounds mess all over the counter.

Josh and Holly came in together, bickering about the best way to grill steaks. At this point the argument had a good-natured flavor, but that could vanish in a flash, so I skedaddled back up to my office to continue what I'd been doing for the last three hours: using the library's way-faster-than-the-marina's Internet access to learn what I could about the properties on that dead-end road in the middle of nowhere.

The obvious step that Rafe had referred to last night was to drive out to the road—which I'd now learned was technically named 158th Street, in spite of the fact that everybody called it the road to Brown's—and poke around to see what we could learn.

However, Rafe had already committed to helping a friend for a couple of days. This help was to reshingle the friend's hunting cabin in the

Upper Peninsula. The timing was good, because Rafe had just finished the last big drywalling project, and the drywall mud would take time to completely cure.

All of this meant Rafe would be out of town and unavailable for investigative efforts, and he'd made me promise not to go out there on my own. At the time of the promise, I had not had any problem making it, but I'd woken in the middle of the night and heard rustlings from the front of the houseboat.

"Kate?" I'd called. The rustlings continued. I'd eased out from underneath Eddie and padded forward. Kate was tossing and turning in her sleep, her hands over her face, murmuring, "No, no, no."

I stretched out a hand, but pulled back, not wanting to scare her. "I wish I could help you," I whispered. "I know this summer isn't what you thought it would be. You have no idea how sorry I am about that. But I love you. So very, very much."

Kate's tossing and turning went on. I continued to murmur words of love and comfort, and at some point she fell into a deeper, more peaceful sleep.

Though I went back to bed, sleep didn't return, and as the sky brightened, I gave up and headed into the library after leaving what I hoped was a cheerful message for Kate on the whiteboard.

Now my research was done and I wasn't sure I'd learned anything useful. Yes, thanks to the search capabilities of the county's website, I had a list of the current property owners and the dates the properties had last been sold. And thanks to Google Earth's imagery, I could see . . . not much. The satellite had flown over in summer and the only things visible were leaves, leaves, and more leaves. Tree cover that dense could conceal anything from small barns to decent-sized houses, especially if they'd been there a long time.

I sighed and tried to refocus my attention on my immediate surroundings and on the work I should be doing, but my thoughts stubbornly remained elsewhere. Kate needed me to find the killer and I wouldn't fail her. Would. Not.

So at lunchtime I opened a blank spreadsheet and typed in the ranking numbers Rafe and I had assigned, hoping that a different view of the data would give me some ideas. But at the end of the exercise, I sighed. "This is so not useful." I slouched in my chair and looked at the names and numbers. "Names," I said. "Names and numbers and names and numbers and—"

A flash of inspiration struck. If I couldn't figure out who killed Rex and Nicole, maybe I could figure out who hadn't, which was almost as good. Little of my theoretical lunch hour had expired, so I grabbed my purse and headed up the hill.

The noon hour at Lakeview Medical Care Facility was a busy place. Visitors were ambling in and out, residents were being escorted to and from lunch, and employees were walking to and from the parking lot on their own lunch hour.

I hurried inside and stopped at the front desk. "Is Heather working today? I have a question for her, if that's okay." After a brief consultation with his computer, the receptionist said, "She's here, but she might be on lunch."

After thanking him, I pivoted left. Heather's summer lunchtime spot of choice was outside in a small courtyard, under the picnic table umbrella if it was hot, out in an Adirondack chair if it wasn't.

I pushed open the door and immediately spotted her sitting in the sun, her face tipped up to its warmth. "Hey, there. Are you awake?"

"Mmm." She watched with slitted eyes as I dropped into a chair next to her. "Not really. What's up?"

"How do you feel about tattling on a coworker?" Then, seeing her face darken, I quickly went on. "Okay, that sounded bad. What I should have said was . . ." What, exactly? Once again, I'd jumped in without being prepared. "I'm trying to figure out the movements of some people on the Fourth of July. To help the police figure out who murdered Rex Stuhler."

Heather's eyes opened wide. "You think someone here is a killer?"

"Of course not. But it can happen that one person's movements confirm someone else's, and that person's confirms another's, and so on, if you see what I mean." I didn't know exactly what I meant, but either Heather was humoring me or I'd sounded at least vaguely convincing, because she was nodding.

"Sure, I get it. Who are you wondering about?"

"Lowell Kokotovich. Do you know if he went to the fireworks on the Fourth?" I was trying not to get my hopes up; there were a lot of employees at Lakeview, and the odds of her happening to know were—

"His wife did," Heather said. "I only remember because of that murder. Their youngest is scared of fireworks, so they hadn't planned on going, but some friends of hers from downstate dropped in unexpectedly, and she went with them."

"Exactly what I needed to know." That put Lowell in the clear for Rex's death, and making a case for Lowell's wife being a killer seemed beyond far-fetched. "Thanks, and sorry for interrupting your lunch."

"Glad to help," Heather said as she clambered out of the chair. "And now I have to go train a new CNA. Hope I can break her of habits she learned when she was a home health aide."

That was a problem I'd never thought about. "I figure you're talking about bad habits?"

Heather shrugged. "Every organization is

different, and what's okay in one place is against the rules in another."

That didn't make sense to me. "Aren't the rules about health care the same no matter where you are?"

Heather had been about to open the door, but she paused. "Let's just say in some places the procedures are more relaxed."

"Like what?" I asked, frowning.

"Medications are a big one. I hear some places, like assisted living facilities, let CNAs distribute medications, but we certainly don't."

"And home health aides? Can they?"

She sighed. "I'm sure it happens."

"But they shouldn't?"

"Not in a million years. They shouldn't be touching any medications, they're not trained for it. Um, Minnie, are you okay?"

"Fine," I said automatically. "Just . . . thinking. Thanks for your help."

The entire time I walked back to the library, all I could think about was Courtney doling out Rupert's medications. It worried me so much that when I got back to my office, I dug out Rupert's application for outreach services and called the phone number he'd put on the form.

"Hello," Ann Marie said.

"Hi, this is Minnie Hamilton, and—"

"Sorry, but we can't come to the phone right now . . ."

308

I waited through the message, then left one of my own. To call me as soon as they could.

At six o'clock sharp I left the library, making the day an occasion of sorts—the first day in recent history I'd actually left work at the time I was scheduled to be done. I'd also traded hours with Donna so I could take most of the next day off, sacrificing my Sunday afternoon for the sake of Friday investigative efforts.

This was not as much a sacrifice as it sounded, because the upcoming weekend forecast of cloudy with a serious chance of rain was not nearly as attractive as the forecast for the next two days, which was abundant sunshine with the ideal summer temperature of seventy-six degrees.

I took the long way back to the marina, skirting downtown and its accompanying crowds. Another couple of weeks and the people would start to thin out, but now it was still full-bore tourist season.

"Huh," I said out loud. In the six years I'd lived in Chilson and the many summers I'd spent here as a youngster, I'd enjoyed the crowds. Welcomed them, even. The tourists and summer people brought an energy with them. Added excitement. Created an atmosphere that was completely absent in winter. But this summer I'd been annoyed by the masses of humanity.

A broad smile spread across my face. It had taken a while, but I was becoming a local! Not to other locals, of course, because I hadn't been born in Chilson, but to the unknowing outsider, I would be tagged as Being from Here.

"What do you think?" I asked Eddie, shutting the houseboat's door quickly to keep him from slipping outside. Of course, if he'd been determined to get out, nothing I could do would prevent that, but I felt a need to make the effort.

My furry friend, who was curled in the middle of Kate's sleeping bag, lifted his head half an inch. "Mrr?"

I smiled and rubbed the side of his face with my index finger. "What's your opinion on tourism? A boost for many local businesses and therefore we should do our best to increase the numbers? Or are tourists changing the very fabric of our community and we should do our best to diversify the economy?"

Eddie sighed and sank deeper into his nest.

"Yeah," I said, leaning down to kiss the top of his fuzzy head. "The answer to both is yes, isn't it?"

"Mrr," he said, yawning.

I patted his hip and stood. "Hope you're okay that I leave you alone again. But . . ." My voice trailed off, because I'd turned while talking and was now reading Kate's whiteboard message.

Working late at Benton's. Closing and doing end-of-month inventory, so don't wait up.

This was followed by a drawing of a curly-haired stick figure lying in a bed. I peered at the sketch, trying to make out what was on top of my stomach, then smiled. It was a stick figure Eddie.

I was still smiling when I parked in the side lot of Mason Hiller's convenience store. It lasted as I walked to the front, and remained stuck on while I opened the door and walked inside. Then it dropped off.

"Oh," I said. "Um, hello."

The kid I'd met the first time I'd stopped looked up. "Hey." As I approached the counter, he put down what he'd had in his hands, which wasn't his cell phone, but a graphic novel.

This, of course, distracted me completely. I nodded at his choice of reading material. "Is that *Mooncop*?"

He eyed me, suspicion clear in his expression. "Yeah. You know it?"

"Sure." The bookmobile carried a healthy stock of graphic novels, and I enjoyed reading them. "I won't tell you the ending, but it's great. Have you read the *Sandman* series?"

The kid's face lit up. "Neil Gaiman is, like, the best ever!"

I did not disagree, and we launched into a rousing discussion of his work. "This is so cool," he eventually said. "My parents tell me to read a real book. I can't wait to tell them the bookmobile lady reads graphic novels, too."

"If they don't believe me, have them give me a

call," I said, laughing. "But I have to confess that I stopped by to talk to your cousin."

"Mason?" The kid made a face. "Yeah, he almost fired me that day after you were here the first time. Sorry. I was nervous about being here on my own and it came out all wrong."

I nodded. Understandable. Not commendable, but understandable. "Is there anything else you remember?"

"About Mr. Stuhler and Ms. Price?" He shook his head. "Nah, I didn't know them. Mason, though. He's worked here for a long time, and I think he said he knew them both."

I tried to remember exactly what Mason had told me. Hang on, he'd said he didn't know either one of them. And that's when he'd turned all cranky on me. "You sure?"

The kid shrugged. "Pretty sure. But it's hard to hang with Mason these days. All he talks about is money, money, and again, money. And how he doesn't have it."

Though we chatted a little longer, he didn't have any more information. As I drove toward Chilson, I thought about what I had learned.

Mason was focused on money, which seemed like a red flag, at least of a sort. But why would that make Mason nervous to talk to me about Rex and Nicole?

Did any of it connect to murder?

And if so, how?

CHAPTER 18

Halfway to town, my cell phone beeped with an incoming text. When I saw it was from Rafe, I pulled into an old-fashioned roadside park and read the message.

Rafe: *Cars*

Minnie: *What about them?*

After a moment, the dots started blinking, then up popped a message.

Rafe: *Suspect*

Minnie (typing while frowning in a puzzled manner): *Complete sentences, please. What do you suspect about cars? That mine needs new struts? That the one my mom is thinking about buying is nice? That we'll be able to buy completely autonomous ones in ten years?*

Rafe: *Check out the vehicles of our suspects to see if anyone is driving a new truck. Maybe that was Luke driving ahead of Courtney that day on Brown's Road, but maybe it wasn't. Doesn't hurt to look at the others.*

Minnie: *Three whole sentences inside a single text message. A new record! I'm so proud.*

Rafe: *1 off—later*

I laughed, sent him a thumbs-up emoji, and, with help from Google Maps, drove around looking at cars. By the time I got back to Chilson, the gas tank was low, so I stopped for gas. Since the air temperature was mild and the sky was clear, I set the gas to flowing and started inching away to stand in the sunshine.

"Thanks anyway," said a semi-familiar male voice.

I turned and saw Mason Hiller walking out the gas station's front door. I edged back into the shade as he crossed the asphalt parking lot and got into a slightly dirty and slightly battered SUV.

He started backing up his vehicle as I thought about possibilities. So far my Car Mission had yielded only negative results. Neither of the Vannetts' cars had been noteworthy in any way, or particularly clean. Same with the vehicles parked next to the Prices' cabin, same with the car in Violet's driveway. But Mason's cousin had said Mason was always talking about money. And Mason had acted oddly when I'd started talking about Nicole and Rex.

I released the gas lever and whirled around to put the nozzle back into the pump. Did I want a receipt? Not this time, thanks. Jumping in the car, I started the engine and sped after Mason.

Happily, he'd turned toward downtown, and it was easy to follow his vehicle. He parked in a public lot far enough from the retail district that the city hadn't installed parking meters. I pulled into a space on the other side of the lot, waited until he'd walked away, then got out and hurried after him.

"This isn't stalking," I muttered, though I was pretty sure it was. I pushed that uncomfortable concept to the back of my mind, where I hoped it would fade away.

Mason was walking briskly, and I found myself almost trotting to keep up. Two blocks later, at the first store we came to—a new place that sold T-shirts—he went inside.

I couldn't very well go in with him, so I stopped and pretended to be interested in an accountant's window display. This was difficult, because the display was a sign with the name of the business, but fortunately Mason was back outside before I had time to look truly stupid.

Mason ducked into the next place, which sold sunglasses. He was back outside quickly, and went on to the shoe store.

By this time I'd decided that the key to an innocent lurk was to pull out your cell phone and tap away while surreptitiously keeping an eye on your subject. Mason had left the shoes and was entering a men's clothing store when I heard my name.

"Minnie."

I looked up at the forty-ish woman who'd called to me, and smiled. "Hi, Rianne. How's business at Benton's been this summer?"

"Amazing!" She grinned. "And part of it is due to your niece."

"Um, that's . . . great."

"She's such an asset, you wouldn't believe it. No, of course you'd believe it; you're her aunt, so you know how great she is."

"Um . . . you bet."

Rianne nodded. "You know, if all of my staff were as fun and cheerful and hardworking as Katie, I'd be able to take a full day off in the summer without thinking my grandparents would roll over in their graves."

Fun? Cheerful? Hardworking? "So glad it's working out," I murmured.

"If she comes back next summer," Rianne said, "I'll give her as many hours as she wants. I'll even pay her overtime. With her sales skills, it's worth it."

I managed to pick my jaw up off the ground without Rianne noticing anything was wrong.

She waved and headed off, and while I was standing there, trying to rearrange my concept of the universe, Mason walked out of the men's store and into a fudge shop. It was time to figure out what he was doing, so I retraced my steps back to the T-shirt place. A twenty-something man with a scraggly beard and a backward ball cap greeted me. "Can I help you?"

"Hi," I said. "I'm looking for a friend and he's not answering his phone." I rolled my eyes dramatically. "I was wondering if you've seen him? Thin, long-ish hair, a little older than you. His name's Mason."

The guy nodded. "He was in here a few minutes ago, asking about . . ." He paused.

I smiled. "Asking about what? Please tell me he lost his phone again. Because that's the only reason he should have for not answering text messages."

Laughing, the guy said, "No, he was asking if we were hiring."

Eddie and I were watching the sunset. His back half was on the chaise and his front half was on top of my legs. The humidity had gone up again, so I wasn't exactly enjoying the heat his body was kicking out, but he was purring, so that made it okay.

"It was the same at the other businesses," I told him. "Mason was looking for work." But late July could be a bad time for that. There was little more than a month left in the official summer season, and business could start dropping in mid-August.

Eddie tipped his head back and yawned, giving me a fine view of the roof of his mouth.

"Not your most attractive feature," I told him. "Though I still wonder what those ridges do."

"Mrr."

"Yeah, that's what I figured." I scratched the side of his face and got the purrs going again. "And I've also figured out that Luke, that's Luke Cagan, from the hardware store—"

"Mrr!"

I stopped with the scratching. "Sorry. Was I doing it wrong? Of course I was. Anyway, I stopped at the hardware store and Jared told me Luke bought a late-model truck and keeps it immaculate. But I also learned from Darren—you remember, the mechanic who loves the bookmobile almost as much as I do, but from a completely different point of view? Anyway, I stopped by Darren's garage and it turns out that he takes care of the Jaquays' vehicles, and they have a new pickup. Still, all things considered, it was probably Luke out there that day with Courtney. But I'm so horrible with car identification, I could have it all wrong."

"Mrr!"

"I'm a sorry excuse for an amateur investigator, aren't I? And I'm not a very good aunt. Plus I can't think of the last time I saw Aunt Frances and Otto, and I haven't been up to the boardinghouse in—"

Eddie thumped down to the deck, jumped up onto the railing, and up onto the houseboat's roof.

"Mrr!"

I slid deeper into the chaise. "You got yourself up there, you can get yourself down. I'm not coming up after you."

"MRR!!"

"Forget it."

There we sat, me down below trying to enjoy

the stunning sunset, him up above staring holes into the back of my skull. And we might have stayed that way forever except for an unexpected visitor.

"Nice night," Ash said, stepping aboard. "What's up with you, Mr. Ed, besides everything?"

"Funny." But I smiled, because it kind of was. "Any chance you can convince him to get down from there?"

"Think about what you just said." Ash dropped onto the other chaise. "Convince a cat? Or more to the point, convince Eddie?"

We turned and looked up at the cat in question.

Eddie looked down. "Mrr."

"That settles that," Ash said comfortably, turning back around.

"Once again, the cat gets what he wants." I glared at Eddie. He glared back. "Tie," I said, then whipped around before he could claim to win the staring contest. "So, a Friday night and you're not working? That hasn't happened in months, seems like."

"Yeah," he said. "And now I don't know what to do with myself. Where's Rafe?"

"In the UP." I frowned, trying to remember which of his friends he'd gone off to help, and came up dry. "With a buddy, fixing up a hunting cabin. He should be back tomorrow. But since you're here," I said brightly, "I can fill you in on what we've found out about our murder suspects."

Groaning, Ash closed his eyes and leaned his head against the chaise's back. "I'm not working. Not working at all right now. Barely even breathing."

He did look tired, but that was endemic to the Up North population in summer. With daylight sticking around past most children's bedtime, we tended to stay up late and not get enough sleep until mid-September.

But I hardened my heart and told him everything Rafe and I had learned. About identifying Courtney Drew's car as one I'd seen on the road that day. That we'd been trying to locate the second vehicle, and that we were pretty sure Luke Cagan owned it.

"Then again," I said, "it's possible those vehicles had nothing to do with the murders at all. But . . . it just seems like a huge coincidence. Courtney and probably Luke driving down Brown's Road the same day Rex and Nicole were on the bookmobile. And then an air conditioner almost falls on me."

"Wouldn't Violet and Julia also be in danger then?"

I eyed him, looking for evidence of sarcasm, and found nothing but fatigue. "Maybe. But it just seems weird. I think someone should go out to Brown's Road and see if there's anything

320

at the dead end. That could tell us a lot. Maybe they're cooking meth down there." I shivered. "Or they've been stealing guns and are storing them in a . . . in a cave or something." Even to my own ears, that last possibility sounded stupid.

"Sure," Ash said, with his eyes closed. "I'll get right on it. But don't you have a bunch of other suspects?"

"Well, there are the Jaquays. And Mason Hiller, who owns the gas station out there."

"What about Violet Mullaly?" Ash asked. "Wasn't she on your suspect list once upon a time? Or has she been shifted over to the possible victims list?"

"Not yet." Then I remembered he'd been looking into her background. "Is there a connection between her and Rex? Or Nicole?"

"Mrr!"

I turned just in time to see Eddie launch from the houseboat's roof, aiming himself directly for . . .

"Hey!" Ash sat upright as Eddie landed on the chaise, right between Ash's flip-flopped feet.

"MRR!"

"You're in his spot," I said.

"There's room for two." Ash patted the upholstery. "Have a seat, little buddy."

"Or over here." I patted the space next to my knees. "Lots of room."

With a distinct curl of his lip, Eddie jumped

to the deck and stalked off, his tail twitching mightily.

"Don't go far," I called. "It's almost bedtime."

"Mrr!"

Ash laughed. "You two crack me up. Sometimes it really feels like you're having a conversation."

Of course we were. I wasn't sure we were communicating, but we certainly talked to each other.

"So you'll look into Courtney and Luke?" I asked.

He sighed. "Sure. And the Jaquays and Violet Mullaly and who else? Oh, yes, Mason Hiller."

I felt a pang of sympathy, but did my best to squash it. Kate needed a resolution to this more than he needed sleep. And if someone truly was trying to kill me—something I'd mostly tried to forget—well, that needed to stop, too. Preferably sooner rather than later.

"Have you heard about the burglaries?" Ash asked, then described a string of cottages that had been broken into in the last few days.

This was odd, because most area robberies happened in winter, when the vast majority of expensive lake cottages were empty of people, though not of their expensive contents. "I'm sure you'll figure it out," I said.

"Eventually, sure. But meanwhile half the lakefront owners in the county are calling us, wanting extra patrols, wanting us to keep their property safe. Basically wanting us to be their security guards." He sank deeper into the chaise and muttered something about a deputy vacancy in Alaska.

I knew he wasn't serious. Ash was too much a part of Chilson to ever move very far away. But I also understood the realities of law enforcement. He and Hal would continue with the murder investigation, but they also had to deal with the immediate needs of the community. Which meant finding the killer could take some time.

Luckily, I had an idea.

My niece stared at me. "You want to do what?"

It was Saturday morning, breakfast was done, a beautiful summer day stretched ahead, and the first step in my plan was about to commence. "For the two of us to go pick raspberries."

Kate shook her head and went back to her tablet. "It's my first full day off in I don't know how long. I don't want to do anything. Besides, why go to the trouble of driving to the other side of the county, standing in the hot sun, getting your arms all pricked by those nasty raspberry vines, getting mosquito bit, and driving all the way back here? Because I'm pretty sure you can walk into the grocery store and buy raspberries."

As I'd often made similar comments about fishing, I should have understood her argument. Instead, I found myself getting stoked up anger-wise, and the conversation I'd so carefully prepared the night before, after Ash left, vacated my brain completely.

"The entire time you've been here," I said, "you haven't done anything you couldn't do in Florida. No, don't talk. Right now I don't want to hear anything from you. You're in northern Michigan during a gorgeous summer and you haven't done a single thing to take advantage of it."

"I have, too," Kate said. "Remember the Fourth of July? When I fell on top of a dead guy?"

Right. Well, there was that. But she wasn't going to dwell on that particular incident any longer, not if I could help it. "All the more reason to get out and do something else." Which didn't quite make sense, so I kept going. "You won't even go swimming in Lake Michigan! Okay, it's cold, but there are only five Great Lakes in the world, and you haven't even put your feet in."

"Don't see why I need to," my niece said, shrugging. "It's just water."

" 'Just water,' " I repeated incredulously. "Just water? You're kidding, right?" I asked, in spite of the fact she clearly wasn't. "That's it. We're going to pick raspberries, because the cherries are already done, and then we're going to the beach. Pack a bag with swim stuff, or I'll pack it for you."

Kate suddenly seemed to realize the direness of her situation. "You're serious."

"As a tax return. You have five minutes to pack a bag. And get some real shoes." I nodded at her flip-flopped feet. "Those aren't going to be comfortable in the raspberry patch."

"But Aunt Minnie—"

"Don't 'Aunt Minnie' me," I said, trying not to recognize the timbre of my mother's voice. "Five minutes."

Less than ten minutes later, we were in the car and headed out of town.

Kate was slouched in the passenger's seat next to me, and Eddie was in the carrier in the back seat, a location that he was unfamiliar with and clearly did not like, judging from the howls that were emanating from the carrier every two and a half minutes.

"Why didn't you leave Eddie at Rafe's house?" Kate asked. "Or with Aunt Frances?"

I was beginning to wonder the same thing. "Because Eddie and Otto's adorable little gray cat don't get along, and Aunt Frances and Otto are driving up to see that historic state park, Fayette, and won't be there to referee. And I couldn't leave him at the house because that drywall mud in the downstairs bathroom isn't dry and you know how Eddie can be."

Kate sighed, but didn't protest, because a few days ago she'd left a glass of milk out and woke up in the middle of the night with half of it spilled on her sleeping bag. Eddie could have stayed on the houseboat, but both Eric Apney on one side and the Axfords on the other were having work done on their boats and Eddie was not a fan of power tools. It was easier for everyone if I removed him for the duration.

My niece continued her slouch. A few miles later, she muttered, "Where are we going?"

"To a farm out past Brown's Road."

She sat up a little. "Isn't that the road where the bookmobile stopped that day?"

Frowning, I asked, "How do you know that?"

She rolled her eyes. "Because I'm not stupid, even if you think I am."

What was she talking about? "What on earth makes you think I think you're stupid?"

"Besides everything?" She made a rude noise in her throat. "Can we drive down that road? Brown's?"

My knee-jerk reaction was to say no, and my mouth opened to say the word, but before I could say it, I remembered that this was, in fact, the plan I'd come up with last night. Rafe had made me promise I wouldn't come out here by myself, and I wasn't. Kate was with me.

"Fine," I said tightly. "There's nothing to see, but let's have at it."

And I turned onto Brown's Road.

CHAPTER 19

Kate and I sat in my car near the same spot the bookmobile had parked less than a month earlier. Deeper in the shade, though, because it was getting hot. We were so far underneath a maple tree's low-hanging branches that the car was probably invisible to the casual glance. Our activities, however, were far different than that of bookmobile day; my niece was looking through the windshield with no interest in anything and I was texting Rafe.

Me: *On Brown's Road with Kate. All fine, see you soon.*

I hit the Send button and immediately turned the phone off, just in case he was paying attention to his own cell and shot off an immediate text of protest.

"There's not much out here," Kate commented.

She was correct. There was not. Well, not if you equated structures created by humans with "much." On one side of us was a lovely northern forest of maples, beeches, and birches, a depth of green that reached as far as the eye could see. On the other side was a field that had once been cleared for farming, but had been abandoned years ago. Scrub trees and shrubs dotted the acreage and it wouldn't be long before there was little difference between the two sides of the road.

Less than a hundred yards south of where we sat, the field came to an end and the trees closed in, filling both sides of the road. I studied the narrowing roadway and wondered how far it went before it petered out to nothing. The map function on my phone showed it going another half a mile, but my phone's map had led me astray before.

"We should talk to those people," Kate said. At my puzzled look, she pointed across the field to an old farmhouse.

I shook my head. "No. It's—"

She cut me off. "Why not? Oh, wait. I know. It's because all my ideas are stupid, right? Sure, you called them melodramatic, but I'm pretty sure that's another word for stupid," she said, crossing her arms over her chest.

"Mrr!" Eddie said from the back seat.

Over my shoulder, I sent him a glare that was meant to convey the message of "Cut that out because I don't need you adding to my woes right now, thank you very much," but the effort was lost on him because he'd turned around in the carrier and all I could see was his hind end.

I turned back around and faced my niece. "What I was going to say was that I looked up the ownership of that house and it's under foreclosure. No one lives there, and hasn't for over a year."

"But maybe someone is living there anyway," she persisted. "Someone could have broken in."

"Do you see any signs of that?" I asked.

She peered through the windshield. "Well, no, but if anyone was hiding out, it only makes sense they'd try to hide all the signs."

I wondered when kids learned about Occam's razor. Not that I could remember when I'd figured it out. Last week, perhaps? "You're right," I said. "But if someone is hiding out there, I don't want to walk up and knock on the door. Isn't that when things start to go bad in horror movies?"

Kate shrugged, muttering, "Mom doesn't let me watch stuff like that."

"Wise woman," I said, earning me a Look from Kate.

"Why, because this way I never know what anyone is talking about?" she demanded. "What is it with grown-ups? Don't you remember what it's like to be a kid? Always being told what I can't do, what I have to do, what I should be doing?" She flung her hands about. "Mom and Dad keep telling me I need to act like an adult before I get treated like one, but how will I ever learn how to act grown up until they treat me like I have half a brain in my head?"

At long last, I was clueing into the fact that Kate's frustrated anger didn't necessarily have anything to do with her kindly aunt Minnie. "Kate, sweetie," I said, "don't you see? They're treating you this way because they actually do remember what it's like to be young."

"That doesn't make sense," she said flatly. "If they remembered, they'd be . . . I don't know . . ."

"Be what? Nicer to you?" I smiled. "Unfortunately, that's not the way it works."

"It should!" she practically yelled.

I was torn between two competing reactions. The first one was to murmur sympathetic noises, to coo auntly endearments, and to give Kate a comforting hug. The second one, which was the wrong one, was to laugh out loud. Sadly, it was also the stronger reaction and Kate saw my mouth twitch.

"You're laughing at me." Her eyes narrowed.

I shook my head. "No, I'm not. Laughing, yes, but at myself, not you. See, I remember having almost this exact conversation with Aunt Frances the summer I turned seventeen."

"Not sure why that's funny," Kate muttered.

It probably wasn't, not to her, so I changed tactics. "Growing up is hard. You think you're an adult because you're so much smarter and more capable than you were a year ago. But you'll think the same thing next year. And the next and the next. And about the time you hit thirty, you'll realize it never stops."

"Thirty?" Her eyes bugged out. "Mom and Dad are going to treat me like a kid until I'm thirty?"

That hadn't been what I meant. Then again,

she wasn't ready to hear the truth; that parents tended to permanently think of their offspring as children, no matter how old they were.

"Let's go for a walk." I tied my car key to my shoelace and opened the car door, though walking hadn't been my intention when we'd driven down here. At the time, I thought we'd take the car as far down the road as the road would go, see what we could see, then turn around and head for the raspberry patch. Now, however, I thought a walk in the woods might do Kate some good. Aunt Frances and I had taken lots of walks during my youthful summers, and I was finally realizing that those hadn't happened by accident or because my aunt was such a friend of the outdoors. "Open your window a little, will you?" I asked. "Eddie could use the—"

"Mrr!!"

"—the fresh air."

"You're not supposed to lock animals or small children in the car during the summer," Kate said.

Now why did her saying that irritate me? I took a deep breath, which didn't do as much to calm me as I'd hoped, so I took another one. "The point," I said, "is making sure they're not in an overheated vehicle long enough to endanger their health. If you look at where we're parked, you'll note that the car is completely shaded by trees, and will stay that way until"—I looked up at the sky—"after lunch. And since that's a couple of hours from now, I can't come up with any likely scenario putting Eddie in danger."

Kate tossed her head. "You don't have to sound so much like a librarian."

Since I was a librarian, I figured everything I said made me sound like one, but for once I was smart enough to keep my thoughts inside. "He'll be fine." The risk of theft out here on this deserted road felt so low as to be nonexistent. "The car is locked and the windows are rolled down to allow for airflow. I don't see how even Eddie will be able to find a way to damage anything in the short time we'll be gone, do you?"

She shrugged, but didn't say anything, so I considered that a win for Minnie. Not that it was a contest, of course.

I looked in at Eddie through the slightly opened window. "See you later, pal. We won't be—"

"MRR!!"

"Yes, I'll miss you, too," I said soothingly. "I'm so glad we have this kind of bond. Back soon, okay?"

"Is he going to be okay?" Kate asked, looking backward as we walked down the side of the gravel road, listening to the sound of Eddie's unhappiness.

"He's fine," I said. Eddie's howls could be prodigious, but as James Herriot might have said if the Yorkshire veterinarian had found himself with Eddie as a patient, if he could howl that loudly for no real reason, he probably didn't have anything wrong with him except recalcitrance. "He'll get tired soon. When we get back, I bet he's sound asleep."

Kate didn't look convinced, but she kept walking alongside me, and by the time we reached the part of the road that was bounded by trees on both sides, we could barely hear him at all.

"Oh, no!" Kate slapped the pockets of her tight shorts. "I forgot my cell phone."

"You can live without it for a few minutes, can't you?"

"What if we need to contact someone? You have yours, but what if it breaks? What if the battery runs down?"

Sighing, I knelt down, untied my car key, and handed it over, because some things aren't worth arguing over. Her light feet ran off, the car door opened, there was a pause, the car door shut, and she hurried back. I took the proffered key and tied it back on my shoe. At least she'd come back. Some kids might have driven off, leaving their poor aunt stranded.

We started walking again. Fifty yards later, the road took a slight turn and we couldn't hear a thing except the sough of wind in the leaves and our own footsteps. It was quiet and peaceful, and I was just beginning to enjoy myself when Kate said, "So this is where that Courtney drove that day?"

I stared at her. "Excuse me?"

My niece sighed heavily. "Really? I can hear, remember?"

"But . . ." I tried to recall what conversations I'd had with whom that she might have overheard and quickly came to the conclusion that I hadn't a snowball's chance of pinning down anything specific.

"I. Was. In. The. Room," Kate said, loud enough to startle any nearby wildlife. "Just because I don't say anything doesn't mean I'm not listening."

"Well, sure, but . . ." I stopped talking, because my brain was catching up to the circumstances. At some point Kate would realize she might have been better off keeping that tidbit to herself. I, however, wasn't going to be the one to bring it to her attention. That sounded like a sibling's job.

"So this is where she went?" Kate asked.

I blinked, pulling out of my mini-reverie. "Has to be," I said. "This road doesn't connect to anything. It dead-ends just up ahead." I'd confirmed this by peering at the county's aerial photography and Google Earth. The road proper petered out quickly, narrowed to a two-track, then faded into a vanishing trail.

Kate swiveled her head, looking left and right and left and right. "And there was a second car?"

"A truck. It was ahead of Courtney's."

"Is this like a hangout place? For kids." She

paused. "You know. For . . . stuff some of them like to do?"

I laughed. "Kate, I know what kind of stuff teenagers get up to. I was one once, remember?" Not that I'd been invited to those kinds of parties, but I'd known who went, where they were, and what happened. "And if you're thinking Courtney and whomever came out here to do whatever, they didn't need to. Courtney has an apartment of her own."

Kate managed to shove her hands in her shorts pockets. "There are still good reasons she could be meeting someone out here. The guy could be married and doesn't want to be seen going into her apartment. Or maybe she's meeting another woman. Maybe her family will disown her if they find out she's not straight, and her grandmother is dying and the last thing Courtney wants to do is disappoint her granny, so she's hiding her true self for now."

Staring at my niece, I said, "Kate, that's—"

"Dumb?" she cut in, her chin up. "Stupid? No, wait. Melodramatic?" She drew the word out long.

"What I was going to say is that both of those sound plausible."

"I figured you'd say that, and . . ." She paused. "Wait, what?"

"Both of those scenarios are reasonable and possible." Kate continued to look at me blankly, so I went on. "As possibilities, they're sound. The next step is to find a causal link. Some concrete fact," I hastened to add, since I'd heard myself lapse into jargon that some might call librarian-y, "that gives credence . . . that makes a good case for one of those theories being true."

"Or both." Kate almost grinned. "Don't you see? Courtney could be hiding her lesbian self from her family, *and* her lover could be married."

Another possibility I hadn't considered. Still, if I'd given a nod to the separate theories, it wasn't going to go well if I put the brakes on now.

"Lots of could be's," I agreed. "But to get the sheriff's department to take any of this seriously, we have to come up with something more than a theory." Due to my prior interactions with personnel from said department, this was something I understood at a bone-deep level. "How about . . ." I mentally tacked over to another point of view. "What do you think we should do next?"

"If you seek a pleasant motive, look about you," Kate said.

Her statement was amazing in two ways; one, that my Florida-bred-and-born niece knew that Michigan had a state motto, and two, that she could misquote it so aptly. I made a mental note to look up Florida's state motto. "There are lots of trees about us, but not much else."

"We're not at the end of the road yet," Kate

said, striding forward. "Courtney and whoever came out here for a reason. All we have to do is find it."

She made it sound easy. But since I'd been thinking pretty much the same thing when I'd decided to drag her out here, I shouldn't be harboring so churlish a thought. "Bad aunt," I muttered, hurrying to catch up with Kate's longer legs. I was, however, thrilled that Kate was finally enthusiastic about something while in my presence.

"What's that?" Kate asked. "Do you see something?"

"Nope." I fast-walked to her side. "Do you?"

"Not yet. But it has to be here."

She spoke so confidently that I didn't have the heart to tell her the harsh truth: that it was possible—even likely—that we wouldn't find a thing other than old tire tracks, which weren't proof of anything other than an extended stint of parking.

We walked through the dappled sunlight, looking down at the road, looking deep into the forest, even looking overhead. But all we saw were trees, trees, and more trees. All pretty, of course, in their various stages of growth, but none of it could be interpreted as a clue.

Just as my research had indicated, as we walked, the road became two tracks of dirt bisected by a low grassy hump. Though we studied the gravel and dirt, too much time had passed to see anything more than the vague outlines of vehicle traffic, and even those disappeared as the two-track became a narrow meandering trail, then a deer-wide trail, and eventually there was no trail at all.

"Kate," I called, for she'd taken the lead and was ten yards ahead of me. "Come on back. There's nothing to find up there."

"You don't—*slap!*—know that. Maybe something's just ahead. Maybe all we have to do is go a little farther. Wouldn't it be too stupid to give up just before—*slap!*—dang these mosquitos!"

"Come on back," I repeated more firmly, and this time she did so. "Tell you what," I said. "I'm as disappointed as you are that we didn't find anything. But"—I held up my hand to silence her upcoming protest—"maybe you're right, and what we want to find is just ahead. However, we need to come prepared. We need mosquito repellant. Plus water, a compass, and a decent pedometer to tell us how far we walked. And we need to tell someone where we're going."

She sighed, but it sounded less a teenage sigh of the-world's-so-unfair and more a sigh of resignation. "Fine," she said, but the surliness was mostly absent. "That makes sense."

I let out a small breath. "Now let's get back before Eddie starts to worry."

Side by side, we traipsed our route in reverse.

"Isn't it funny," I said, "how things can look so different depending on the direction you travel?"

Kate glanced around. "Not sure what you mean."

"Well," I said, gesturing. "I didn't notice that tree on the way out. See all the holes? That means it's old, or diseased, and insects are starting the decay process."

Her eyes went wide. "*Bugs* did that?"

"No, but yes." I laughed at her expression. "Sorry. But the bugs are in there, eating away at their dinner, and that's what attracts the pileated woodpeckers. They're big birds, and—" I stopped.

"And what?" Kate had continued walking, but now saw I'd fallen behind. "What's the matter?" Then she saw what I'd already spotted, the faintest hint of a trail, which we hadn't noticed before because of a log blocking the view from that direction.

"Well," I said. "It seems we've found something."

"Yeah. And look at this." Kate pointed at the log. "Its bark is different from this tree." She thumped the woodpecker's lunch buffet.

"Or," I said slowly, "any of these other trees." Not that I was Nature Girl, by any stretch—the pileated woodpecker's habits was pretty much my full knowledge of woodland creatures—but even I could tell the difference between the bark of deciduous trees and that of conifers. Given that we were surrounded by maples, birches, and beeches, why were we looking at a pine log? "And," I said, "it's been cut. You can see the saw marks."

Kate squatted down to get a closer view. "Okay, I see them now." She popped upright and looked at me.

I looked back.

The conclusion was obvious. Someone—read Courtney and her cohort—had created this path and hidden its entrance. The big question now was, where did the path lead?

I tucked my curiosity away and put on my Aunt hat. Two people had already been killed and I was not going to put my niece in danger. "We need to leave," I said. "Now that we have something solid to tell Detective Inwood, he and Ash will follow up on this and—Kate, wait!"

Because she had bolted away from me faster than a runner out of starting blocks. She tore through the trees faster than her aunt could follow, which I was doing, of course, because I wasn't about to let her go down that trail all alone, but she had youth and—yes, I can admit it—fitness on her side, and her lead on me grew longer and longer.

"Kate!" I called. "Stop!"

She didn't.

I summoned the biggest, best Librarian Voice

I could muster. Through my panting breaths, I yelled, "Katrina Abigail Hamilton! Stop right now!"

To my surprise and shock, she did. At least the noise of her crashing through the underbrush stopped, and I suddenly found that I could run a little harder and a little faster, and my thoughts ran along with me.

Please don't let her be hurt. What happened up there? Please, please, don't let her be hurt. I'll never forgive myself. Please, please, please . . .

I rounded a bend in the path and saw my niece, sound and whole, standing next to a small building. It was a classic Up North structure: a patchwork siding of half metal and half plywood, with a complicated roof that from a distance looked like a bunch of rusty highway signs tossed up every which way. Bigger than an outhouse and smaller than most sheds, its solidly wood door might or might not have had ancient barn origins, but the chain and lock that fastened it shut were bright and shiny.

Hmm.

"Aunt Minnie?" Her voice was unrepentant. "You need to look at this."

With relief, I slowed to a walk for the last few yards. "What I need to do," I said firmly, "is get you out of here and back to the car. Let's go. Now."

"But look!" She pointed. "See?"

And since I was human, I felt compelled to look. What I saw was a small and dusty window, just high enough off the ground that I couldn't see inside, even standing on my tiptoes.

She saw my difficulty and took a knee. "Here. You can get up on my leg."

"Kate—"

"Just a quick look. Then we can go."

Thinking things that would instantly disqualify me for the Aunt of the Year Award, I grabbed the edge of a piece of plywood and clambered on top of Kate's leg. As the shed's interior was illuminated only by the light that came in through that window, it took a moment for my eyes to identify what was on shelves.

And I suddenly understood everything.

Because on those shelves were hundreds of short plastic bottles.

Prescription medications.

"What's in there?" Kate asked.

"Pills," I said. "Lots of them." I flashed back to that day at Ann Marie and Rupert Wiley's house. Courtney's over-the-top reaction when I'd walked into the room. How she wasn't supposed to be handling medications at all.

"They're stealing them, aren't they?" Kate's voice was high and excited. "Selling them on the black market."

I slid off her leg and hit the ground with a bump. Nicole. She'd had back problems. Could she have been addicted to opioids? Had she been buying from Courtney?

Even though Up North lacked many Big Box types of shopping opportunities, there were avenues for selling stolen goods. It was my guess that Courtney's stash had a high percentage of opioids and she was making a pretty penny on sales, enough money that she and her partner were willing to kill to keep the operation going.

Only . . . who was the partner?

A metallic *click* made me freeze, and a male voice said, "Hold it right there."

CHAPTER 20

Kate and I stared at each other, then, as a single unit of Hamiltons, turned to face a twenty-something man, his thick blond arm hairs visible even in the mottled forest light.

Luke Cagan.

Though the very fact of his presence was disturbing, even more troubling was the handgun pointing directly at my niece's midsection.

I stepped in front of her. "Hey, Luke," I said as easily as I could. "It is Luke, right, from the hardware store? How are you doing? I'm pretty sure you can put that gun away. We were out here hiking, is all, came across this cool little shed. Do you happen to know who owns it?"

"Cut the crap." He gestured with the gun. "I saw you looking inside. You know what's in there."

I put on an expression of innocence and shook my head. "Not really. It's so dark in there I couldn't make out a thing. All that reading I do, it messes up my night vision." This wasn't true—at least not yet—but I figured flat-out lies to get Kate away from a guy with a gun wouldn't count against me in a final life tally. And even if they did, I didn't care.

"So there's no problem here, right?" I turned my

hands palms up, smiling, being agreeable, being friendly, being accommodating. "We'll move along and I'll see you around, okay?" Nodding a cheerful good-bye, I took an angled step forward, intending to go around Luke, keeping my body between that nasty gun and my niece.

Luke stared at me and didn't move. I watched carefully, ready to knock Kate aside the instant his finger started to tighten on the trigger, the instant his eyes started to focus.

We made it one step. Two steps. And just as I was wildly hoping that my pretense at innocence might actually work, footsteps pounded toward us and Courtney Drew appeared.

"What are you doing?" she called.

I wasn't sure to whom she was talking, Luke, me, or Kate, but I jumped ahead of anything either one of them might say. "Hi, Courtney," I said, smiling broadly, edging closer to the gun. "Remember me? It's Minnie Hamilton. I drive the bookmobile. We met at Rupert and Anne Marie Wiley's house a few weeks back. My niece and I were hiking, but now we really need to be getting back. Our friends are expecting us soon, and—"

"Stop talking, already," Courtney said. "And you're not going anywhere."

"Um." I stopped and reached backward. Kate grasped my hand and I gripped hers tight. If I'd been smart a long time ago, I would have learned

345

Morse code and taught it to my nieces and nephew during holiday gatherings, thus providing a current means of communication. Sadly, all I knew were the letters for SOS, but even then I wasn't completely certain I wouldn't be spelling OSO, and neither sequence would help much, anyway.

Courtney stood next to her boyfriend. "You know who she is, right? That librarian. The one we almost took care of with the air conditioner."

"That's her?" Luke frowned down at me. "But she's so short."

I knew this wasn't the time to mention that good things came in small packages. And from a lifetime of being underestimated due to my size, I also knew nothing I could say was going to change his point of view of my capabilities. What I could do was bide my time and hope an opportunity presented itself that would let me take advantage of his prejudice.

Behind me, I heard Kate suck in a breath. I squeezed her hand as hard as I could and said, "There's no information I have that the sheriff's office doesn't already know, so there's no point in hurting my niece. She doesn't know anything anyway."

"Do, too!" Kate said. "I know that—"

My hand squeezed Kate's so hard I heard her knuckles crack. "She doesn't know anything," I repeated. "So how about it? Let my niece head back to Chilson. Nothing will change if she leaves."

Neither one glanced my way.

"This is a problem," Courtney said, crossing her thin arms. "I wasn't prepared for this."

"We can put them in the shed." Luke tipped his head in that direction. "That lock is pretty good."

"You think?" Courtney rolled her eyes. "And five minutes after we leave, they kick a piece of siding off and wriggle their way out. She's short, remember? And that girl is skinny. With a boost, I bet she could get out the window."

Luke studied the shed. "Yeah, I guess." He looked over at Courtney. "You want me to shoot them, right? Now or later?"

But Courtney was shaking her head before my brain freaked out. "We have a delivery to make, remember? And if these two really are meeting up with friends, they might have said where they were going."

"We need time to hide their bodies, then." Luke shifted the gun from one hand to the other. "Do you think we need to kill them somewhere else?"

Courtney frowned. "That's a good question."

I thought it was a horrible question, but I was fairly sure my opinion didn't count, so I kept quiet. A better question would have been when had Rafe headed home? Or would anyone think to read the houseboat's whiteboard? I'd written an itemized list—*Brown's Road, King's raspberries,*

Lighthouse Park—but did anyone other than my mother know that's where I wrote my where-abouts? I couldn't think, couldn't remember.

My mind whizzed at a million miles an hour. There had to be a way out of this. I had to think of something. I had to get Kate away from these two. I had to get her safe.

"Got an idea." Courtney dusted off her hands as if she'd handled something dirty. "Keep them here a minute."

"You going to put the delivery together?" Luke asked. "Because you're right, we need to get moving. Last time we were late out there, he said if we did it again, he'd find another supplier."

Courtney sighed. "I know. Well, I have one idea, but do you have any?"

"One idea is better than none, right, babe?" He grinned at her.

Thieves/killers/black marketeers who internally managed their enterprise through collaboration and cooperation? Who knew? But that meant my first instinct, to figure out a way to divide and conquer, wasn't going to be easy. I needed another plan, and I needed one fast, because I was fairly sure I wasn't going to care for any of Courtney's ideas.

"Distract him," Kate whispered.

I frowned, but before I could turn my head to whisper a puzzled reply, she'd slipped out of my grasp.

"Hey!" Luke yelled.

"Kate, no!" I called.

Instead of paying attention to her aunt or the guy with the gun, she launched herself at Courtney, arms out, fists flying.

Luke took one step, lifted a hand, and yanked her backward by the hair. "Stupid kid," he said, disgustedly. "What did you think you were doing?"

"Trying to escape," she said through gritted teeth. "What did it look like?"

Courtney glared. "Like you were trying to earn yourself a faster death. Luke, hang on to her. I'll be right back." She marched to the shed and pulled a key out of her shorts pocket. One click, and the padlock dropped open.

Kate shot me a look. "Why didn't you—"

"Shut up." Luke, who was holding my niece by the neck with one hand and pointing the gun at me with the other, rattled Kate hard enough to make my own teeth hurt. "I don't want to hear a word out of you. Like ever."

He smiled, and that's when I was certain that Luke Cagan had shot and killed Rex Stuhler. Whether it was Luke or Courtney who'd killed Nicole Price, I didn't know, but if Luke had killed once, what was there to stop him from killing again?

Well, nothing except a vertically efficient librarian and her contrary niece.

"A very determined librarian," I murmured.

"You either," Luke growled, pointing the gun between my eyes.

Having a gun aimed at me had happened once or twice before, but that familiarity did not decrease my heart rate. Or loosen my suddenly tight throat. Or stop my forehead from sweating.

I nodded and, as the gun dropped, started to breathe again.

"This will work." Courtney came out of the shed and showed him a handful of twine. "Do the kid first, then her," she said, nodding at me. Either she didn't remember our names, or was already demoting us to non-name status. Neither possibility boded well.

Luke gave her the gun, which she handled with unfortunate familiarity. So much for my short-lived plan of shoving her to the ground while simultaneously grabbing the gun away from her. Anyone that at ease with a firearm would almost certainly have the impulse to hang on to the thing.

"How tight?" he asked, shoving Kate around and hauling her hands behind her back.

Courtney shrugged. "All I care about is they can't get loose."

"Works for me." He wrapped the twine around Kate's wrists, pulled it hard enough to make her gasp—and grinned.

Which was when I started to hate him. This was

not a calm, detached hatred. No, this was more the Captain Ahab and the Great White Whale kind of hatred, the kind that could consume you.

"You will regret that," I said quietly, making it less a vow and more a personal goal.

Courtney narrowed her eyes and used the gun to gesture at me. "Tie her hands next, I want to make sure she doesn't go anywhere." A pause. "And get it good and tight. She's smart and I don't trust her."

I felt myself twirled around and did what I could to flex my hands, to make them bulgy and muscle-y, but I was pretty sure my efforts didn't make any difference.

"Oh, hey, look at this," Luke said as I felt my cell phone sliding out of my shorts pocket. "Forgot to look in their pockets." He tossed the expensive rectangle on the ground and, with one heel, smashed it to tiny bits. "Check the kid."

Courtney eyed Kate's pockets. "She doesn't have room in there for half a sheet of Kleenex."

I didn't know where Kate's phone was, but having them look for it wouldn't be good. "She doesn't have one," I said. "I took it away from her last week when she didn't make curfew."

Courtney snorted. "Curfew? I moved out of my mom's house because she made me come home by midnight."

"Now what?" Luke asked. "Tie them to a tree?"

"We're going to use the shed," Courtney said.

"But you said—"

"Yeah, I know what I said. We can take care of that, though. I'll show you."

The two of them walked over to the shed. Kate looked at me with wide eyes and a white face. "Aunt Minnie—"

"We'll be fine," I said. "Don't worry. She's not the only one with ideas." This was true. I had lots of ideas. None of them useful at this particular point in time, but Kate didn't need to know that.

"Let's go." Courtney returned and prodded me in the back. "Into the shed."

"You realize," I said conversationally, "that I'm friends with the entire sheriff's department, including the sheriff. They won't stop looking until they find me."

"Much good it'll do them." Luke laughed.

"Shh," Courtney hissed. "Don't engage, okay? Inside," she said, and gave me a shove.

I stumbled forward, losing my balance in the process and tumbling toward the dirt floor. As I fell, I managed to rotate and hit the ground hip-first. This was surprisingly painful and I *oofed* a grunt of pain as I landed.

"Aunt Minnie, are you okay?" Kate awkwardly knelt next to me.

Luke kicked my legs to the side. "Shut up and lie down. No, you here and you here. Oh, for crying out loud . . ."

He dragged me to one side. Dragged Kate's

feet around. Rolled me over. Rolled Kate around.

The entire thing was an exercise in frustration and humiliation, and I could tell that my face was aflame with fury. At the end of it, Kate and I wound up tied together with more twine, my nose touching her knees and her nose up against my ankles.

"Done," Courtney said, dusting her hands again, a mannerism I was finding very annoying. "This has taken way too long. We're going to be late."

Luke stepped over the top of the Minnie-Kate assemblage and, from the sounds of it, started grabbing pill bottles. "They've reopened that county highway already, so we don't have to take the detour. We'll be fine."

Bottles went into whispery plastic bags. They crossed the shed and slammed the door, causing motes of dust to drift down through the small slats of sunlight. We heard the click of the padlock, and just before their footsteps faded away, we heard Luke ask, "When do you think we should come back to finish the job?"

"Good question," Courtney said. "How about later on today?"

"Let's do it after dark."

"Ooo, romantic." She laughed. "I like the way you think."

And then they were gone.

CHAPTER 21

"They're going to kill us, aren't they?" Kate asked.

I tried to moisten my dry lips. Didn't accomplish the goal. "They want to. But it's not going to happen."

"No?"

The hope in her voice made me want to weep and comfort her at the same time.

She sighed. "Really? And how, exactly, are you going to keep that from happening?"

I found myself, of all things, smiling. This was the obstreperous Kate I knew and loved. "First, let's work on your use of pronouns."

"What are you talking about?"

She sounded annoyed. On a normal day, I would have become annoyed in return, which would have been obvious, and her annoyance would have increased, and the escalation would have gone on until one of us (Kate) stomped away in a sulk. Today, however, things were different. The fact that she had the gumption to be alert and critical when a pair of stone-cold killers were intent on ending our lives was a sure indication she'd have the courage to take action when needed.

"I'm saying the two of us need to come up with a plan."

"Me? What makes you think I can do anything?"

Well, almost sure.

I opened my mouth to give her words of wisdom, a message that would give her confidence, a nugget of gold to help her get through the next hours, but she wasn't done talking.

"You didn't want me to say anything to that Luke. You didn't want me to run. You didn't want me to do a thing back then when our hands were untied and we were standing up, but here we are stuck and about to get shot to death, and now is when you want to do something? Now?"

And back to being sure. "Kate, my dear sweet niece. I wanted you to keep quiet and not do anything because right then it wasn't going to help."

"I could have—"

"No," I interrupted, "you couldn't. Neither one of us could have."

"But they say getting away from kidnappers before you're moved to another location is important. That running away is your best defense. If you'd run in the opposite direction I did, we would have split them up and I bet one of us would have gotten away, called nine-one-one, and by this time Those Two"—she made the phrase a capitalized one—"would have been in handcuffs. Why didn't you run?"

Because that would have meant leaving her behind, and there was no way I would have done that. "You're missing one pertinent point," I said. "Luke was holding a gun. I doubt either one of us is fast enough to outrun a bullet."

"It's not like on TV," she argued. "Unless he was an awesome shot, which kind of seems unlikely, he wouldn't have been able to hit us once we got running."

"Unlikely, yes. Because . . ." I stopped, not wanting to say the words out loud.

"Because what?"

I shut my eyes briefly, saw how the situation could have spun out, then shook my head against the images and opened my eyes. Looking at packed earth was far more soothing than what I'd just pictured. "Because," I said, "Luke Cagan is a man, and a fit young one at that." Kate started to say something, but I talked over the top of her.

"Those TV shows and movies with heroines kicking butt and taking the names of men half again their size are fantasy," I said. "The only real exception is a highly trained female against an out-of-shape couch potato. Men are bigger and stronger and faster and no indignant proclamations of equality are going to change that."

"So what are you suggesting? That we lie here like sitting ducks and wait to be murdered?"

I rolled my eyes. "What, you think direct

attacks and quiet acceptance are the only two choices?"

"At least I tried something," she said sulkily. "I don't hear you coming up with any ideas. All those college degrees and you're lying here next to a kid who doesn't even have a high school diploma. Guess you're not really any smarter than I am, are you?"

Oh, for crying out loud. "What makes you think—" I forced myself to stop. This was not the time to deal with Kate's misinterpretation of everything I'd ever said to her.

"We'll talk about that later," I said. "What we need to do now is untie ourselves."

"Really?" she asked, sarcasm dripping off the syllables in great big glops. "Wish I'd thought of that."

"Then it's time to catch up. Take a look over there." And before she could make a snide comment about not knowing where "there" was, I added, "In the corner closest to your head, someone nailed up a bunch of old license plates." I felt her twist around to see.

"Yeah, what about them?"

"Take a close look. What do you see?"

"A bunch of old license plates."

Patience, I told myself. *You must maintain patience.* "How are the license plates hanging on the wall?"

"Nails?" She paused. "I guess?"

"Don't guess," I said. "Look harder."

"It's dark in here. I can't see."

Patience. "Then let's move closer."

"We're tied together," she reminded me, because obviously I must have forgotten. "We can't move, right?"

"Courtney and Luke assume we can't move. But I think we can." At least I hoped we could. Because if we couldn't, there wasn't a chance we'd get out of this alive. "No, I *know* we can. All we have to do is figure out a way."

"How?" she asked sarcastically. "Wriggle like a couple of worms?"

"If that works, sure."

"Seriously, Aunt Minnie?"

That's when I heard the despair lurking underneath her question. She was scared, and it was my fault. Which meant I had to fix this. "Yes," I said. "Let's be a couple of worms. Come on."

So we wriggled. And rolled. And grunting with the effort, squirmed. I used every muscle with which I was familiar and many whose names I hadn't thought about since high school physiology class. Our body parts bumped against each other in awkward and occasionally painful ways, and it wasn't long before sweat was dripping down my face.

This, I found, was amazingly annoying when you couldn't wipe it off, and I added it to the long mental tally I was making of Reasons to Imprison Courtney and Luke, but we kept going, heaving and wheezing with the effort. And an eternity later, we weren't any closer to our goal than when we'd started.

"This. Isn't. Working," I gasped out and stopped.

"No, I think it is." Kate continued to move, playing inchworm to the slug I'd suddenly become. "Honest, Aunt Minnie. I'm super sure we've moved."

I didn't think she was right, but since I'd always been spatially challenged, I was willing to believe her. Plus, what was the alternative?

"Okay, then." I summoned a breath. "Let's keep at it."

And we did. And after a few more heaves and ho's, I realized we were actually moving. Not very fast or very far, but moving. "Kate," I said, "you're right. When we do this"—I leaned my shoulder and feet into the floor—"we move a teensy bit." Only a fraction of an inch, because we were tied together so tight I wasn't sure our circulation systems would ever be the same, but still. "See? Feet and shoulder, then slide."

"Yeah, I get it. And if we did it at the same time?"

"Great idea. On three, then. One, two . . . *oof!* One, two . . . *oof!*"

The hamstrung Hamiltons slowly, oh so slowly,

made their way across the packed dirt floor, getting closer and closer to their goal. "Need. A. Rest," I panted out. "Can you . . . see?"

Kate slumped, catching her breath. "Give me a sec." I felt the weight of her as she rested and I did my best to communicate courage and strength by laying my forehead against her knees.

After a moment, she pulled in a breath. "Okay," she said, picking up her head. "We're like five feet closer than when we started. Let's see. That lowest license plate isn't that far away now and . . . Yes! It's hanging off a couple of nails! And they look wobbly, I bet I can work them free. One for you and one for me!"

She immediately started the shoulder-feet shuffle again, and I hurried to catch up to her. A few more one, two, *oof*s later, Kate said, "Hold it, I think we're close enough. I just have to . . ." She grunted and *oofed* and I found myself pulled around by her strength. Yet another advantage of being compact in size; the ability to be hauled around by your niece when tied together in a dark shed.

"Okay." She twisted around. "Now I reach up and pull out the nails, right? Then we'll use the points to start cutting these strings. It'll take a while, but I think this will really work!"

"Go slow," I cautioned. "We don't want to—"

A tiny *Thud!* noise was followed by a howl from my niece. "I dropped it!" she sobbed.

"We're fine," I said soothingly. "Don't worry. Can you see it?"

Kate sniffed, and I felt her head twist around. "No . . . hang on, yes." She sniffed again. "But it's rolled under the edge of the wall. It's outside and I can't reach it."

"That's okay. There's another nail, remember?"

Sniff. "Yeah. There is. But with two nails we could both have been working at cutting us apart."

"We'll be fine," I said. "Work on the other one."

"Okay." She sniffed again and shifted a bit. "Um, there's something I should tell you. That guy my parents kept telling you I was messed up over? I got over him months ago. I don't know why Mom and Dad think I'm still thinking about him."

"Um," I said. "That's . . . good. I mean, that's great. That you're over him."

"And there's another thing." Her shoulders shifted as she reached for the nail. "My tablet? What I'm doing on it mostly is Moon Time."

I frowned. "Um . . ."

She sighed. "It's a video game for little kids. It's embarrassing to be caught playing it. My friends make fun of me."

"I read middle grade books," I told her. "And not for work, but because I like to."

"Yeah? But I have to tell you one other thing. I

361

don't really get sick at the smell of food cooking in a restaurant."

Such a surprise. "No?"

"No." She sighed. "I was just nervous about working in one. A restaurant, I mean. All those people on TV, they really know what they're doing, and I don't know how to do anything. I'm not sure I even like to cook," she said, sounding ashamed. "I mean, I can, but . . ."

So she was my flesh and blood after all. "Not sure if you've noticed," I said, "but I'm not overly fond of cooking, myself."

"Yeah?"

"Yeah."

"Wow. I just thought you were too busy. I thought all grown-ups liked to cook."

As if.

"Okay," she said. "I can feel the nail, only—" She stopped. "This one's in deep," she whispered. "I can't get it out. Not without a hammer or something."

"Next plan," I said calmly, as I tried to think of one. "That license plate. Can you get it down?"

"Um, maybe. Let's see . . ." She lifted her head. "What was that noise?" Kate asked.

I went still. "What noise?" Because if Courtney and Luke were back early, our chances to escape had dwindled to basically none. "I didn't hear anything."

"Shh!"

And then I heard it. A rustle of leaves that wasn't the wind. An approaching rustle. I couldn't hear any footsteps, but someone— something—was making that noise. I flexed my hands, trying once again to break the twine, and again didn't get anywhere.

The rustle came closer. And closer. And then:

"Mrr."

I let out the breath I hadn't realized I was holding. "Eddie, what are you doing here?"

"Mrr!"

Kate laughed. Actually laughed. "He missed us. Well, you, anyway. Maybe me a little."

"But his cage was latched!"

"Yeah, about that."

"Mrr!"

Eddie's well-being had been at the back of my mind since Courtney and Luke had appeared on the trail, but now I had to face this new reality. And I didn't like any of the possibilities of what might happen to my fuzzy little friend any more than I liked what might happen to Kate. Or me.

"Right," I said. "Back to the license plate. Its edges will be relatively sharp. The sooner we can cut ourselves free, the sooner we'll get out of here and not have to listen to him anymore."

Because Eddie was whining. And scratching at the shed's siding. And giving the occasional howl.

Kate shifted some more, tightening the twine

around my body. "Okay, I can feel the corner . . . got the corner . . . the edge . . . got the whole thing!" she called triumphantly.

"Great," I said, blowing out a breath. "Now see if you can use that to—"

"I know what to do." Kate contorted herself and started sawing at the twine binding us together. "I'm not stupid, you know."

I swallowed my initial response. "If you want me to move so you can get a better angle, just let me know."

She grunted and I waited, hoping and praying that the strands would part under the plate's rusty metal edge like the proverbial knife through butter. I looked up at the window. While it had always been dark in the shed, the faint light coming in seemed even fainter. Dimmer. Which either meant a cloud was passing overhead, or that we'd been in here for hours and it was getting dark.

I stared at the window. The forecast had been for clear skies and no clouds had been in sight the entire day. *Hurry,* I silently said to my niece. *Please hurry hurry hurry—*

"MRRR!!!"

This time the howl came so close to my head that I wished for earplugs. "Eddie, geez Louise! Could you lighten up already? And what are you scratching at?" Not that I cared if he damaged the shed—have at it, pal—but the noises his paws were making weren't of the scratching variety.

And then I caught on.

"Kate," I said. "I bet Eddie thinks your nail is a cat toy. Is there any way you could entice him to push it our way?"

"The nail? Why would he think that's a toy?"

"Because he's a cat. Now if you could—"

"Don't need to," she said. "He's already pushed it back this way."

No wonder he was howling. He wanted his toy back. "Hang on to the license plate, and we'll move around so I can get the nail."

"Or," Kate said, "I pass the plate over to you and I start using the nail. The plate's bigger, so even if we drop it, we could find it again."

It was a good plan, and we carried it out immediately to the accompaniment of an occasional quiet "Mrr" from Eddie. It was hard work, far harder than I'd expected, and it took some time to saw ourselves loose from each other.

When the last piece of twine parted, we rolled away from each other, and lay there, breathing deep and free. "Is this what the parting of conjoined twins feels like?" Kate asked.

I smiled. "Next time I run into some, I'll ask. Can you stand?"

Standing with your hands tied behind your back is a trick, but with the support of each other, and the shed's walls, we managed to get upright. "Okay,"

I said. "I'm holding the license plate. You turn around and rub the twine on your hands against it."

Kate, for once, did as I said without putting up a fuss. I held the plate as tight as I could, bracing its sharp edges with my fingers, but it took way longer than I could have liked for the twine to break apart.

"Free!" Kate shouted, throwing her arms high in a victory salute. I wanted to shush her, but since I also didn't want to worry her about the possible imminent return of Courtney and Luke, I quietly said, "Nicely done."

She whirled around and took the plate out of my hands. "You know," she said, sawing away, "this thing isn't nearly as sharp as I thought it was. If I'd known how dull it really is, I might never have tried."

"Well, sometimes it's better not to know."

"Ignorance is bliss, right?" she asked.

I wondered if anyone ever quoted Thomas Gray accurately. "Well, that's not—" I stopped as my wrists came apart. "That didn't take long."

"You'd already picked half of it away." Kate came around to my front and studied my hands. "Aunt Minnie, you're bleeding. We should put something on it."

"Later. We need to break out of here." I eyed the shed's interior. "That piece of plywood looks pretty weak." And it was the side most out of view of the trail. "Shall we?"

The two of us kicked and shoved and heaved and hip-checked, and it didn't take long for us to loosen a corner that looked Kate-size. "Go," I said, and she went out ahead of me. Then she held the corner of the plywood up, and I crawled out . . . and realized that the light was gone out of the day. Dusk was here and darkness fast approaching.

"Let's go," I said, scooping Eddie into my arms. "Quietly."

"Wait." Kate scurried to a nearby tree, shuffled around in the carpet of last year's leaves, then crouched. "Got it!" she said triumphantly, holding up her cell phone.

"What . . . how?"

She grinned. "Just before I jumped at that Courtney, I tossed it over here."

I gave her a quick hug. "Do you want to call nine-one-one, or shall I?"

"Aunt Minnie!" Kate whispered. "Up ahead!"

But I'd already seen the bobbing lights. It had to be Courtney and Luke, coming back to finish their list of chores.

"Follow me." I took a hard right off the trail. This deep in the woods, there was no understory to hide us and no handy shrubs to hide behind. What we needed was a big rock, or anything big. But what out here was big enough? And then I saw it.

"Here." I pushed her down behind a fallen

tree and dropped to my knees next to her, with Eddie in my arms. As I moved to flatten myself, Eddie squirmed out of my arms and took off.

I wanted to call him, but I couldn't. Courtney and Luke were only a few yards away and any noise now would give away our position. All we needed was for the two of them to get past, then the three of us could scurry off. But now one of us was gone.

Eddie! I shouted silently. *You get back here right now!*

He didn't, of course.

"That's weird," Luke said. He stopped where we'd taken the turn off the path and danced his flashlight around. "I don't remember seeing this before."

Courtney's flashlight joined Luke's. "I don't see anything."

"Because you're not a deer hunter. Those leaves there? They've been turned up in the last few hours. You don't think—"

"Mrr!!" Eddie streaked into and through their fields of light, disappearing into the dark on the other side.

Courtney jumped. "Geez, he scared me!"

"Just a stupid cat," Luke said. "Want me to shoot it?"

My heart froze.

"Nah." Courtney turned away and started

walking. "Let's get going. If we want to watch that movie tonight, we need to get this done."

When they were around the bend, I tugged on Kate's hand. "Time to go," I whispered.

"But what about Eddie?"

"He'll catch up." At least I hoped he would. If he didn't, I'd be out here at first light. "Don't worry about him."

I trotted off, measuring in my head the time it would take Courtney and Luke to find the shed empty of Hamiltons. Five minutes? Maybe less. As soon as we left the trail and hit the two-track, I increased my speed and was soon running flat out, with Kate at my shoulder.

Eddie galloped up behind us as we burst out of the narrow part of the road and onto the gravel proper.

"Where did he come from?" Kate gasped.

The better question was, where had he been, but I didn't have the wind to say it out loud.

"Hey!" Luke called. "Stop! Stop or I'll shoot you in the back!"

"Just do it, Luke," Courtney shouted. "They're getting away."

"They're right behind us," Kate cried. "How can that be?"

I didn't know. "Keep running," I panted out. "Keep running until you get to the road. Someone will help you."

"Aunt Minnie—"

"Run!" I yelled, and slid to a stop. Then I dropped into a crouch and turned to face Luke Cagan.

Three sets of blindingly bright headlights flashed on all around me. "Police!" a megaphone boomed out. "Hold it right there! Put your hands up!"

"Not you, Minnie," Ash said, walking into the light cast by the sheriff's vehicles. "Those two."

"Oh. Right." I dropped my hands and watched as deputies hurried forward to handcuff Luke and Courtney. I looked around for Kate, and saw her being attended to by a female deputy.

"Minnie!" Rafe ran out of the darkness. I bleated a bit as he hugged parts of me that hurt, but not very loudly. "You haven't answered your texts for hours," he said. "I knew something was wrong."

"So you called out the cavalry?" I nestled my face into his shoulder. "So romantic."

"I'll show you romance." He dropped to one knee and took my hands. "Minerva Joy Hamilton, I love you, you love me, and we belong together like . . . um, like . . ."

"Peanut butter and jelly?" Ash suggested.

The female deputy talking to Kate said, "Bogie and Bacall."

Another deputy laughed. "With Niswander, it's more like Abbott and Costello."

I looked around. At the deputies, at Kate, at Ash, at the empty expressions of Courtney Drew and Luke Cagan. This was a night that would forever be shadowed by how close Kate and I had come to being killed.

Putting on a smile, I tugged Rafe to his feet as Eddie, who had again appeared out of nowhere, bumped his head against my shin. "Don't you dare propose to me like this. I want a marriage proposal we can tell our kids about. Besides, I'm a filthy mess. What I want more than anything else is a long, hot shower."

He pulled me tight. "You got it."

Two hours later, after all the questions were answered, all the papers signed, and all the necessary phone calls made, I fell into bed. And I never did get a shower that night.

CHAPTER 22

Aunt Frances added another piece of bacon to my plate. "But where did all those medications come from in the first place?"

Rafe, Kate, and I had walked up the hill for an aunt-cooked breakfast, and I was almost hoarse from telling the story of what had happened the day before. It was now clear that I had to eat before answering any more questions, because if I didn't, everything would get cold and that was no way to treat my aunt's cooking.

I ate a bite of bacon and took another gulp of coffee. Aunt Frances's question was a good one. The array of prescription medications in the shed had rivaled a pharmacy's, and it had taken Ash, Hal Inwood, and the sheriff herself a fair amount of time in the interview room with Those Two to get the full explanation. They'd been interviewed separately and Courtney had remained silent until Luke had started talking. And talking. And talking.

I'd been long asleep by that time, but an hour earlier, Ash stopped by the houseboat to give me an update. He'd looked exhausted but satisfied, and what he'd told Kate and me had made the final pieces of the puzzle click into place.

"Courtney is a home health aide," I said, adding jam to a piece of buttered toast. "She's been stealing pills, a little bit at a time, from her clients. Just one or two at a time. Small amounts so you'd think you dropped one, or accidentally took a double dose."

She encouraged that, too, Ash had said. If a client mentioned missing medication, Courtney would look all concerned and mention that the client had forgotten something just the other day, and had the doctor checked for signs of senility?

Ash's face had hardened. "Ms. Drew laughed," he'd said. "Said old people are so easy to take advantage of. All you have to do is scare them a little and they're putty in your hands."

"There's more," Kate said, glancing at me. I was busy getting the right ratio of maple syrup to pecan pancakes, so I nodded and she continued. "Courtney is apparently well known within her company for lending a hand with end-of-life care. A lot of people don't want to do that, but she was always volunteering."

Otto sighed. "And pocketing all those medications instead of disposing of them properly."

"When did Luke Cagan come into it?" Aunt Frances asked.

I swallowed a spoonful of raspberries. "They've known each other since they were kids, so it's hard to say. The shed was on property owned by Luke's uncle on his mom's side, and the uncle is only there during deer hunting season."

Aunt Frances nudged the bacon in Kate's

direction. "So the uncle wouldn't know a thing."

"Yep. The shed was originally a sugar shack, but no one in the family has made maple syrup for years." I eyed the stack of sourdough toast and reached for another piece. "According to Courtney, Luke kept pushing her to steal more and more medications because he wanted to go on guided hunting trips all over the world." I considered jam options. "Of course, Luke said Courtney was the one who was pushing him to get better prices because she wanted to buy a house on Lake Mitchell."

The sadness of the entire saga had weighed heavily on me when Ash had described it. However, coffee, good food, and even better company were combining to push back the darkness, and my spirits were on the upswing.

"I'm still struggling with the why of it," Otto said. "Not the drugs, that I understand. It's the murders."

"That's what was so confusing," I said. "Nicole, from her back pain, had ended up with an addiction to opioids, and she'd found an Up North supply courtesy of Courtney and Luke. They often sold their pills out on Brown's Road, right where the bookmobile stopped that day, not far from Rex's house."

Otto nodded slowly. "And Rex saw an exchange?"

"With Nicole, on the Fourth of July." Not that Luke was confessing to the murder, but now that his handgun was in evidence, there'd be a

374

ballistics test. "That last day on the bookmobile, Nicole had stayed late on our stop because she'd wanted to connect with Courtney to get more pills. They set up a purchase on the Fourth of July. Rex had wanted to explore more of that road on his bike, and he went back on the Fourth. He saw Nicole with Courtney, and he stopped to talk."

"So sad," Otto said.

"But why didn't Rex tell anyone?" Aunt Frances asked. "If I'd seen a drug deal, the first thing I'd do is call the police. Did he even tell his wife?"

"No," I said. "But Rex confronted them, right on the spot. And Courtney and Luke and Nicole spun some story that apparently Rex said he'd believed. And maybe he was going to tell the police the next day."

"What about Nicole?" Otto asked. "Why on earth did they kill her?"

"Different reason altogether." I ate a bite of marmalade-laden toast. "She had to be downstate for some family things after the Fourth of July and didn't hear about Rex's murder right away. When she did, she figured straight off that Courtney and Luke had killed him."

I put down my toast and spoke quietly. "Nicole was using Rex's murder as a way to get free pills."

Aunt Frances reached over and squeezed my hand. "Addiction is a horrible thing, my dear. We can only hope that someday there will be a better way to cure it."

I nodded agreement and tried to focus on breakfast.

It had been thanks to my own big mouth that day at Rupert and Ann Marie's house, that Courtney had known I was curious about Rex Stuhler's murder. Which explained why she and Luke wanted me out of the picture, and probably explained the air conditioner episode, but the timing didn't work for my fall into the street, so maybe that had been an accident after all. And it had turned out that neither one of them had known of Violet or Julia's existence, a fact for which I was extremely grateful.

Ash had also followed up on the other information I'd passed along. What he'd seen that day on his phone was that Violet had a criminal history. It was a college shoplifting prank, done on a dare during sorority pledge week, but she attributed all the things that had gone wrong with her life to that single episode.

"She plays the victim card like a champ," Ash had said, shaking his head. "Not at all like Mason Hiller."

Turns out that Mason had intentionally shorted customers on their change on July 3 because he'd just got the news that he needed to purchase new gas tanks to stay in compliance with some new state regulations. He'd come to his senses the next day, had already paid the people back, and was trying to find a second job to afford the hideously expensive tanks.

"So it's all over?" Aunt Frances asked.

"Mostly," I said. "Hal Inwood and Ash are trying to track down the people who were buying from Luke and Courtney." I had no idea what crime they might be charged with, but Ash had seemed determined to follow the trail wherever it might lead.

Rafe held up the coffee carafe. I smiled at him gratefully, and stood to pick up my newly filled mug. "Aunt Frances," I asked, "would you mind coming out on the porch with me a minute? I want you to see something."

My aunt gave cleaning-up directions to the men, grabbed her own coffee mug, and followed me outside, trailed by Kate, who'd opted for two generations of aunts instead of kitchen chores.

"Can I sit?" Aunt Frances asked, a smile quirking up one side of her mouth.

"Sure. This might take a few minutes."

The three of us settled down, Aunt Frances and Kate on the cushioned love seat facing the street, me on a rocking chair. It was late morning with a glorious blue sky above; birds were singing, the sun was shining, people were out and about. I breathed deep of the fresh air and thought grateful thoughts.

Last night Kate and I had come far too close to death, and it would likely change both of us in ways we now couldn't imagine. Upon my insistence, she'd called her parents before she'd gone to sleep and she'd tearfully told them the entire story. My brother had sighed and said something along the lines of, "I suppose all's well that ends well." Jennifer had cried, but not for very long, and she'd laughed when Kate had said she'd have the best ever "What I Did on My Summer Vacation" essay when school started.

"Nice morning," Aunt Frances said. "But what are we doing out here?"

I used my tiptoes and started my chair rocking. "Waiting."

"For what?"

Partly for an opportunity to fit Florida's state motto of "In God We Trust" into the conversation. "Just waiting." I nodded in the direction of her coffee. "All will be revealed before that gets cold." At least I hoped so.

She shrugged and raised her mug. "Hope this isn't an odd aftereffect of yesterday's trauma. That you can't stay indoors for more than an—" She stopped talking and squinted across the street. At the boardinghouse. "Well, that's interesting," she murmured.

The three of us watched a thirty-ish couple laden with backpacks hurry down the front steps, climb into a car topped with two stand-up paddle boards, and drive away.

"Wasn't that Amy and Zach?" Kate asked.

"It certainly was." I watched their taillights

378

disappear. "A couple of weeks ago they were kiteboarding, but they've moved on. I hear they're talking about renting a catamaran next weekend."

Another couple came down the stairs. In their mid-fifties, they went at a more sedate pace, but they, too, had their hands full. Though they had picnic baskets, not backpacks, the contents were undoubtedly similar.

"Bert and Yvette," I said, and waved. "Have a good day!" I called.

They waved back as they placed their baskets into the bed of Bert's pickup truck. Yvette smiled. "We're taking that road you recommended, the one out past the state forest land. Think we can get lost this time?" she asked Bert, turning her face up for a kiss.

"Get a room, you two!" Canary called as she walked out the front door. She was followed by Walter, who closed the door behind them.

"Well, if it isn't Minnie." She beamed. "Walter and I are headed to that wonderful toy store. Your friend Mitchell ordered us a new jigsaw and we just got a call that it's in."

"Better get going," Walter said, "or someone might buy it out from under us."

Canary laughed, but let herself be pulled along, and the elderly couple headed off briskly in the direction of downtown.

"Hmm." Aunt Frances sipped her coffee, which was still steaming.

"Exactly," I said. "Despite the appearance of no matchmaking, there is a significant amount of pairing going on."

"How . . ." My aunt shook her head. And laughed. "You know what? I don't care how. But you know what? It makes me happy."

And if my aunt was happy, I was, too.

The three of us sat there for a few minutes, breathing in the morning air, feeling the easy peace of summer.

"So what are you two doing today?" Aunt Frances asked. "After yesterday, I'd say nothing is in order. And if you want to include me in that, I'm ready and waiting."

Kate smiled. "I can do nothing until noon, but I'm scheduled to work at Older Than Dirt."

"You sure you want to go in?" I asked. "I can call Pam and explain."

"Aunt Minnie, I'm fine. What would I do all day anyway? And please don't tell me pick raspberries." But she said it with a smile.

Soon, she went off, as did Rafe, who said he had things to pick up before working on the house, and though Graydon had texted that I could take the day off, I decided to stop by the library to check e-mail. Three days of unanswered e-mails and I'd spend half of Monday reading and answering. As it was, I'd spend a good share of Monday morning telling the Shed Story, and there were things I needed to get done.

I slipped in the side door and, looking left and right, scurried into my office, closing the door without anyone seeing me.

Knock, knock.

Then again, it was entirely possible I wasn't as stealthy as I'd thought. I'd have to ask Eddie for lessons.

My door opened and Graydon poked his head in. "Morning." He glanced at his watch. "Yes, still morning, barely. Glad I caught you, I didn't think you'd be in today." He gestured at my office's empty chair and, mentally waving good-bye to the productive hour I'd planned, I nodded for him to sit.

"This won't take long," he said, getting comfortable. "Did you know the board had a special meeting this morning?"

"Did not." I felt my brow furrowing. They'd heard about yesterday's escapade. Once again, I'd made a name for myself and not in a good way. Moral turpitude was included in my employment contract's termination-for-cause section and they were going to fire me. What was I going to do? I hadn't finished paying off my student loans, I needed to help Rafe pay for the house, and I didn't want to sell my houseboat. Plus, I had the best job in the world and couldn't imagine doing anything else, ever.

Graydon crossed an ankle over his knee. "It was an emergency meeting. Trent called it yesterday morning."

I put my hand to my forehead and tried to smooth out my skin. Okay, not going to fire me. At least not for what had happened out on Brown's Road. The library board's bylaws allowed for emergency meetings, but they were only allowed under special circumstances. "What was it for?"

My boss inspected the sole of his deck shoe. "The attorney advising the board on Stan Larabee's bequest is in town this weekend, and she wanted to give the board her final recommendation." Graydon smiled. "Which they voted to adopt, all in favor."

"You look pleased," I said cautiously.

"Every penny will go into the Stan Larabee Endowment. There's enough capital to generate healthy annual dividends and the board, with oversight from Mr. Larabee's attorney, will make decisions on how to use that money, with Mr. Larabee's wishes regarding the bookmobile a guiding principle on disbursements."

I tried to do the mental math on how long it would take to get enough dividends to buy a new bookmobile. Failed completely.

"It's the wisest possible use of the bequest," Graydon said.

"Sounds like something a lawyer would say."

"Direct quote," he agreed. "There's just a couple of things. Mr. Larabee must have been quite a character, because his will included two, ah, interesting requests. He wanted to have the next bookmobile painted in his favorite color, purple."

"And that sounds like Stan," I said softly.

Graydon eyed me. "Minnie, I thought you'd be happy."

"Oh, I am. It's just . . ." I smiled, albeit sadly. "It's just this was the last thing Stan left behind. Now it's over and Stan really feels gone."

"Au contraire." Graydon stood. "Mr. Larabee's endowment will last essentially forever. The way I see it, this is only the beginning."

He was right, and by the time he'd left my office, I was ready to say so. "You're right," I called after him, and received an "I know. See you tomorrow" in reply.

"Well, there you go," I said to the empty air. "It'll be a little like Stan is watching over us." And somehow, I got the feeling of a nod from Mr. Larabee himself.

An hour later, I tiptoed back outside. Donna spotted me, but she averted her eyes when I held up my index finger in the universal "Shh!" gesture.

"See you tomorrow," she said as I went by. "Hope you're bringing provisions, because I anticipate a long story at break time."

Small towns being what they are, how she knew about the shed less than twenty-four hours later was a mystery only in the specifics. "I'll stop at Cookie Tom's," I promised, and escaped into the sunshine.

Half a block later, my phone beeped with an incoming text.

Rafe: *had lunch?*

Minnie: *I was planning on stopping at Shomin's. Do you want me to get you something?*

Rafe: *don't buy food all here*

Minnie (while smiling at her phone): *Could you please spell that out in proper English, with punctuation to ensure proper communication?*

Rafe: *can but not gonna-see U soon*

Laughing, I shut down my phone and started walking faster as I wondered what Rafe was planning. Fat Boys subs were always a winner, but maybe he'd gone all out and fired up the grill. We hadn't had hamburgers in at least a week so he was probably on the edge of withdrawal.

My brain was so full that I didn't pay much attention to where my feet were taking me until I was all the way downtown and mired in late summer pedestrian traffic, heavy this weekend because of sidewalk sales.

Instead of being annoyed, however, I found myself smiling at the gamboling children, the sunburned parents, and everyone who was crowding the sidewalks with bulging shopping bags. All would be gone in a month and Chilson would, once again, be a place where you could find a parking spot anywhere you wanted.

"How has your summer been going?"

I stopped and looked around, but the question

hadn't been asked of me; it had been asked of someone behind a rack of vintage linens outside Older Than Dirt. The questioner sounded familiar, though, and I hesitated as I tried to place the name.

"Great," said a young and very familiar voice. "I'm so glad my parents let me come up here to stay with Aunt Minnie. I've been begging them for years, but this is the first year they thought I was old enough."

"So you're enjoying the houseboat?"

I almost snapped my fingers. Bianca Sims, now Bianca Koyne. Mitchell's wife, which was a two-word phrase I still couldn't wrap my head around.

"You bet. And Eddie is like the best cat ever." Kate's hands appeared over the top of the rack as she tidied the goods. "Aunt Minnie talks to me like a real person, you know? Not like I'm a little kid, but like I'm an adult. She asks my opinion on stuff and really wants to know the answers."

Bianca murmured something I couldn't hear.

"Let me know where to send the nomination," Kate said, laughing. "She's the Best Aunt in the World if you ask me. You know what happened yesterday? She literally saved my life!"

My cheeks burned with embarrassment and I cut across the street, staying out of their view. No way did I want them to know I'd been eavesdropping, but I wasn't sorry I accidentally had. Now I knew that Kate didn't hate me and maybe, just maybe, there was hope of an Aunt Frances–type relationship in our future.

"All is not lost," I said out loud, smiling up at the sun.

By the time I got to the house, my stomach was telling me that breakfast, while large, had been a long time ago and it was past time to eat something. I hurried up the steps and opened the front door. No food smells or cooking sounds emanated from the dining room or kitchen. I wandered through the rooms and found nothing, and no one. Then a faint noise from up above my head gave a clue as to Rafe's whereabouts.

"Hey!" I called. "Where's all that food you promised?"

"Up here!"

I traipsed up the stairs, thinking about the phone call I'd just finished with Kristen, who had been in line to get the Shed Story. With her atrocious restaurant hours, I hadn't wanted to bother her much before noon. But as it turned out, she'd already heard a large percentage of what I'd told her.

"How did you know all that?" I'd asked.

"You seriously think I'm going to give away my sources?" she'd scoffed.

"It's not like you're a reporter, trying for first amendment protection."

"There are parallels," she'd said. "But let's get

to the good stuff. Tell me again how you and Kate wriggled your way across the floor. No, wait. Tomorrow during dessert you can demonstrate."

She'd howled with laughter, then said softly, "I'm really glad you and Kate didn't get shot."

Remembering, I was sorry for the catch I'd heard in her voice, sorry for the pain she would have suffered if last night had included a nasty death or two. Which was a weird thing to be sorry about, but there you go.

I reached the second floor hallway and looked around. No food. No Rafe. "Where are you?"

"Keep going!"

Where? I wondered. But his voice was still coming from above my head, so that was a clue. I turned and saw that the small, narrow door at the end of the hall was open. "Are you in the attic?"

"Come on up."

Huh. I'd been in the attic all of twice—once to note its existence, a second time to reassure myself there was room for the boxes of books that were in the boardinghouse attic, from whence they would eventually be shifted, but not yet, as Rafe and I were still working on bookcase design. I'd considered not moving until said bookcases were installed, but I wasn't sure I wanted to wait that long.

I climbed the narrow stairway and peered at the cobwebby gloom. Still no Rafe. But . . . hang on . . .

A window at the end of the gable facing the water was wide open. I walked over, stepping around the broken chairs, tables, and toys, and poked my head outside. "You're on the roof," I said.

Rafe reached for my hand and helped me clamber through the window frame and onto the balcony. It was an odd part of the house, because it could only be reached via defenestration, and I hadn't been sure we would ever use it. But since I'd known Rafe for more than twenty years, I should have known better.

"And why not? It's a beautiful evening." He ushered me to one of two low chairs. "Have a seat. I'll be right back."

"Um . . ." But he'd already ducked back inside. I leaned forward, resting my elbows on my knees and my chin in my hands. More than nice, really. The view was spectacular. From here I could see every boat in Uncle Chip's Marina, half of Janay Lake, and over the line of trees and to Lake Michigan. Seagulls wheeled about, ducks scurried, sailboats fluffed. It was late summer in Chilson and all was well with the world.

Rafe came back laden with two of the biggest picnic baskets I'd ever seen.

"How hungry do you think I am?" I asked, laughing.

He plopped both baskets near my feet. "Basket number two contains your favorite meal from your favorite restaurant, and no, I'm not talking about Fat Boys. This is courtesy of a certain chef from a restaurant that is getting almost too popular for its own good."

"But I just talked to Kristen. She didn't say anything about this. And it's lunch hour. They don't serve that whitefish until evening."

"If you know the blonde like I do," he said, "anything is possible."

The undeniable smells of whitefish stuffed with crabmeat wafted my way. "The blonde can be sneaky." I smiled. "What's the occasion?"

"Ah. That calls for basket number one." He dragged it closer, and I heard a faint "Mrr."

"Eddie?" I opened the basket and saw the cat carrier. Half of Eddie's whiskers and his nose were visible through the wire door.

"Mrr."

I looked at Rafe, who was looking extremely pleased with himself. "Eddie's fine with heights," I said, puzzled, "but why on earth did you bring him up here?"

My beloved leaned forward and pulled the cat carrier out of the basket. "Mr. Hamilton," he said, "I love your Minnie very much and I would like your permission to marry her."

"You're asking my cat for my hand in marriage?"

"No interrupting," he said. "I have this all memorized."

389

"You do not."

"No, but I'm on a roll. Mr. Eddie, yesterday your Minnie told me she wanted a marriage proposal we can tell our kids about. I'm not the most creative guy in the world, but I can't think of anyone who's been proposed to on a roof. So what do you think? Will this fit the requirement? And do I have your permission?"

"Mrr!" Eddie said. "Mrr!"

"Double yes." Rafe patted the carrier. "Thanks, buddy. You're the best."

"Rafe," I said softly. "You don't—"

"Minnie." He took my hands in one of his and kissed them. "You are the love of my life, holder of my happiness, and keeper of my dreams. You make the sun shine when clouds are gray. We are better together than we are apart. Though you have horrible taste in music—"

"Hey!"

"—we laugh at the same things, and since we laugh a lot, nothing else really matters. So. Minerva Joy Hamilton. Will you marry me?"

Crying and laughing at the same time, I said, "Of course I will."

Rafe kissed me soundly. Pulled away, then came back for another one. "Double version for Eddie's double yes."

It was classic Rafe from top to bottom, and I wouldn't have changed a thing, not the roof, not the food, and certainly not the cat. After we ended the Second Kiss, Rafe opened the picnic basket and I glanced at Eddie.

He was sitting meatloaf-style and looking directly at me. When our gazes met, he opened and closed his mouth in two silent "Mrr's." More doubles. And then my eyes opened wide. In all the fuss after last night, I'd never had the chance to think about the implications.

"You know what? Eddie saved me and Kate last night. Twice."

"How's that?" Rafe handed me a china plate from Three Seasons laden with whitefish, roasted Brussels sprouts, and redskin potatoes.

"The nail in the shed," I said. "If Eddie hadn't pushed that back inside, we would have been still in there when Courtney and Luke came back. And if he hadn't distracted them by running through their flashlight beams, they might have looked closer at the trail we'd left."

We exchanged a glance, then Rafe stared at Eddie and slowly said, "He really did, didn't he?"

I leaned forward and kissed the tip of his furry nose, which was still poking out through the wire door. "You're the smartest cat in the whole wide world," I said. "Anything you want, all you have to do is ask. We'll get it for you. Anything at all."

Eddie looked at me. At Rafe. Back at me.

Then closed his eyes.

And fell asleep.

Center Point Large Print

600 Brooks Road / PO Box 1
Thorndike, ME 04986-0001 USA

(207) 568-3717

US & Canada:
1 800 929-9108
www.centerpointlargeprint.com